T0011923

**It would probabl[...]
now, but this cou[...]
see him before a[...]**

Having convinced herself that easily, she said, "You could dance with me, Oklahoma. Make this a real celebration."

He looked at her for a few stilled moments before his smile grew into a laugh and he held out a hand. "I can do that, Nebraska."

She laid her hand in his, and her heart had never felt more full as he led her across the lanai and onto the dance floor. There, she was transported back in time, to the dance contest and once again became Ginger Rogers and he was her Fred Astaire. A complete fantasy, where she had no worries or fears. Was free to just dance.

Author Note

Thank you for picking up a copy of *A Dance with Her Forbidden Officer*. The basis of this story came to me while I was in Hawaii and read about the competition of navy bands called the Battle of the Music, which took place the night of December 6, 1941. I could clearly see the characters in my mind—Wendy Smith, a Red Cross volunteer nurse, and K.T. McCallister, an underwater welder in the navy—enjoying a night of music and dancing the evening before the historical attack on Pearl Harbor. It was a night that changed their lives as much as the following morning.

I hope you enjoy reading about Wendy and K.T. as they journey to their happily-ever-after.

LAURI
ROBINSON

—

A Dance with Her
Forbidden Officer

HARLEQUIN
HISTORICAL

HARLEQUIN®
HISTORICAL™

Recycling programs for this product may not exist in your area.

ISBN-13: 978-1-335-59604-8

A Dance with Her Forbidden Officer

Copyright © 2024 by Lauri Robinson

For questions and comments about the quality of this book, please contact us at CustomerService@Harlequin.com.

TM and ® are trademarks of Harlequin Enterprises ULC.

Harlequin Enterprises ULC
22 Adelaide St. West, 41st Floor
Toronto, Ontario M5H 4E3, Canada
www.Harlequin.com

Printed in U.S.A.

A lover of fairy tales and history, **Lauri Robinson** can't imagine a better profession than penning happily-ever-after stories about men and women in days gone past. Her favorite settings include World War II, the Roaring Twenties and the Old West. Lauri and her husband raised three sons in their rural Minnesota home and are now getting their just rewards by spoiling their grandchildren. Visit her at laurirobinson.blogspot.com, Facebook.com/lauri.robinson1 or Twitter.com/laurir.

Books by Lauri Robinson

Harlequin Historical

Diary of a War Bride
A Family for the Titanic Survivor
The Captain's Christmas Homecoming
An Unlikely Match for the Governess
A Dance with Her Forbidden Officer

Southern Belles in London

The Return of His Promised Duchess
The Making of His Marchioness
Falling for His Pretend Countess

The Osterlund Saga

Marriage or Ruin for the Heiress
The Heiress and the Baby Boom

Twins of the Twenties

Scandal at the Speakeasy
A Proposal for the Unwed Mother

Visit the Author Profile page
at Harlequin.com for more titles.

To Justin, Connie and Karlee, my Hawaii traveling partners. Love and thanks for an amazing trip that couldn't have been better!

Chapter One

"Don't you just love Saturday nights?" Helen Collins asked with excitement in her voice, a gleam in her dark brown eyes, and a smile on her bright red lips as she scanned the occupants filling the dance hall at the Bloch Arena. "Music and a never-ending supply of handsome men. What more could a girl want?"

"Nothing," Lois Adams agreed, while fluffing her poofy curls with a hand and setting her gaze on the bar at the far side of the room. "Absolutely nothing, and I believe I see an anchor-clanker who wants to dance with me."

Giggling, Helen said, "More than one anchor-clanker."

Music and gaiety surrounded her, and filled with her own excitement, Wendy Smith smiled as she watched Helen and Lois cross the crowded room, swinging their hips that were highlighted by their pencil skirts, heading straight for a lively group of sailors in their white uniforms and blue neck scarves. She loved Saturday nights, too. Every nurse did. So did every armed services man stationed in Hawaii.

Besides the navy, there were army, army air force,

marines, and coast guard all stationed on the island. It was amazing seeing so many men walking around in their uniforms everywhere she went.

There were times when she pinched herself, just to make sure she really was in paradise and not back on the Nebraska plains, where this time of year a person had to be bundled from head to toe because the wind and cold had the ability to leave exposed skin frost-bitten.

Her mother would be so happy to know she was here.

The sun was always shinning on the island, and even when it rained, it was over within a short time and the sun was back again, dried things out like it had never happened. In the four months that she'd been here, she'd rarely needed a sweater, and never a coat. Answering the Red Cross's advertisement for nurses' aides had been the best thing she'd ever done. After completing her two months of training in California, she'd accepted an assignment in Hawaii. The sandy beaches, blue ocean, colorful birds and flowers, lush green landscape, was indeed a paradise.

As a young girl, she'd been told there was more to life than living on the Nebraska panhandle, and had promised her mother that as soon as she was old enough, she'd leave. That had happened on her twenty-first birthday. That's the minimum age the Red Cross required of recruits—between the ages of twenty-one and forty and unmarried. She figured if the government was willing to pay her while she was seeing more of the world, she'd gladly repay them by giving every man, woman, and child who needed nursing the best care possible. Having the time of her life while doing that was an added bonus.

Checking that the red belt was even around the waistline of her white and red polka dot dress, with a full skirt because she found pencil skirts too confining to dance in, Wendy walked toward the dance floor. That's where she'd be spending the entire evening. Dancing until her feet hurt inside her white slingback shoes and she was so exhausted that she'd fall into bed hours from now tired and happy. That may not happen until sunrise. It so happened that her day off this week fell on Sunday. Tomorrow. There would be no need to be up and ready to relieve the night shift at the hospital by eight in the morning.

Facility 161, as the arena was known on base, was a huge octagon building that hosted, amongst other things, two bowling alleys, a boxing ring, movie theatre, and a circular dance room that had one open side, letting in the fresh island air.

Tonight, the Battle of the Music was happening, where navy bands from the ships homeported in Pearl Harbor would compete. The USS *Arizona* band had won the preliminary round of the battle back in September, shortly after she'd arrived in Pearl Harbor, and they were very good. However, she'd also heard the USS *Pennsylvania* band, as well as those from the USS *Tennessee*, the USS *Argonne*, and the submarine base band at different dances since then. They were all good and she wasn't rooting for one over the other, would simply cheer for all of them and be happy for the winner.

The music was already in full swing and the dance

floor filled with couples, including Lois, whose blond curls were bouncing as she danced with a tall sailor.

Wendy checked that the white plumeria flower she'd attached to a bobby pin that was holding back her hair was still in place behind her right ear. Behind the left ear would mean she was in a relationship, and she wasn't. Nor did she want to be. That was another thing she'd promised her mother. To never let some man trick her into believing that love and marriage was what every woman wanted and needed.

Not her. She was the one in charge of her life, and would keep it that way.

That was something else that was so wonderful here. Back home, men were looking for a wife. Someone to clean, cook, and have babies—that would never be her. Here, many of the men had girlfriends and wives back at home, and weren't looking for anything other than someone to dance with them. That was all she wanted to do, too. Dance.

Dance the night away!

Biting down on her bottom lip at the giddiness filling her, she found an open spot along the sidelines of the dance floor, and glanced about, looking for a partner. There were an unlimited number to choose from. Men greatly outnumbered women on the base.

A sailor with short dark hair—although they all had short hair—caught her eye. He was taller than most, his shoulders broader, and had an amazing smile that filled his face as he listened to another sailor, leading her to believe he would be a fun dance partner.

However, he appeared far more interested in whatever the other sailor was saying than dancing. She was disappointed, but with so many others clearly looking for a partner, she continued to scan the room.

Her gaze landed on him again, a couple of times, until she reminded herself that she was here to dance and smiled at a shorter, thinner sailor with blond hair who was looking at her expectantly. She nodded and met the blond sailor at the edge of the dance floor, and within seconds, was being sashayed around the wooden floor. He had happy blue eyes and was a fair dancer. She enjoyed the two songs they danced to, but was glad when another sailor tapped his shoulder, because she was looking for a livelier dancer.

She was again a bit disappointed that it hadn't been the amazing smile sailor who tapped the other one's shoulder. That wasn't like her. She cared about a man's dancing ability, not his looks. Dancing was when she felt completely free, like a bird let out of its cage, and she wanted to find a partner to match that freedom on the dance floor.

Her new partner was a bit taller than the last one, and she danced with him until another sailor tapped his shoulder. Thus it continued, with her dancing with so many sailors she no longer found anything distinguishing between them, other than none of them had been the lively dancer she was looking for, therefore, she decided to take a break from dancing. She made her way over to the beverage station, chose a bottle of soda, and walked through the open wall to the concrete lanai, where the slight coolness of the night air was welcome. Lifting the hair off the back of her neck, so the air could evaporate the sheen of sweat from dancing, she admitted to having noticed that the amazing smile sailor hadn't danced with anyone. It was too bad.

Some people just weren't dancers. She could understand that, yet there was something about him that made her want to dance with him.

She hadn't fully realized how much she enjoyed dancing until she'd started attending the dances every Saturday night here at the base.

There had been dances back home, but because everyone knew everyone, she'd had to subdue her enjoyment and be careful to not dance too often with the same person, because that could imply things that she hadn't wanted implied.

Here she could dance with anyone without worry and she would find the perfect dance partner tonight. A real ducky shin-cracker. One that would make Fred Astaire jealous.

Kent Thomas McCallister, known as K.T. since birth because his father was Kent Edward McCallister, watched the woman walk out onto the lanai with a soda pop. He'd never seen someone having so much fun dancing in his life. He'd felt sorry for her a couple of times because her partners hadn't been able to keep up with her. Maybe he should have felt sorry for them, instead.

With a white flower tucked behind one ear and a white and red polka dot dress, she was eye-catching, but it was her spirited behavior that was impossible to ignore. He made it a habit to not notice women. Yet, she'd captured his attention and held it for the last hour or so, despite his best efforts to overlook her and her dancing.

Betty Nelson had been his girl since grammar school, and had hinted that they should get married or engaged before he left home, but he refused to do that to her. The world was at a precarious point and he didn't want her waiting on a husband who might not return. That was a chance every serviceman took. That would also be the ultimate broken promise.

However, he had promised to return to Oklahoma and to her if he survived his four years and would hold true to that.

Betty's brother Wayne was one of his best friends. Wayne had joined the armed services, too. The army. Last K.T. had heard, Wayne was in Great Britain. That's where his cousin Ralph Johnson was headed, too, or at least that's what his mother had said in her last letter.

K.T. had chosen the navy because of the advertisement in the newspaper seeking welders. Due to the welding skills that he'd learned from living on a farm in Oklahoma during the Great Depression, when everything had to be repaired with whatever was available because there was no money to buy new parts, and even if there had been the money, parts had been hard to come by, he'd advanced up the ranks quickly. He'd been teaching others the skill practically since the first weld he'd made early on in his training.

He'd also mastered diving—an instructor had claimed he must have gills—and now the underwater welding unit that he supervised was highly sought. He and his unit had traveled up and down the West Coast, repairing navy ships in all the ports. That's why he was here, at Pearl Harbor, which was scheduled to quickly become the Pacific homeport of the US Navy fleet. The United States had been dancing around the edges of the conflict that had been going on overseas for the last two years, and knowing it was inevitable that the States would eventually get pulled in, all of the armed forces were being fortified. At home and abroad.

Three years ago, with Oklahoma still dredging its way out of the Dirty Thirties, he'd enlisted in the navy, answered that ad, because he wanted a future. Betty hadn't been keen on the idea, but he'd explained how everyone was struggling to make ends meet, and this was not only a way for him to serve his country, it could provide him with the skills he'd need to some-day provide for a family.

She'd accepted it, and he'd assured her that the four years he'd enlisted for would go by quickly. They had so far, and during his two short trips home, she had agreed that he'd chosen correctly. She was proud of him, and he was proud of her for understanding.

The ad had said that the navy had been looking for welders, but he hadn't planned that his training would also focus on diving. Yet, it was something he enjoyed more than he'd thought he would. There was an en-tire new world under the water and he reveled in the challenges of welding while under water.

The girl moved further across the concrete lanai, to the edge that didn't really give much of a view other than the construction happening around the base. However, the moon, which was a little more than half, but not quite three-quarters, was enough to brighten the night and give her a golden glow silhouette.

Nothing about Oklahoma had prepared him for Cal-ifornia. The West Coast was a sight to see, the lush green landscape, the hillside cliffs, and the ocean. He would have been satisfied to remain there, but with things escalating overseas, the powers that be deter-mined Hawaii would serve better as a homeport, and since his unit was charged with ship maintenance and repairs, this is where they'd been deployed. At that time, he'd thought the sights of California had prepared him for Hawaii, but he'd been wrong.

Though basic in some aspects and sparsely populated, with red dirt roads and huge fields of sugar cane and pineapple, the island of Oahu was an enchanting place, beautiful. That woman standing beneath the moonlight reflecting off the tall palm trees overhead, proved just how beautiful. What he was looking at could have been a postcard picture. There were other people on the lanai, and he looked back toward the dance floor, wondering if she was waiting for one of her dancing partners to follow her outside.

This was the first dance he'd attended. Not because he didn't like dancing, but because he usually watched the boxing matches at the arena on Friday nights, and one night out was what he allowed himself. He liked things planned and orderly.

He'd come tonight because of his unit. Several of them had placed bets on who would win the battle between the bands, and for no other reason than camaraderie, he'd decided to join them.

The others he'd come with tonight were on the dance floor, and he watched them for a moment, but his attention kept going back to the polka dot dress woman. What was it about her that he couldn't get past? Or was it just him? Was the dance reminding him of home and all the people he missed? His mother would love to see this woman dancing. That had to be it. His mother loved dancing and he would write her about the dance.

Turning his attention back to the dancing didn't help; his mind was still on her. Saying hello to a woman wasn't going to change anything about him, but it would get her off his mind. He picked his bottle of beer off the table and walked out onto the lanai, didn't stop until he was standing next to her. He looked up into the sky as she was, at the millions of twinkling stars. "Nice night."

"It is. I think I could live my whole life here and never tire of the weather," she said. "There aren't even any bugs."

"That's because of the wild chickens, they eat the bugs." Chickens? That's all he could think to talk about? It was odd how the chickens roamed free, but the truth was, standing next to her had turned him brain-dead.

She twisted and looked up at him. "We had chickens in Nebraska, and still had bugs."

He'd never seen eyes sparkle like that before and it took a moment before he could speak, "Well, then, I guess my theory has been proven wrong, because we had chickens in Oklahoma, too, and we still had bugs."

"Biting flies?" she asked. "The ones that looked all innocent, then just like that—" she snapped her fingers "—they'd bite you with the sting of a hornet."

He chuckled at her description, because he suddenly did remember those flies. Just as suddenly, the subject made talking with her easy, normal, like someone he'd have talked with back home. "I haven't thought about those flies in a long time."

She took a sip of her bottle of soda pop. Looking at him the entire time. "How long have you been here?"

"Three months," he answered. "You?"

"Four, but I was in California for two months before that."

"I was in California for almost three years."

"Nice place, but this…" She let out a soft sigh. "Have you gone to Waikiki Beach yet?"

"No."

"Hiked up to see the waterfall?"

"No."

"The Blowhole?"

"No," he replied again. He'd heard about all of those sights, and men in his unit had gone to see them, but he was here to work, not sightsee. He didn't tell her that because she must live life like she danced, with an adventurous spirit.

"Surely you've at least gone up to the top of the hill and looked down at the harbor at night. Seen all the ships lit up bow to stern with strings of lights? It's a sight to see."

"Yes, I have walked up to the top of hill to see that." She was right about it being something to see. All those ships lit up and the lights reflecting off the water was quite spectacular.

Her smile grew and dimples formed in each of her cheeks as she tilted her head to one side and shook her head. "Three years wouldn't be enough for me to forget those biting flies. A person couldn't even sit outside on nice evenings because of those pesky things. They'd even find a way to sneak in the house come winter." She nodded, as if answering her own thoughts. "That's another thing I don't miss. The cold. The snow. The wind. I get cold just thinking about it."

"What do you miss?" he asked.

"People," she said. "Family."

That was enough to remind him that it wasn't like him to start up a conversation with a woman, and there'd been no reason for him to do so this time. It had been against his better judgment and he still questioned why he'd done it. All it had accomplished was make him want to know more. Learning more about her could never happen. He gestured toward the building, where music and laughter were floating out into the night air. "I'll let you get back to your dance."

"It's not my dance." She drank the last of her soda pop. "It's a dance for everyone to enjoy, have some fun with people they'll probably never see again."

There was solid truth in that, and there were plenty of men who would jump at the opportunity to cut a rug with her. If things were different, he wouldn't mind dancing with her, just because, unlike her other partners, he knew he could keep up with her.

"Ships, people, come and go every day," she said. "Can't blame them for wanting to have a little fun when they can."

That, too, was the truth. "No, you can't." Tipping his bottle toward her, he added, "Nice talking to you, Nebraska."

Her soft giggle floated on the air as she tapped her bottle against his. "You, too, Oklahoma."

He turned, walked back toward the building.

She caught up with him almost instantly. "Aren't you here to dance?"

"No. I'm just here to listen to the bands."

"You can do that while dancing."

He shook his head, mainly because he could easily give in and dance with her. Men with girls back home, with wives back home, danced all the time. He chose not to, and would continue to choose not to.

"You don't know how, do you?"

The hint of teasing in the depths of her blue eyes increased her cuteness, and he questioned what was happening to his immunity to women. It had always been there in the past. Women wanted promises and he didn't make any that he couldn't keep.

"That's too bad," she said. "Not knowing how to dance."

The open wall was right before them, as was the dance floor, filled with hundreds of people. "I know how to dance."

She set her bottle in the trash bin, then planted her hands on her hips. "Prove it."

He shook his head. "You'll just have to believe me."

She laughed. "I don't have to believe anything." Holding up a single finger, she continued, "One dance then I'll have proof. Or are you chicken?"

Her grin said she knew that no one called a sailor a chicken.

If his first mistake had been to walk over and start up a conversation with her, his second one was his own competitive nature. She wanted someone who could match her energy, and he could do that. Prove it with one dance. What she'd said was true. Everyone was here for fun and no one could blame them for that. Not even him. He tossed his beer bottle in the trash bin. "Let's go."

Her laugh was light and carefree as she skipped onto the dance floor ahead of him. "That's what I wanted to hear! And you're going to have fun! I guarantee it!"

He was amused by her, and accepted that. They probably would never see each other again after tonight. He grasped her hand, held it over her head as she performed a perfect pirouette, then dipped into a graceful, perfect curtsy. Laughter rumbled in his chest as he bent at the waist in a bow, then he grasped her other hand and proceeded to lead her across the floor with a fast two-step dance. "You guarantee it, do you?"

"I do! That's what life is for!"

It had been over three years since he'd danced, since leaving home, but it all returned quickly. She was graceful, her steps smooth and in perfect time with his, and again, he thought how he'd never seen anyone enjoy themselves so much. Her enjoyment was contagious, because he felt it seeping into him. He was having fun. There was no harm in dancing with someone. He'd danced with many different women back home and Betty had never minded. Nor had he minded when she'd danced with other men. This was no different.

Ready to convince her just how well he could cut a rug, he lifted their clutched hands, so she could twirl again, and this time, caught her behind her back with his free hand and dipped her over his arm. She laughed aloud, kicked one leg in the air as she popped upright and spun again in the opposite direction. He caught her around the waist again and dipped her over his other arm.

"Aw, Oklahoma," she said with a cheeky grin as she popped upright again. "You are quite a ducky shincracker!"

He danced her backward in the fast two-step. "I told you."

She pivoted on one toe, making her skirt swirl, and ended up with her back against his shoulder and her head tilted so she was looking up at him. "Yes, you did, and I hope you don't tire easily."

He laughed and held her waist as she spun around to face him. "You are full of challenges, Nebraska."

The shimmering overhead lights filled her ocean-blue eyes with sparkles as she danced closer. "You love challenges."

"How do you know that?"

"You're in the navy!"

She not only had a point, she was right. He did love a challenge and hers was filling him with a delight he hadn't felt in years.

"You just need to learn to have fun!" she said, grasping his hands and dancing him backward.

"I know how to have fun," he replied, once again taking the lead.

The music was loud and the high spirits of the men and women filled the air, but her words rose above the noise as she said, "Prove it!"

He grasped her around the back with one hand, and with their other hands clasped and straight out in front of them, he put his cheek against hers and danced the catlike, stealthy steps of the tango with her, back and forth across the floor.

Her laughter was also contagious, because before long, he was laughing along with her as they continued to challenge each other with step after step.

As the band struck the final notes of the song, he gave her one last spin and ended the dance with her dipped over his arm again.

While the music faded, the crowd clapped, and after she popped upright, she did, too, but then also stuck two fingers in her mouth and let out a whistle that rivaled all the others echoing across the dance floor.

K.T. laughed. He'd never met anyone as full of life as her.

"Folks! Folks! Listen up!" the emcee shouted into the microphone, coaxing the crowd to quiet down. "We have a surprise for you! A jitterbug dance-off! The winners will be the last couple still on the floor after twenty minutes of nonstop dancing!"

She spun and looked at him with a mixture of anticipation and enthusiasm, and a clear challenge that was emphasized by the way she once again had both hands on her hips.

What could he do?

Except nod.

Wendy had danced plenty back home, the town hall had been next door to her aunt and uncle's store and had hosted dances once a month or more, and she'd danced even more since arriving at the base—yet, she had never, ever, found a partner so skilled, so in tune with her every move. She'd been surprised when it had been him, the amazing smile sailor, who had stepped up beside her on the lanai. What hadn't surprised her was how handsome he was up close. His eyes were an iridescent brown, darker in the center and lighter around the edges, and topped with dark lashes and full eyebrows. His nose was straight, and his jaw was well-defined. There was also a slight wave in his thick, short hair. Over all, she'd say he had the most perfect male face that she'd ever seen.

The rest of him wasn't far from perfect, either. She'd had no fear that his strong arms would keep her from falling when he'd dipped her. His shoulders were broad, easy to hold on to, and he was just the right height. Not too tall and not too short.

It was a thrill to dance with him. He was energetic and knew a few dance steps that she hadn't, but had figured them out by easily following his lead. His timing and rhythm were perfect, and tremors of exhilaration ran over her skin at the chance to dance with him again.

As the band struck the first notes of the dance-off, she threw her head back in laughter at how he bent down and crisscrossed his arms and knees in the Charleston dance style.

She loved the Charleston! Copying his movements, she grasped his hand when he caught a hold of hers and danced side by side with him, kicking their legs high and in time with each other.

He gave her hand a tug, and held their hands overhead as she twirled, and then, side by side, they launched into the fast side kicks of the jitterbug while holding hands.

Christopher Columbus, but this guy could dance! Unlike the other sailors she danced with, he held all of her attention. She'd known he would, right from the start. There was something about him that had caught her attention from that first glance, like when a person is window-shopping and sees something that they can't forget.

They danced forward and backward while kicking their feet, and twirled about, met up and tangoed cheek to cheek before starting it all over again. He was in tune with her every move, and she his. They never missed a beat, never slipped a step as they danced across the entire dance floor, from the open side, to the band, and back again.

At times, they danced around other couples, and at other times, they'd release hands and separate, each of them slide-stepping around other sets of dancers in between them, all the while keeping their eyes on each other, silently communicating. When they'd meet back up after passing another couple, he'd grasp her hand and she'd twirl until her back met his chest, then loop an arm around his neck as he danced them forward.

She felt like Ginger Rogers and he was her Fred Astaire.

The Fred Astaire she'd been looking to find.

The music continued without a break, and even though her legs were getting tired and she was breathing hard, she never slowed. Couldn't because her partner never slowed. That was fine with her. She didn't want to slow down. The way he continued to catch her around the waist every so often and dip her over his arm was too much fun.

Every time he did that, or she would twirl into his shoulder and look up at his face, her heart did a tiny flip. He was more than a ducky shin-cracker, he had an appeal about him. A genuine appeal that might have left her breathless if she wasn't already having a hard time catching her breath.

"They are dropping out like flies," he said.

She glanced around, noting that there were only a few couples left on the floor. "Biting flies?"

He laughed.

Sweat was trickling down the back of her neck, her heart was hammering, and she had to suck in a breath of air in order to ask, "Getting tired?"

"I'm not quitting until the last dog is hung," he replied.

"Me, neither." Although she had to admit, "Twenty minutes is a long time."

He lifted their hands, she twirled, and he dipped her over his arm. "Think of the band. They've been playing nonstop. That can't be easy."

"You're right." If the band could keep blowing their horns and beating their drums, she could keep dancing. Back upright, she caught the edges of her skirt with both hands and swished it playfully around her knees as she danced all the way around him.

Laughing, he grasped her waist when they came face-to-face again, and lifted her off her feet. She planted her hands on his shoulders, and as he held her so her face was above his, he danced in a circle before setting her back down on her feet.

She kept her hands on his shoulders as they danced a bit slower until it felt as if she'd caught her second wind, then she let go, hooked arms with him and they side-kicked their way across the floor.

Along the way, she counted other couples on the floor. "Five."

"That's what I counted, too," he said.

They pivoted about, and started back in the other direction, this time facing each other and holding hands as they kept their feet moving in time with the music.

"What do we win, if we win?" he asked.

"I have no idea, but we will win," she answered.

"I like the way you think, Nebraska," he said, releasing one hand.

There was no doubt in her mind that they would triumph; she did, however, wonder why he'd never seen all the places she'd mentioned earlier. She'd done all of that, and more, within her first couple of weeks here.

Every day she had off was another adventure. Tomorrow, she planned on taking the jitney to Honolulu to see the Iolani Palace. She'd never seen a palace before, and even though it was now the capitol building of the Territory of Hawaii, she figured it would still count. That was worth the forty cents it would cost for the jitney ride there and back.

She wondered if he'd like to see the palace. Probably not if he hadn't seen all the other things, unless he hadn't seen them because he didn't have anyone to see them with. Not everyone liked going places alone. She didn't mind it, but company was always nice. He would be fun, she was sure of that, but she'd never gone anywhere with anyone except other nurses.

He tugged on her hand, and she twirled beneath their clutched hands and kicked a leg in the air as he dipped her. Then, with both feet back on the floor, she laid one hand on his shoulder, and still holding his other hand, matched his steps in a quick, almost waltz-like flight across the floor.

She had never laughed so much in her life. All it took was one look at the smile on his face, and the happiness inside her exploded, simply burst and had to be let out.

As they reached the other side, a loud crash and clanging sound from cymbals being clapped together filled the air. It was a moment before she realized the music had ended.

Looking at her, with a huge smile, he said, "Congratulations."

She twisted her neck, looking around him, and behind her, and realized they were the only ones on the dance floor.

As the emcee pronounced them the winners, she looped her arms around his neck and let out an excited squeal. He grasped her waist and lifted her off the floor.

She kicked her feet in the air, while hugging him. "I've never won anything!"

"Now you have!"

He let her down as they became surrounded by people, including the emcee who handed them each a small gold-painted cup trophy. Helen and Lois were there, congratulating her, and someone handed her a bottle. She was so thirsty that she drank half of it before realizing it was a beer. She'd never liked the taste of beer, but drank the rest of it, because she was still thirsty, and continued thanking people who were congratulating her.

The emcee was soon on the loudspeaker again, talking about the next band that would start playing soon, but Wendy wasn't listening, she was looking for Oklahoma.

She didn't know when or how they'd become separated, and scanned the crowd that was now clearing off the dance floor. He was taller than most and she spotted him already on the other side of the room.

He caught her gaze, lifted up his trophy, and gave her a nod, before turning back to the sailors surrounding him.

Wendy let out a long sigh, happy they'd won, but sad it was over.

"Who is that?" Lois asked, staring across the room.

"Yes, what's his name?" Helen wanted to know, eyes in the same direction.

Wendy held the trophy against her chest, where her

heart was thudding in a peculiar way. "I have no idea what his name is," she admitted.

If she'd ever had a regret, that might be it. Not knowing her Fred Astaire's real name.

Chapter Two

K.T. sat at his desk, spinning the square wooden base of the little gold-painted trophy around in circles. For the life of him, he couldn't wipe the smile off his face. Nor could he stop thinking about Nebraska. He'd tried every waking moment since leaving the dance last night, and since crawling out of bed earlier this morning. She'd even snuck in on his dreams.

Her joy of dancing, spirited nature, and her womanly curves were damn hard to get out of his mind. He'd thought writing a letter to Betty would help, but all he'd managed to pen was the date and greeting. Though there had been no engagement before he'd left home, there was the expectation it would happen when he returned. She'd been his girl for years, and he imagined spending the rest of their lives together, but he knew that not all men returned from war, and refused to make a promise that could turn her into a widow. He didn't expect anything to happen to him, nor want it to, but he was a realist. If anything did happen to him, he wanted Betty to go on with her life, not pine over a dead husband.

He'd changed tactics then, thought he'd write his mother a letter, tell her about the Battle of the Music, but the paper before him was completely empty, because he was afraid that if he mentioned the bands, he'd start writing about the dance-off, and how he'd won. She'd like to hear about that. The radio in their house had always been playing music and he imagined it still was that way. His mother loved music and had taught him to dance shortly after he'd learned to walk. As well as all of his siblings. Saturday nights was dance night at their house, unless of course there was a real dance happening elsewhere.

Not a single one back home could have compared to the one last night. Nor could another dancer compare to Nebraska.

It was concerning how a peculiar flicker happened inside him whenever he thought about her, and dancing with her. That had never happened before, and he'd met a lot of women since leaving Oklahoma. Betty, and knowing she was back home, waiting on him always won out, and it confused him as to why that hadn't happened last night.

He'd never been doll-dizzy. Ever.

He probably just needed a bit of time. Last night had been more fun than he'd had in years and that was sure to stick with him for a day or two. Accepting that had to be it, and that the smart thing to do would be to just let it fade away, was exactly what he'd do. He'd been in Pearl Harbor for three months and hadn't run into her before, so it was unlikely that he would again. Unless he attended another dance. That was an easy enough thing to avoid.

Without knowing anything except her love of dancing, and her hate of biting black flies, and a few other things, he wouldn't even be able to find her if he went looking.

Flustered by his inability to control his own thoughts, he pushed away from his desk, rose, and strolled to the door. His unit was unique in the sense that they weren't assigned to any ship and therefore lived in a barracks located within the navy yard's industrial area that was still being built as part of preparation for war. His was a private room, hosting a bed, dresser, and desk. He didn't need anything more, and would gladly bunk with his unit when construction of the upper floors was complete and these lower rooms were used for other things. He had no need for housing as other supervisors received, or even some of the married men in his unit, because he had no need for a home here. Had no family here. They were all back in Oklahoma. That's where his home was, too.

Wearing a pair of navy-issued white shorts and button-up shirt, he walked down the hall and out of the main door. The USS *Pennsylvania* was in dry dock and that's the direction he headed, to take a look at how the overall repairs were coming along. That was another thing he loved about his job. The opportunity to engineer repairs. Come up with ways to make things better than new.

Though many would still be sleeping, for that was permitted on Sundays, there was already movement happening around the base. The faint sounds of morning songs being played by ship bands could be heard, and his smile was back, remembering last night.

She was the best dancer he'd ever met. It was as if they'd known each other's moves before they'd even happened. The way her eyes sparkled, and those dimpled cheeks, why, any man would have been enchanted dancing with her. That's all he'd done, was dance with her, so there was no reason to dwell on it so deeply.

There was work to be done here, and that's what he needed to focus on. Every ship had to be ready for action.

He arrived at the ship, waved to the civilian drydock worker who was already manning the massive crane beside the ship that moved the iron in place, and made his way aboard. The familiar, yet odd buzz of aircraft coming closer caused him to look over toward Ford Island, wondering why the flyboys were at it so early. Especially on a Sunday.

Ford Island looked quiet, and he shifted his gaze, scanning the air.

As if out of nowhere and looking like a flock of angry birds, a massive group of aircraft came into view over the ocean, heading straight for the harbor. More than he could count. His guts knotted with an odd sense of premonition, even before he saw the red dots on the planes.

He ran, shouting, and pointing to the sky. "Command battle stations! We're being attacked!" He pounded on anything close at hand to make more noise all the while running. "Command battle stations! This isn't a drill! Attack! Incoming!"

He ran toward the stern of the ship, to the turrets housing the battle guns as the ship came to life. Men wearing nothing but their underclothes were soon racing alongside him, shouting about the attack.

Within seconds, all hell broke loose.

The incoming planes fired at everything in sight,

and bombs fell from plane bellies, creating an explosive, fiery pandemonium.

Focused on acting, not thinking, K.T. manned a gun, and began firing at the planes overhead. They flew low enough he could see the pilots. See the whites of their eyes and the smiles on their faces.

It was a full-blown attack. A life and death attack. War.

The war had reached America, and all he could think was to defend. He had to defend his country. His compatriots. His homeland!

Men around him were firing guns, too, and the sounds filling the air were deafening, but he heard someone say something about the crane.

K.T. saw the crane boom moving back and forth and realized the cab of the fifty-foot boom gave the operator a vision they didn't have. "He's signaling us! Showing us where to aim! He can see the fighter planes coming before we can! Keep firing!"

Within no more than a matter of minutes since he'd first seen the planes, black smoke surrounded him and everything else, encompassing the entire harbor, making it nearly impossible to see anything. The sounds of plane engines, bombs hitting their targets, gunfire, and more, so much more, merged into thunderous mayhem.

Through breaks in the black smoke, he saw chaos, too.

Flames were everywhere, including in the water from the fuel oil being spewed by bombed ships. The water, the ships, the ground shook from the assaults that just kept coming. Plane after plane. There seemed to be no end to them.

American planes were taking flight, battling the

incoming enemy planes midair, and every battle station on the ships and the ground were manned, firing back at the enemy.

Next to Ford Island, the USS *Arizona* took a direct hit, and exploded with a fiery inferno. Through the billowing black smoke, all he could see was the stern, sticking out of the water at a ninety-degree angle. Also hit, the USS *Oklahoma* had rolled onto her side and was going down. The USS *California* was on fire, and sinking, and other ships were ablaze.

K.T.'s gun clicked. He tried again, and again, but was out of ammunition.

The entire harbor had become a raging firestorm. Smoke, fire, explosions, in every direction. And men. Hundreds of them on the ships and in the water, trying to swim to safety through the blazing oil-coated surface while planes continued to fly overhead, firing bullets, and dropping more bombs.

He told himself to focus, not on the calamity, but on what he could do. He wasn't a gunner. He was a diver, and could do more good in the water than up here.

K.T. turned his weapon over to a gunner who was ready to reload and ran all the way down to the dock, and leaped into one of the many lifeboats going out into the harbor to save as many as possible.

Ships were sinking, with men in them, and he had to get them out now, while there was a chance to save them. Flames raced over the top of the water, yet men jumped off ships, taking a chance on diving through the flames rather than becoming entombed in a sinking ship.

He started pulling oil-coated men into the lifeboat. Some didn't have the strength to get in the boat, and he dove overboard to hoist them up over the edge. There was over a foot of oil on top of the water, and more men beneath it. Men who needed his help.

Time ceased to exist as K.T. dove under the water, swam downward, found men trying to swim to safety, and others attempting to escape through holes blasted in the massive hulls of the ships. One by one, he dragged them to the surface, to a rescue boat, then dove down again for another one. And another one.

And another one.

He refused to quit until every last one he could save, was saved.

The day had started out so normally, so commonplace, until a buzz had sounded. Then, just like the biting black flies back home, the attack had come out of nowhere. Totally unexpected, and far worse than imaginable.

Wendy had gone from shaking and scared out of her wits when she'd heard the first blasts of bombs striking and the blaring sirens, to being too busy to worry about what was happening outside of the hospital. She entered a machinelike routine of laying down blankets and pillows on the floor of the hallways for the men being carried in by the dozens. At first, she'd had gurneys, then cots and pads, but quickly ran out of them. When a spot opened up, all she had was a thin blanket to pad the floor and a pillow for their head.

A clearing station had been set up near the docks, to take care of the minor wounds and injuries, those sent to the hospital were the most severely injured. Injuries like she'd never imagined.

People who were injured themselves helped carry others in, and some would collapse on the spot. Despite the calamity and the speed of needed response, the hospital remained composed; everyone instinctively knew what needed to be done, and did so in a quick and orderly manner.

Wendy remained true to that, too. Tears stung her eyes, but she kept them at bay because it would be selfish to cry when so many were suffering. Many of the injured were burned. The smell of singed hair and burnt skin permeated the entire hospital. As did the smell of the fuel oil that coated the men who'd been in the water. Her heart ached for each one of them and she tried to offer comforting words and solace while seeing to their needs.

There was no time for paperwork, or to even learn the names of the injured. Charge nurses triaged patients by marking their foreheads.

Wendy, following orders of the nurses in command administered morphine shots to those marked with an *M* and tetanus antitoxin for those marked with a *T*. Those they marked with a *C*, for critical, she'd assign to an operating bay, and for those with an *F*, meaning they were fatally wounded, she'd administer sedatives as instructed and find another pillow or blanket in hopes of making them as comfortable as possible.

The nurses who weren't able to find a marker, because they were all being used, made do by using the tubes of lipstick in their pockets to mark foreheads.

Bright red lipstick.

She'd never be able to wear that color again without thinking of today.

She also assisted the charge nurses in starting IVs, and lost count of the times that while swabbing alcohol on a man's arm, his skin would peel away. She could only imagine the pain the patients had to be in, and it made her work harder, faster, to see each and every one of them received care as quickly as possible.

She tried her hardest to not search each patient, looking for a familiar face. Any one of them could have been someone she'd met since arriving here, or a sailor that she'd danced with, just last night even. She didn't want to recognize any of them. Truly didn't.

Each time she carried soiled linens to the laundry and collected clean ones to lay down in the hallways, she told herself that they'd stop coming soon.

It was a lie.

Wives and family members of sailors had come to the hospital to volunteer. Many delivered food and drinks to not only the patients, but the nurses and doctors, to keep them going.

The pace didn't slow down all day, and when night fell, it brought along another set of concerns. A blackout was issued. There again, volunteers took on the job of covering every window in the hospital. Flashlights were the only lights allowed, and due to being limited in numbers, only specific people had them, but that didn't stop Wendy from doing what needed to be done.

It was after midnight, when Nurse Manning told Wendy to return to her quarters, get some sleep, and return by eight in the morning for the day shift. She hated leaving, knowing there were so many who needed care, but the halls were empty, which in itself seemed implausible when she remembered how they'd been lined with the injured mere hours ago.

She left the hospital and once outside, questioned what good the blackout would do. The entire harbor was ablaze, leaving a smoky red haze in the air, along with the scent of burning oil.

It was a short walk to her living quarters, yet there were armed guards every few steps.

"That way, miss." One of the sentries gestured with his gun, pointing it toward the opposite side of the building from where she'd been heading.

It was too dark to see beyond him. "Can't I use the outside stairway?" Her berthing room was on the second floor, in the back of the building, close to the outside stairway.

"No," he said quietly. "The vacant quarters building was hit, burned to the ground. The fire's been put out, but the plane that crashed into it is in the field next to it. The area is off-limits."

Her heart began to race. She hadn't been aware of a plane crashing. The vacant quarters building was directly behind her living quarters. Knowing how close the hospital had been to being destroyed was frightening. Her aunt Ella's voice sounded inside her.

"Things could always be worse."

Aunt Ella had said that very often, and though it was hard to imagine after all she'd seen today, Wendy knew it was true. The hospital could have been hit, as well as many, many other buildings.

"Do you think there will be another attack?" she asked.

"Hard to say, miss, but our boys are in the air and any ship that could sail is out on the water. We won't be taken by surprise again."

Again.

She had never imagined that there would have been a first time. The repercussions of what had happened were very real. She felt guilty that she'd once looked at all of this as a vacation instead of the dire straits that it truly was and would continue to be for a long time to come.

"Good night," she said, though it was doubtful that anyone on the island, or elsewhere, would have a good night.

The inside of the building was eerily quiet. It was always quiet this late, but tonight, everything felt eerie. The exact opposite of last night, when she'd been on top of the world carrying home her little gold-painted trophy.

Lois and Helen were asleep in their beds, and she quietly collected her nightclothes and walked down the hall to take a shower. The smell of fuel oil and other things couldn't be washed away, and would live with her forever, but a shower now would save time in the morning. It would also allow her to shed the tears she'd kept bottled up all day without anyone hearing.

She had taken her training in California seriously; learned how to take temperatures, blood pressures, pulses, wrap bandages, and give shots, as well as the training she'd continued to receive since arriving in Hawaii while working at the hospital, but she'd felt so inadequate today. There had been so many times when she'd wished that she could have done more for the patients.

Beneath the warm water of the shower, she let the tears flow. All the training in the world wouldn't have been able to save many of the men she'd seen today. It was all so sad.

So very sad.

Although exhausted when she climbed into bed,

sleep still took a long time coming because her mind wouldn't shut off. Thoughts of so many things kept circling, including wondering about people. Those she knew, those she'd recently met. Wondering and wondering if they had survived the attack.

When morning arrived, she dressed in a bleached-white uniform, including apron, hose, and shoes, attached her hat with two bobby pins, buckled her watch on her wrist, and walked to the hospital. The devastation of the base that couldn't be seen in the darkness last night was there this morning, and though she tried not to look, it couldn't be unseen.

Nor could the scent of burning fuel oil not be smelled.

The destruction and loss increased her determination to do all she could for those who needed help now. That was why she was here and that was what she would do.

She entered the hospital, and went to the main nurse's station for her daily assignments.

"Good morning, Nurse Smith," Nurse Manning greeted. "I'll need you to assist me this morning."

Though she was technically a Red Cross aide, they were all addressed as nurse. Wendy wanted to ask Nurse Manning if she'd been there all night, for it appeared so. Her hat was slightly askew and her hair that was peppered with gray was falling from the pins holding it up in the back, but that wasn't her place, and she silently fell in step beside the nurse.

"A sailor was brought in after midnight last night," Nurse Manning said. "He'd refused to come in before, insisting that others needed care first. The skin on his upper back and shoulders was severely burned by the fuel in the water, but he wouldn't stop until others were rescued. He used a torch to cut holes in hulls of sunken ships to get trapped men out, until he collapsed and they brought him in. His burns are deep and need special attention. I used a tincture of green soap and water to cleanse the wounds last night, it was a tedious and painful process for him, even with the morphine. He will need to remain on his stomach in bed for at least two weeks and will need specific care."

Wendy nodded as she listened. Yesterday, she'd been taught how to spray tannic acid solution on burn victims, the fastest way to cover large burns.

"We will be using a different method on this patient," Nurse Manning continued. "I will show you the ingredients that will be mixed with mineral oil. Dressings will be soaked in that solution, then laid over the burned areas, and changed every four hours."

"Yes, ma'am," Wendy replied. Everyone agreed that Nurse Manning was the best charge nurse at the hospital.

They entered a working station, and Nurse Manning paused near the table. She drew in a deep sigh and squared her shoulders in a way that piqued Wendy's nerves.

Nurse Manning turned and there were unshed tears in her eyes. "I requested permission from the ward officer to be able to see to this patient personally, and I requested that you be my assistant, because I've seen you work. I know how precise and unwavering you are in tasks. Both requests have been granted."

Wendy nodded, taking in how the middle-aged nurse's hands shook. "Is this patient someone you know?" There were nurses who were married to sailors, or dating them, or had brothers and cousins stationed here with them.

"No, I've never seen him before last night." Nurse Manning lifted her chin a bit higher. "But I've seen burns like this before. Many others in the hospital are just as serious and they will all receive the best care possible. I asked for this patient because though his burns are severe, they are confined mainly to his upper back, shoulders, and upper arms. I believe with the proper care, he will heal quickly and return to duty."

"I see," Wendy replied.

Nurse Manning gave her head a small, quick shake. "I will tell you what I told the ward officer this morning. Something I hadn't told anyone in a very long time. Over ten years ago, I was living in Kansas, and I kept a small can of kerosene behind the stove, to help me light the stove fires. My son was four years old and inside taking a nap. I was outside washing clothes and don't know what happened exactly, but I heard him screaming. I ran inside and he was completely engulfed in flames. The tin of kerosene was empty and the fire box door on the stove was open." She paused and wiped at the corners of her eyes with her fingertips.

Wendy had a hard time breathing, imagining the scene just described.

"We didn't have a telephone or automobile. Just a tractor and my husband had taken that to town. I wrapped my son in a wet sheet and ran two miles to the neighbors. They gave me a ride to town, to the doctor who worked out of his house. We stayed there for three days, then he told me to take my son home. That there was nothing more that he could do for him. I kept putting lard on the burns, like the doctor had done, but infection had already set in, and within days, my son died."

"I am so sorry," Wendy whispered, holding back her own tears.

"Three months later, my husband took me to town, where I signed divorce papers that I had known nothing about, and then he took me to the train station, purchased a ticket, and gave me three one-dollar bills." Nurse Manning cleared her throat. "He said that he couldn't be married to a woman who would let her own son die."

"But you didn't let him," Wendy whispered, her voice shaky. She couldn't imagine a husband treating a wife like that. Couldn't imagine anyone being so cruel. Until she remembered her own father, who had left her mother before she'd been born. A bitterness filled her at how a man could ruin a woman's life. Turn it into something she'd never wanted. "You did everything you could."

"But it wasn't enough—my son had died." Nurse Manning drew in a breath. "I ended up in Kansas City, went to work at a hospital and earned enough money to put myself through nursing school, so I could save lives. When I heard nurses were needed for the war effort, I enlisted immediately. And though I would never have wished that all of my studying of burn patients would be needed, it is now. If I can prove my therapies work with this one patient, they may be incorporated into the care of others, helping many, many more."

Wendy's determination to help increased tenfold and she listened carefully as Nurse Manning explained they'd work overlapping sixteen-hour shifts, with each of them working eight hours alone while the other one slept. She also gave permission to call her by her first name, Gloria, and said they both would still need to complete duties with other patients.

"Of course," Wendy replied. "I fully understand."

Nurse Manning then turned to the table. "All right then, I'll show you what needs to be mixed with the mineral oil. We will be using sulfa drugs, tannic acid jelly and solution, picric acid, gentian violet, and triple dye, with and without silver nitrate, and sulfanilamide powder, but not all together and in different quantities."

Wendy paid very close attention, and made a few notes while watching the process so she'd be fully prepared when the time came for her to do the applications by herself. She also listened carefully as Gloria told her about their patient. He was from a specialty unit. Underwater welding and his ability to return to duty was critical for the rebuilding of all the damaged ships. His name was Lieutenant Kent McCallister, and he had saved numerous lives yesterday, even after his clothing had been burned off his body. Besides his shoulders, arms, and back, he had smaller burns on the backs of his calves.

After the sterile dressings were put to soak in the mixture, Gloria instructed Wendy to collect another basin for the dressings they would remove and to follow her. The patient was in one of the smaller wards, with only three other patients, who would also be under their care.

Rolling white curtain walls separated the four patients. An IV bottle was hung on the pole at the top of his bed, which was near the wall, and he was lying on his stomach, with both arms laid at his sides, bent at the elbows so his hands were on the mattress near his ears. His upper back, shoulders, and upper arms were draped with dressings, and a sheet covered him from his lower back to the back of his knees, then more dressings covered his calves.

"We'll keep him strapped to the bed so he doesn't try to roll over in his sleep," Gloria said, lifting the sheet enough to show that two sets of bed straps went across his lower back and thighs. "And will keep administering morphine for several days to keep the pain from being too excruciating. Which means he'll sleep most of the time."

Wendy pushed the wheeled cart up next to his bed and the moment she looked down on the man's face, her breath stalled in her lungs. Even with one side of his face lying on the pillow and his eyes closed, she recognized him, and her heart constricted tightly inside her chest.

"Oklahoma," she whispered to herself. "Oh, Oklahoma."

He had been the main sailor that she hadn't wanted to recognize yesterday. Refusing to let tears form or think of other outcomes, she sucked in a deep breath and vowed that she now had even more reasons to make sure that Gloria's treatments worked. She would have wanted that for any sailor, but as selfish as it seemed even to her, she wanted it even more for Oklahoma.

As gently as possible, Wendy assisted Gloria in removing the dressing from the backs of his arms, shoulders, and neck. The severity of the burns had the ability to take her breath away, but she didn't let it. This was her job, therefore, she examined his injuries carefully, so she could keep track of healing, and watch closely for infection.

She and Gloria discussed his condition, including how having his head turned to one side wouldn't allow the back of his neck to heal well. Through their conversation as to what could be done about that, Wendy had the idea that a hole needed to be cut through the mattress for his face.

The idea had come to her because several years ago, Mrs. Gardner, their neighbor back home, had slipped on the ice and broken her tailbone; Aunt Ella had sewn Mrs. Gardner a pillow with a hole in the middle for her to sit on and take pressure off her tailbone. It was an odd comparison, and she and Gloria agreed to not tell anyone from where the idea had originated.

"It'll mean moving him again," Gloria said, "but it's necessary for proper healing."

After they'd seen to all of Oklahoma's needs, they went over the other patients in the ward before Gloria took her leave to find out about having a mattress equipped.

Wendy completed a round of the other three men, and made a point of getting to know a little about each one of them.

John Taylor was nineteen, with a happy-go-lucky personality from New York, and had a broken left leg and arm, caused by being blown out of his bunk. He'd had surgery early that morning to have the bone set in his leg.

Wes Henderson was thirty-two, nice and polite, from Wyoming, with bullet holes in his shoulder. He'd been hit while reloading his machine gun and had gone through surgery yesterday to have three bullets removed. He was married, his wife, Faye, lived on the base with him and was an active volunteer at the hospital. Wendy shared that she'd met his wife on numerous occasions in the past and liked her bubbly personality. Wes grinned from ear to ear, hearing that.

The last patient was eighteen-year-old David Gomez, from California, who had a long and deep gash on his right thigh from shrapnel when the USS *West Virginia* had been hit. His brother Robert had also been on the ship, and David was still waiting to hear if his brother was alive or not.

Once Wendy made sure all of their needs were seen to, she walked back over to Oklahoma's bed, checked that his dressings were still all in place, and then leaned down, whispered in his ear, "Expect another trophy, Oklahoma. We are going to win this one, too. I promise."

Then, although she would like to wait by his side, just in case he needed something, he was only one of the many patients in the hospital and she left the room to complete other duties while awaiting the arrival of the new mattress.

She'd never had a personal connection to a patient before, but already recognized that it made her job more difficult. Waiting for healing to occur wasn't an easy task for anyone, not patient or nurse, and right now, she wanted nothing shy of a miracle.

K.T. tried to open his eyes, but they were too heavy. The room was spinning. Or maybe he was spinning. Or just being moved. He wasn't sure. His head was foggy and his body ached. More than ached. It hurt, a lot. Parts of it. Other parts, he couldn't feel. It was as if they were numb and he didn't have the ability to concentrate enough to know what was numb and what hurt. All he knew was the sensation of being moved made the pain unbearable and he gave in to the darkness pulling him downward.

There was no relief in the darkness. He was under the water, searching for a way into the submerged hull where he could hear men knocking on the other side. They were trapped and he had to get them out. But he couldn't. He tried and tried, but couldn't. Couldn't save them because he was being held down. Held down under the water.

His lungs were burning, in need of air, and he had to surface, but when he broke through his confinement and swam upward, he was no longer in the water. He was back at home. In his family's living room, with the radio playing. His mother was dancing with him. They waltzed around the furniture, laughing.

She was happy, as usual, which always surprised him considering her unhappy childhood. She'd been eleven when her father had left. Just up and left his wife and five children. Ran off with another woman, is what his mother had said, and that they never heard from him again. His mother had never been shy about sharing that story, and said that a man like that wasn't worth spit. She'd told all of her children how difficult that had made her life. How she'd had to leave school and work as a laundry maid to help feed her siblings.

She'd drilled into them how important it was to keep promises, and remain committed to those who depend upon you, and she'd told them to never forget that they were a McCallister. As if the name held great significance. It was why he couldn't promise to marry Betty when he knew he might not return.

Then, suddenly, he was dancing with Nebraska. Having the time of his life, until the dance floor became flooded, then he was trying to find her, to save her.

He couldn't find her, couldn't save her, there were too many people.

His heart was pounding, his lungs burning, and he tried harder, but he couldn't move.

It had to be a dream. He had to be dreaming and he tried to wake himself, but his eyelids wouldn't open. He couldn't breathe either; it was as if something was holding him down, keeping him lying on his stomach. Even his head was confined.

He fought harder, tried to move, tried to wake up, until he heard Nebraska's voice. It had to be her because she was calling him Oklahoma, and telling him to lie still, that everything would be okay. That he just needed to sleep.

Her hand was holding his, and his entire body relaxed, knowing he'd found her. He gave up his futile attempts to open his eyes and let the overpowering darkness surround him again. This time, though, it was more like a heavy, warm blanket that offered comfort and a dreamless sleep.

That occurred over and over again. Where he tried to wake up, only to be sucked deep into nightmares filled with water and fire, and dancing, and trying to find people.

He had no idea how many times that happened before he'd finally been able to open his eyes, only to wonder if he was deep inside yet another nightmare. Attempting to clear his vision, he blinked several times. Nothing changed. All he could see was a tile floor, through a grid of springs.

That's what they appeared to be, but it was dark;

there was barely enough light to see more than shapes. He tried to move, but sharp pain, concentrated across his upper shoulders, stopped him. He was lying on his stomach, and couldn't lift his head more than half an inch, certainly not enough to see anything besides the floor.

His mind was foggy and he closed his eyes, struggling to focus on what he last remembered. As memories formed, his heart began to race and he tried harder to move. The attack. The entire harbor ablaze. Ships sinking. There still had to be men to save. To find.

"Whoa," someone said quietly.

It was a female voice, but not the one from his dreams.

"It's all right," she continued. "I'm Nurse Manning. You're in the hospital. We've been lessening your morphine doses and waiting for you to wake."

"Why am I in the hospital?"

"You have burns on your neck, back, shoulders, and the backs of your arms and legs. That's why you're on your stomach."

His throat plugged. It had happened. This was why he'd never made promises he couldn't keep. "How bad is it?"

"Serious," she said quietly, and then continued to explain his burns in detail.

While taking it all in he said he remembered rescuing men, and more, but he still needed to collect all of his bearings. "Can I sit up?"

"No, not for a while yet, and then only for short times. How bad is your pain?"

He questioned what to say. If he said it wasn't bad, would she let him up?

As if reading his mind, she said, "You aren't getting

up whether you lie or tell the truth. I need to know in order to regulate your morphine doses."

He'd heard enough about morphine to know that was part of the reason for his strange dreams. The other part was simply his mind. Reliving what had happened. "The others. The men in the ships, have they all been rescued?"

"From what I heard, you rescued a fair share all by yourself," she replied.

There were still more. He knew that for certain. Growing more frustrated, he asked, "How long have I been here?"

"This is your fourth night," she answered. "How bad is your pain and where does it hurt the most?"

"Not too bad," he replied honestly. But as soon as he admitted that, the pain intensified in specific areas. His shoulders and back, but his neck was the worst. "The back of my neck feels like it's on fire."

"The skin on the neck is very sensitive. Nurse Smith came up with the idea to cut a hole in the mattress for your face, and it's worked out very well to keep the pressure off your neck. I'll change the dressings on your neck and the coolness of the solution will help. So will the morphine."

"I don't want more morphine." Though some parts of his memory were vivid, the rest was hazy at best. This woman sounded nothing like Nebraska. His frustration grew even more, knowing he had no way of finding her. No way of knowing if she had survived the attack. "I need to be able to think straight."

Other people and names were entering his mind. Men from his unit and others. So many others that he needed to know about. It was hard to stomach his condition and the fact that he was in the hospital rather than out in the harbor helping to save others. Rather than being out there with his unit, rebuilding ships that needed to be able to sail, to defend America.

"Right now, the only thing you need to think about is getting better," she said.

How could he focus on getting better when there were things he needed to do? He felt her removing something, a blanket, or bandages from his back, but the grogginess was returning. He fought against it, but it soon was enveloping his mind again, and he was losing feeling again, like parts of him were going numb.

Then, he could no longer keep his eyes open.

Chapter Three

Arriving at the hospital a full half hour ahead of time, Wendy went straight to her workstation to prepare the solution for Oklahoma's dressings. She'd had a hard time sleeping last night. They'd been slowly lowering his doses of morphine yesterday, and all night she'd wondered if he'd awakened while she'd been gone.

Several times in the past three days, he'd been restless and mumbling, and she'd held his hand, whispered that all would be okay, because that was all she'd been able to do.

"Good morning," Gloria said, entering the room. "I have good news. Dr. Bloomberg was in to see our patient early this morning and confirmed that there is no infection as of yet."

Wendy instantly knew who Gloria referred to. Even though they knew his name, she called him our patient, while Wendy continuously thought of him as Oklahoma.

"That is wonderful news," she said, pressing a hand to the increased beat of her heart. She was overly pleased for many reasons. Burns became infected easily. Others in the hospital were already experiencing that.

"And," Gloria continued, "he woke up last night."

"He did?" Wendy's happiness grew.

"Yes, he did," Gloria replied with a touch of warning, but her smile showed her delight in what had happened. "He still has a lot of healing to do."

"He does," Wendy agreed while gradually mixing the solution in the basin. "But I fully believe that your procedures are working better than all the others." During her sixteen-hour shifts, she assisted in several other wards and was sure the solution-soaked dressings were working far better than spraying the tannic acid solution on the burns. She sincerely hoped that would soon be proven so that others could receive the same treatments.

"Dr. Bloomberg commented on it positively, but it will be a few more days before we can make any real comparisons." Gloria laid the dressings in the solution one by one. "Dr. Bloomberg said our patient could begin eating solid food this evening, and I'm quite worried that it will be extremely difficult to keep him on his stomach once that happens. He appears to be very strong-willed."

"Well, we'll just have to think of ways to do that," Wendy said, knowing he wasn't one to back down from a challenge. "There is too much at risk not to."

"I agree, and that is exactly why I requested you to be my assistant. We think alike." Gloria picked up the basin and placed it on the rolling cart. "Our other patients all had a restful night."

Wendy listened as they walked out of the station and Gloria filled her in on their other patients. They were each doing well in their own right, and she was working behind the scenes to help find David Gomez's brother,

Robert. She'd sent out inquires as to his whereabouts, but it was a slow process. Many of the fallen and injured had not been wearing ID tags. Along with many other changes put in place, everyone was now required to wear ID tags at all times, including all of the hospital staff.

So many things had changed within the past few days, since the attack. Armed patrol guards were stationed everywhere, foxholes and trenches were being dug, and bomb shelters were being created. Families of servicemen who had been living at the base, all the bases, had been evacuated to Honolulu, and word was that those evacuated would soon be required to return to the States. That had cut down greatly on the number of volunteers helping at the hospital.

Except for Wes Henderson's wife, Faye. She'd refused to be evacuated, as had a few other wives who didn't have young children or were not pregnant. Faye visited her husband almost hourly and was where Wendy received most of her information about what was happening outside of the hospital walls.

They entered the ward, and Wendy's gaze instantly went to Oklahoma, looking for a sign if he was awake again or not. It was impossible to tell.

Arriving at his bedside, she gently touched his hand. "Good morning, Lieutenant McCallister."

He let out a low growl sound. "K.T.," he said. "My name is K.T."

Her heart welled with joy that he was awake. "Very well, K.T." She gave his hand a gentle pat. "How are you feeling today?"

"Bound and gagged."

She shared a smile with Gloria, who was standing

on the other side of his bed, at his response. If nothing else, that answer was a display of his will.

"I can understand how it feels that way," Gloria said. "But it's necessary for your healing."

"I need some water," he said. "My mouth feels like I chewed my way through this mattress."

Wendy had thought of that and had come up with a plan, one that Gloria had approved of considering they needed to keep him lying down as much as possible.

"I'll get you one," Wendy said.

Her hands trembled as she walked around the rolling curtain and across the room to a table holding a pitcher of water and drinking glasses amongst other regularly needed items. She told herself that there was nothing to be nervous about, but she was anxious, wondering if he would recognize her or not. His drink of water would come about in an unorthodox way, but it was imperative that he remained on his stomach as much as possible.

She filled a glass with water and picked up the length of tubing she'd collected from the supply closet yesterday. A paper straw wouldn't be long enough to reach through the bed springs. She was convinced this would work, and was also just as convinced that she would do the same for any patient.

Back at his bedside, she handed the glass to Gloria, then lowered herself onto the floor, and making sure the skirt of her dress was smooth beneath her, she laid down on her back. After scooting a short distance beneath the bed, she took the glass of water from Gloria and made her way over until her face was directly beneath his.

It was odd, looking at him through the grid of the bed springs and the mattress framing his face made him look slightly different, but she still would know that face anywhere.

The way his eyes widened said he recognized her, too, even before he whispered, "Nebraska. It is you."

Her stomach did an odd flip-flop as she nodded. "Hello, Oklahoma," she replied, releasing a smile. She carefully worked the length of tubing through the springs and put the other end in the glass. "I hear you're thirsty."

"I am."

She maneuvered the tubing to his mouth, and held it as he took a long drink.

"That's the best water I've ever tasted," he said.

"Because you were thirsty," she rationalized.

"Still am." He took another long drink. "You aren't Nurse Manning."

It was a statement, not a question. "No, I'm not. I'm Red Cross nurse's aide Wendy Smith."

He grinned. "A Smith named Wendy."

With her very common last name, she'd heard that one before, yet her smile increased. "That is correct."

"You've been here, talking to me while I was sleeping."

"I have been." It was a strange way to carry on a conversation, on her back and looking through the metal bed springs. It was also an odd way to drink water, but it was working. He was emptying the glass. All in all, everything about it made her happy.

"Thank you for that," he said, "and for the water."

"You're welcome." She lowered the empty glass, careful that the tube didn't get caught on the bed springs.

"How long will I be like this?"

"That depends upon your healing. You need to remain on your stomach, but starting this evening, we'll help you sit up long enough to eat." Her cheeks heated up as she thought of other reasons that he'd be able to get up. As an aide, she didn't have anything to do with his catheter, other than emptying the bag on the side of the bed, and would leave it to Gloria to explain when that would be removed.

"Until then?" he asked.

She held the glass up toward the springs again. "It's just water."

"Even prisoners get bread with their water," he said.

Her heart was pounding harder than it should because he was smiling. That amazing sailor smile. It was quite remarkable, and very charming, even with his face surrounded by mattress stuffing. Her heart then fluttered as she realized just how serious his injuries were and how lucky they were that he'd survived. "You're going to heal up just fine, Oklahoma," she said quietly. "And quickly. I'll make sure of that."

"I believe you will, Nebraska." He winked one eye. "You like challenges."

"As do you," she said.

He wasn't just handsome. He was an all-around good man. One who had saved many others and deserved to be saved, too. Blinking at the tears that stung her eyes, she slid out from beneath the bed.

Despite the pain encompassing his neck, shoulders, and back, and the uncomfortable position of being tied on his stomach with his head stuffed through a hole in the mattress, K.T. smiled as she disappeared from his sight.

His heart was still working just fine, because he could feel it pounding. It was good to know that he hadn't been dreaming that it had been her talking to him the past few days. He wasn't exactly sure how long it had been. Time, hours, days, had melded together, and he wasn't sure when he'd asked the other nurse how long he'd been here. Last night, maybe? He wasn't even sure what time it was now.

Morning? Afternoon? The room wasn't dark. Not like the last time he'd awoken. There was no longer the heaviness pulling at him, dragging him back into sleep and he appreciated that.

"Can you get word to Seaman Scott Westman?" he asked. "He's in my unit. Our barracks are just south of the industrial yard." Scott was his second-in-command and hopefully had remained uninjured during the attack. There was so much he needed to know. So much that had to be done.

"He will most likely be in to check on you again this evening," Nebraska said. "He's stopped by the last two evenings."

K.T. had heard her response, and had more questions to ask about Scott, but his thoughts had a mind of their own and were focused on the fact that he now knew her name. Wendy Smith. A Red Cross nurse. That explained why he'd never run into her before the dance. There had been no reason or opportunity for that to have happened. She didn't look any different, except for the nurse's cap pinned in her hair rather than a flower. Otherwise, those cute dimples were in her cheeks and there were sparkles in her eyes, although they hadn't been as bright as the night of the dance.

Her spirited personality was still alive and well, too. He told himself that had nothing to do with him. Crawling beneath his bed to provide him water might be part of her job, but she'd completed it with such an animated smile that any patient would have appreciated the act. He was no more special to her or anyone else than the other hundreds of men who had been injured—or worse—during the attack.

He needed information. Needed to know what was happening. "What time is it?"

"A little after eight in the morning."

He closed his eyes at the disappointment washing over him. The answer hadn't come from Nebraska. It was the other nurse. Nurse Manning.

Whatever bandages were on his back were being removed. It wasn't overly painful, other than the smart of air. As a welder, he'd acquired burns numerous times over the years, small ones and larger ones, so knew the sensation well, but this was multiplied by a hundred at least.

The coolness that followed of new bandages being laid down was a welcomed relief, and the process gave him a clearer picture of just where his burns were located. Overall, the removal and replacement had taken a fair amount of time, and despite the fact that he hadn't moved the entire time, he felt worn out by the time it was over.

Suddenly, he wondered if he was naked. He couldn't tell. Couldn't *feel* if he was or not. He tried moving, parts that he could move, and along with pain, he felt the restraints of the bed straps across his lower back and thighs.

God Almighty, he hoped he wasn't lying there bare-ass naked.

K.T. had no memory of falling asleep, but knew the moment he woke up again. He could hear Nebraska talking. Not to him, but someone else. He listened carefully as she explained that someone had been taken to the hospital aboard the USS *Solace* and was healing, would soon be released.

The hospital ship was docked at Ford Island and hadn't taken any direct hits; he remembered that much. Men from the *Solace* had participated in rescuing others.

"Thank you, Wendy," a man answered. "Does he know where I'm at?"

"Yes, I relayed a message on your behalf," she replied.

The two continued to talk, and K.T. figured out the man was another patient, and the person on the *Solace* was his brother that Wendy had searched for until she'd discovered his location and condition. That didn't surprise him. She clearly took her responsibilities beyond nursing tasks.

Her voice filtered into his hearing again, but this time she was farther away and he couldn't make out what she was saying. He thought he heard another woman's voice, and continued to listen with a high degree of hope that she, not another nurse, would soon make her way to his bed.

The soft footsteps were nearly silent, but the hope inside him was granted to fulfillment when he was sure the steps had stopped beside him. It was overly frustrating to not see anything except the floor, because there was no way to know if it was her for sure.

Until he felt a soft touch on the back of his hand and the tingle that worked its way up his arm. Both of his arms were bent at the elbows, so his hands were lying on the mattress near the sides of his head, and like the rest of him, he was unable to move them.

"Hi, Nebraska," he said, certain that was her touching his hand.

"Hello, Oklahoma. How are you feeling?"

"Trapped."

Her sigh was soft. "I know. I would apologize, but you'll heal faster this way."

Once again, he wondered about being naked, yet didn't want to ask, but needed to know. Really needed to know. "Can I have a blanket?" he asked, hoping that would get to the answer without him actually asking.

"Are you cold?" she asked, with a clear alarm in her tone. "Chills? Sweating?"

Her hands were touching his forearms and the back of his head in a way that reminded him of being little, when his mother would check to see if he had a temperature. "No," he said, feeling guilty for causing her concern. "None of that, I just…" He couldn't say it.

"Wondering if your bum is bare for all to see?"

Her whisper tickled the hair behind one ear. "Yes," he admitted, through his humiliation.

"It's not," she whispered. "Whatever isn't covered with dressings is covered with a sheet and blanket. Other than your feet. I can get you a blanket for them, if you'd like."

Relieved, he said, "No. I'm fine."

"Are you thirsty?"

Her breath no longer tickled his hair, and he did his best to redirect any feelings that left.

"I'll get you some water," she said.

He was thirsty, and wanted to see her face again,

but also felt guilty about her having to crawl under the bed. "Can I sit up to drink?"

"No." She patted his hand. "I'll be right back."

A moment later, he sensed she was back and felt an unusual wave of excitement while waiting for her to appear beneath him. The tunnel vision that the mattress caused was annoying, while uniquely increasing the excitement that was growing by the second.

When her face appeared, wearing her dimple-branded smile, he felt a chuckle rumble in his throat. Yet, he felt the need to apologize. "I'm sorry that you have to crawl under the bed." He was sorry about the bum thing, too, but was trying to forget that.

"Don't be. It was my idea to cut the hole in the mattress, and my idea of how you'd be able to at least have some water. Even after you are allowed to sit up, because that will only be for short amounts of time." She was guiding the tube through the springs as she spoke. "Your dressings won't stay on while you're sitting up, and it's imperative to keep the dressings on for healing to occur."

"Are you doing this for all the burned men?" he asked, before taking a sip from the straw. At that moment, he felt a stab of something that he knew he shouldn't feel. He'd never been jealous or envious of anyone, and sure as hell couldn't feel that way over her nursing others.

"No, just you," she said.

He accepted that, and quit struggling to make sense of anything while taking a long drink from the straw. He'd thought working in the hot sun all day was the true precursor for appreciation of a drink of water, but now knew differently.

Still, other thoughts penetrated his head. "Am I your only burn patient?" he asked around the tube straw.

"No, but you are my main burn patient." Her head twisted, as if she was looking around, before she looked up at him again. "We are trying a different approach to your burns with the solution-soaked dressings and have high hopes that once it's proven to work, that we'll be able to apply it to others."

He let that sink in while drinking more water. It was a bit strange swallowing, took a real concentrated effort. "How are the others being treated?"

"The solution is similar, but applied differently. Sprayed on or applied by hand. Nurse Manning suggested this process for you and we both believe it's working. There are no signs of infection."

Any infection could set back his healing, and he sincerely didn't want that. "I thank both of you for all you are doing, and I will do my best to follow your orders." He took a final sip from the tube, emptying the glass. "But I don't want any more morphine."

"But the pain—"

"I will handle the pain," he interrupted. He wasn't here to lie in bed, he was here to fight for his country. If that meant fighting some pain to get back in the action, he'd do it. He would do whatever it took.

She lowered the glass to the floor. "I can't promise that, but I'll talk to Nurse Manning."

"Thank you. I don't mean to put you on the spot, but there's going to be a lot of work to get the fleet back in the water. I can't leave my unit to that alone."

She pinched her lips together and he was sure she was preventing herself from telling him that he might not be able to do the work he had before. The diving and welding. He would be able to. He'd make damn sure of that. He wouldn't hold her thoughts against her, though. She had a job to do just like him. Sometimes that job probably was telling sailors they would be shipped home rather than fulfilling their commitment.

He wasn't one of those men. Wouldn't be one of those men. Returning home as a burden wasn't any more of an option than not returning at all. "I promised four years of service," he said, "and I will keep that promise." For some reason, he wanted her to understand that, understand him. "My mother experienced a broken promise when she was young, one that changed her life, and not for the good. She raised all of her children, me, my brother, and two sisters, to never break a promise." He let the grin tugging on his lips form over the memories of his mother. "When any one of us misbehaved in any manner, she'd asked if we'd forgotten who we were. Then she'd remind us that we were McCallisters, as if that alone was enough for us to know right from wrong."

Nebraska was smiling.

It was surreal how that smile, those dimples, made him feel better. It probably did that to every one of her patients. "Was your mother like that? Or were you one of those girls who never got into trouble while growing up?"

She shook her head as her eyes widened. "Oh, no. I got into trouble, but not from my mother. It was usually my uncle."

"Your uncle?"

"Yes, he was never mean about it." A tiny frown formed between her brows as she continued, "He'd just set me down and say, *'Now, Wendy, you didn't mean to act that way, did you?'* I'd answer no, and he'd say,

'Good, then don't disappoint me by doing it again.' And I wouldn't do it again, because I didn't want to disappoint him." Her smile was back, full force.

"What about your parents?" he asked.

"My mother died when I was twelve, but we lived with my Aunt Ella and Uncle Sy since I was born."

"In Nebraska?"

"Yes. Bridgeport, Nebraska. It's about fifty miles from Scottsbluff, and not much farther than that from either Wyoming or Colorado. It's on the Nebraska Panhandle. Got its name when the train depot and a bridge over the North Platte River were built."

"What about your father?"

She shrugged. "I never knew him. He left while my mother was pregnant with me. She'd been living in Scottsbluff then, and moved to Bridgeport to live with my aunt and uncle. They were actually her aunt and uncle. My great-aunt and great-uncle. They owned the general store in town. My mother worked there for them, but she always wanted to see the world. She'd read books about places and say that we'd see it someday. Then, when she got dust pneumonia, and knew her dreams wouldn't come true, she made me promise that I'd see the world for her."

"That's why you joined the Red Cross?"

She sighed. "It sounds callous considering all that's happened, but yes that's why, and I got in the navy line because it was far shorter than the army line. I had to make sure I was accepted. My aunt and uncle were getting up in years. I knew they wouldn't sell their store as long as I was there. Their children, three of them, were married and had moved away, Sid and Joe to Scottsbluff and Ellen to Denver, so I was the only one to help my aunt and uncle. Sid, who is a lawyer, wanted them to move in with him and his family, so when I heard about the Red Cross recruiting nurses, I told them all that I was going to sign up as soon as I turned twenty-one. It was the one way for everything to work out for everyone."

"Including for you to keep your promise to your mother," he said. "To see the world."

"Yes."

Seeing the honesty in her eyes, he asked, "So you know about promises, too."

"I do, and I will talk to Nurse Manning about the morphine."

"Thank you."

She held up the glass. "Do you need more water?"

"No, thanks. I'll let you get up off the floor."

She glanced at the watch on her wrist. "I don't have to be anywhere for twenty minutes."

"Where do you need to be then?"

Even her grimaces were charming. "That's when I need to mix up the solution for your dressing change."

"Again?"

"Every four hours."

"I slept that long?"

"A body heals during sleep."

"Is that why I'm strapped to the bed like this? So I'll sleep?"

"No, it's so you don't roll over while—"

"Sleeping," he said at the same time she did.

They both laughed.

"So, what part of Oklahoma are you from?" she asked. "I just told you my life story, which you probably didn't want to hear."

"I wanted to know," he admitted. "I wouldn't have asked if I hadn't." He didn't mind telling her more. "We are both panhandlers. I'm from Guymon, Oklahoma, which is in the Oklahoma Panhandle. My folks own a farm there. My little brother, Jud, is fourteen, my sister Holly is seventeen, my other sister Mavis is twenty, and I'm the oldest. I've been called K.T. since birth because my father's name is Kent, too. Kent Edward, and I'm Kent Thomas. My mother's name is Ruth, and her broken promise was similar to yours. Her father left his family when my mother was eleven. She had four younger siblings, and was farmed out as a laundry maid to help feed everyone. She met my father while working at the restaurant in the train station in Kansas City, when he was heading out to fight in the Great War. He promised her that he'd be back in three years to marry her. And he was, and he did."

His father had been one of the lucky ones. He'd shared many stories about men who hadn't returned. Whose promises to wives and fiancées had been broken by the war. The attack that had happened on Pearl Harbor confirmed how right he had been, how quickly men perished. Those men would never return home to loved ones, regardless of what promises they had made. That could easily have been him. He didn't want to make a promise he couldn't be sure he could keep.

"Sounds like she had good reasons," Nebraska said. "Is that why you joined the navy? Because your father had served?"

He'd said more than he'd meant to, but the words had just kept flowing. "Can't say that was the reason." It hadn't been, and a goodly amount of guilt formed at not having mentioned Betty. They weren't engaged, but that had been his intention upon returning home. "I joined because there weren't many jobs available, the Depression had hit the area hard."

"The Depression hit everywhere hard." Letting out a sigh, she added, "And now we are at war again."

"It was declared?" he asked.

"Yes, the day after we were attacked."

The damage had been disastrous to the ships in the harbor, but he couldn't remember noticing the damage on land. "How did we fare? The base?"

"There was a lot of damage from what I hear. I haven't seen much. I start work at eight in the morning and it's dark when I leave at midnight. But no one is allowed out after dark, and a blackout is being enforced. Cars aren't even allowed to turn on their headlights…"

He listened as she told him about armed patrol guards, foxholes, trenches, bomb shelters, evacuations, and a number of other things, all the while cursing himself for ending up too injured to do his job. He should be out there, rebuilding ships, inspecting the work of the welders in his unit. Instead, he was here, strapped to a bed.

It was more than frustrating. It was unacceptable.

"Would you like me to write a letter home for you?" she asked. "I've done that for other patients. People in the States have heard about the attack and are anxious to hear from loved ones."

Guilt struck K.T. again. People would be worried about him, and he was lying here feeling sorry for himself. Not necessarily feeling sorry for himself, but he clearly wasn't thinking straight. Betty and his family should have been on his mind from the moment he woke up. He was already disappointing himself, and couldn't disappoint them. Wouldn't disappoint them. Promises were meant to be kept.

Chapter Four

Wendy held her breath, waiting for his answer. He'd gone quiet while she'd been telling him about the base. She hadn't wanted to lie to him, but shouldn't have said as much as she had. Things weren't good. The entire island was on pins and needles, waiting for another attack. Everything had changed and the underlying current said that people were expecting the worst rather than the best. She kept trying to remain positive, telling herself that the patients needed to see a smile, not a frown or tears. That was difficult at times, but she refused to let it pull her down. She'd not only written letters for other patients, she'd joined them in prayers, read Bible verses to them, found information about comrades, and completed every other request they asked of her.

"Yes," he said quietly. "If you wouldn't mind."

"I don't mind at all." She glanced at her watch, somewhat needlessly because she was sure it was time for her to crawl out from under the bed. "I'll bring paper with me when I come back with your fresh dressings."

"Thanks."

"You're welcome," she said, and scooted out from beneath the bed. The flock of butterflies that had taken flight in her stomach while lying under his bed were still there, fluttering about. She hadn't meant to tell him about her family, her life. It wasn't like her to be so forthcoming, but it had just happened. Like dancing with him. She didn't regret it, just wondered why she felt so at ease with him. Why she felt differently toward him than so many others. It was confusing because that had never happened before.

"I'll be back in a little bit," she said, and left the room.

Gloria was at the workstation, already mixing the dressing solution.

"Dr. Bloomberg will be assisting me with the dressings this round," Gloria said, while gesturing at the tall dark-haired doctor standing at her side. "You can go have some lunch."

Attempting to hide the infinite amount of disappointment that was washing over her, Wendy said, "All right. Please let our patient know that I'll be in to see him later. I promised that I'd write a letter to his family for him."

"I certainly will," Gloria replied. She then turned to the doctor. "Wendy is taking excellent care of all her patients, going above and beyond."

Wendy knew she wasn't the only one. The hospital was well beyond its full capacity of two hundred and fifty patients, and every single person was doing all they could, as were those at all the other hospitals, ships, and everywhere else. A great spirit of cooperation was felt and emitted by everyone.

"We appreciate your due diligence, Nurse Smith," Dr. Bloomberg said.

She accepted his praise with a nod, then left the room.

Not hungry yet, she checked on some of her other patients before she began making her way to the dining hall. Halfway there, she heard someone yelling for help. Instantly concerned, she ran, and rounded the corner to the main hallway to see an armed guard carrying a woman in through the door.

"Help! She's having a baby!" the guard shouted.

"I'm coming!" Wendy grabbed one of the rolling gurneys that lined the hallways in preparation if there was a second attack and pushed it forward, running toward the man.

"The pains...weren't this bad...when I started walking here," the woman said between gasps as the man lowered her onto the gurney.

"It's okay," Wendy said calmly. "Just lie down. We'll take care of you. We'll take care of everything."

"She collapsed outside," the guard said. "While walking toward the building."

"Thank you," Wendy said to him. "Thank you very much for helping her."

"Thank you," he said, while pivoting on a heel and heading back out the door.

Wendy smiled at how the guard was ready to take down the enemy, but acted as if the pregnant woman scared him to death. "You'll be fine," she said to the woman, helping her get settled on the gurney. "What's your name?"

"Anda Clark," the woman answered.

"Is this your first baby?"

"Yes. My husband is Lieutenant Willis Clark with the

Fourteenth Navy District, assigned to the maintenance yard." She gasped, then let out a groan and grasped her stomach with both hands.

"It's all right, Anda," Wendy said, pushing the gurney down the hallway. "Just breathe. Don't hold your breath. We'll get you in a room and everything will be just fine."

Other nurses had heard the commotion and had also sprung into action. One was at the end of the hall, waving for them to come that way. Wendy knew they'd have to find one of the other rooms that had been turned into makeshift operating stations, because all of the operating rooms were still being used twenty-four hours a day.

"This one is clean and ready," the nurse said, pointing to what had been a supply closet just days ago.

Recognizing the red-headed nurse as Ilene Graham, another Red Cross nurse, Wendy whispered, "We'll need a doctor and charge nurse."

"Helen is fetching one," Ilene replied.

"Good," Wendy replied. "This is Anda Clark." She wheeled the gurney into the room. "It's her first baby. Let's get her in a gown and on the bed."

Charge nurse Moore, who had short black hair and friendly blue eyes, arrived after they had Anda in the bed and Wendy had recorded all of her vitals and contractions on a chart. Upon confirming that it wouldn't be long before the baby arrived, Nurse Moore quickly explained what items needed to be gathered, instructed Ilene to collect a hospital cradle from the second floor, and told Helen to go get a sedative from the pharmacy.

Between contractions, Anda explained that she hadn't evacuated with others because she was due within a couple of weeks, and that her husband hadn't been injured, but he'd been working in the recovery efforts nearly round the clock.

"We'll get word to him," Wendy assured her, while wiping perspiration from Anda's forehead. "Just try to relax best you can." In an attempt to make that happen, she asked, "Do you have names picked out for the baby?"

"Yes. Kevin for a boy and Pearl if it's a girl." Anda's big brown eyes glimmered as she continued, "Will is a diver and thought Pearl was a fitting name, since we're stationed here. But I'm not sure if we should still name her that or not."

"I think it's a lovely name," Wendy assured her. "It's fitting, shows how good things come through thick and thin."

Anda smiled. "You're right. It does show that." Her face scrunched up in pain again.

Wendy held her hand and calmly talked her through the contraction. Once it was over, she gently wiped Anda's brow and whispered words of praise. She had never participated in a birth, was merely going on instinct, and assumed all was going well each time Nurse Moore nodded at her.

Ilene arrived with the rolling metal bassinet draped with a white sheet and positioned it near the bed, and Nurse Moore whispered something to her that sent Ilene back out of the room.

"My husband," Anda said. "Will. Can you get word to him?"

"Yes," Wendy replied, fully understanding that Anda had forgotten she'd already promised that. "Don't worry about that."

"He'll be wondering why I'm not home," she said. "He's a diver and underwater welder."

Wendy's mind instantly went to Oklahoma. "Is he part of Lieutenant McCallister's unit?"

"Yes, he is," Anda replied. "Will and I met in California and K.T., I mean Lieutenant McCallister, approved for me to be able to come here with Will. We heard K.T. was injured, burned while rescuing men from the harbor. Is he here? Will he be all right?"

"Yes, he's here, and I'm sure he'll be happy to hear about the baby's arrival," Wendy said.

Anda smiled, but sucked in air and grimaced again at the pain.

"Nurse Smith," Nurse Moore said from her position near the foot of the bed. "This baby isn't going to wait any longer. We are going to have to do this without a sedative."

Wendy nodded, even as she was encouraging Anda to breathe. The pharmacy could only dispense medication via a doctor's order, which explained why Ilene and Helen hadn't yet returned.

"Okay, then." Nurse Moore folded the covers back over Anda's legs. "Mrs. Clark, it's time to push, I can already see the head."

"It's time, Anda," Wendy repeated near Anda's ear. "Time to push. Push real hard."

The next few minutes seemed to last a lifetime as she encouraged Anda to breathe and push, breathe and push, yet also seemed to be over in the blink of an eye when the tiny cry of a new life filled the room.

"It's a girl," Nurse Moore announced. "A perfect little girl."

The well of joy that filled Wendy was indescribable. She'd done little in the overall scheme of things, but felt so blessed to be in the room at this moment. "Congratulations," she told Anda. "You did it! You have a baby girl!"

"Thank you," Anda said, gasping for air. "Thank you so much."

"Nurse Smith," Nurse Moore said.

Understanding completely, Wendy moved to the foot of the bed and took the baby, so Nurse Moore could see to the afterbirth. In silent wonder, hardly able to believe how absolutely perfect the tiny infant was, Wendy used the basin filled with warm water to clean the baby as she'd been instructed during her training, before she bundled her snuggly in a blanket and carried her over for Anda to see.

"Oh, she is perfect," Anda said.

Wendy's heart was filled with thankfulness for the good fortune of having been here. It was something truly amazing, to have witnessed the true miracle of birth. "Absolutely perfect," she said, and this time, she let a single tear fall, because it was a tear of happiness, not sadness.

K.T. had been disappointed when Nebraska hadn't returned with Nurse Manning, until he realized it wasn't just time to change his bandages. Then he'd been glad for the privacy. Dr. Bloomberg had seen to a few other things, including the removal of the catheter.

He was glad to have that over with, and glad to hear that he'd be able to get up to use the latrine, and to sit up to eat, but the rest of the time would be spent on his stomach, for a yet undetermined amount of time. There was also a goodly amount of discussion about his burns, medications, and the IV, before the doctor and nurse left—with the agreement that he wouldn't have any more morphine as long as he didn't have a setback.

On his stomach again, K.T. stared at the floor. It was a hell of a position to be in, but he didn't regret helping those he'd been able to save. Would never regret that.

What he did regret was not being out there with his unit right now, and he regretted thinking too much about Nebraska. Wendy. Nurse Smith. That's what he had to call her. He shouldn't be thinking about any woman except Betty and returning home to her.

Why was he having such a hard time bringing her image to mind? He knew she had blue eyes and brown hair.

So did Neb—Nurse Smith. Was that why she'd become the center of his thoughts? Because she reminded him of Betty?

No, she didn't remind him of Betty. They were very different. Betty was much more reserved. She would never cut a rug like Nebraska. He grimaced and told himself to remember to refer to her as Nurse Smith.

Betty didn't mind dancing, once in a while. She was happier watching from the sidelines, drinking soda pop and munching on peanuts. She loved peanuts. And chocolate. Years ago, she'd told him that if he wanted to make her happy, all he had to do was give her chocolate. He'd done that as often as money would allow, and she had been happy every single time.

He grinned, remembering more. How Betty could cook. She loved cooking, especially baking, and he loved eating. Everything. He'd eaten over at her parents' house many times.

Why wasn't he hungry right now? Starving hungry.

It had been days since he'd eaten. Was it because of his injuries? Because he'd been lying in bed so long? He needed to get up, get moving. Get his life back in order. All of it. Not just his mind.

He sensed someone coming near before he heard movement, and then saw a white-clad shoulder before a familiar face appeared beneath him. The thrill that shot through him couldn't be ignored, and he did his best to tell himself that it didn't mean anything.

"Brought you some water," she said, maneuvering the tube between the springs again. "And guess what?"

She looked so animated. So happy. Her dimples were deeper, her lips curled up higher in a smile and her blue eyes sparkled with excitement. He couldn't help but smile in return. The tube touched his lips, but before taking a sip, he asked, "What?"

"I just helped deliver a baby," she said, biting her bottom lip, but not so much her smile disappeared. "A perfect, beautiful little girl, and guess what else?"

Women, all women it seemed, were always over-joyed about babies. "What else?"

"You know her, well, you know her parents. Will and Anda Clark!"

It took a split second before what she said clicked in his mind. "Will? Will's wife had their baby?"

"Yes. Just a short time ago. She gave me permission to tell you, and I sent a message to the barracks to let Mr. Clark know where his wife is when his shift ends. They plan on naming the baby Pearl. They'd planned on that before the attack, then wondered if they should after the attack, but Anda decided that she still wanted to name her that. It's the perfect name, don't you think?" She took a breath in and sighed it out. "Pearl. Baby Pearl."

"Yeah, that's a good name. Are she and the baby, okay? Everything good with them?" he asked. Willis was an excellent welder and when it had come time to transfer to Hawaii, he'd been worried about leaving Anda in California. K.T. had requested that anyone in his unit be allowed to bring their families and they had all been grateful when the request had been granted. He would do whatever he could for his men, but would never consider moving his family around the world. If something were to happen to him, then they'd be stuck finding their way back home alone.

"Yes, they are both fine," Nebraska said. "They'll be in the hospital for a few days." She closed her eyes and sighed. "A baby was exactly what we needed here. A new life to show us that despite all the hardships and uncertainty, life goes on, and there are still things to celebrate. Wonderful things."

There was a lot of truth in her statement, and he needed to remember that. Remember her words, especially when his own thoughts became too focused on the bad not the good. "Please give her my congratulations next time you see her," he said.

"I will, and I brought some stationary so I can write that letter for you."

"Letters," he said, trying to pull up the wonderful things about his life. Especially, Betty. Though he hadn't promised to marry her before he left, he had promised to come home if he could and wouldn't go back on that. "I'll need you to write two letters."

"That's fine. I can write as many as you need." Looking at him with a tiny frown between her brows, she continued, "We can do it later if you're tired and want to rest."

"No, I'd like to write them now."

"Okay. Do you want more water first?"

The tube was still next to his lips, and he took a small sip. "That's enough for now."

"Okay." She pulled the tube through the bed springs. "Just give me a minute to put this away and I'll be ready to write."

"Thanks," he said, as she disappeared from sight. He let out a long sigh and forced himself to think about what he wanted the letters to say. They'd be short. Just telling everyone that he was fine. There was no use worrying them with details. He didn't even know details, so couldn't tell them much, anyway.

The scrape of chair legs and the rustling of paper sounded as she settled beside the bed near his head.

"Okay, I'm ready," she said. "Should we start with the envelope? That's what I always do."

"Sure, that's fine."

"Will this one be to your parents?"

"Yes."

"Mr. and Mrs. Kent E. McCallister," she said. "What is the address?"

He told her, and waited until she said she was ready again.

"Dear family," he said. Usually, he addressed letters just to his mother, but he knew she read them aloud to everyone. "I just want to let you know that I'm fine." He questioned what more to say. His letters were usually two or three pages long, telling them about things he was doing, but this one just needed to cover the basics. "A nurse is writing this letter for me, because I'm in the hospital with some burns. They aren't bad, so don't worry. I'll be out soon and will write more then. Love, K.T."

"That's all?" she asked.

"Yes."

There was more paper shuffling sounds. "Okay," she said. "The next one? Who should I address the envelope to?"

"Betty Nelson," he said, and told her the address. Then said, "Just write the same thing for that letter."

"You're sure?"

"Yes." It was disconcerting that he was feeling so detached. This was his family. The people he loved. That was as out of character for him as it had been for him to ask about his bare bum and tell her the things about his family earlier.

"Okay."

"Thanks," he said, and agreed when she told him to get some rest before it was time to change his bandages again. Then, knowing what was bothering him, he said, "Betty and I have dated for years."

There, he'd said it and was glad, except that during the moment that followed, he thought Nebraska might have already left his bedside. Until he heard paper rustling again.

"I'm sure she misses you," she said, sounding as cheerful as ever, "and will be very glad to get your letter."

"I…uh… I don't want her to worry." That was true, but he'd also just wanted to say it out loud, that he had a steady girl, and he wasn't even sure why.

"Would you like me to add a note from me, telling her that you are healing well and we are expecting a full recovery?"

"Sure," he answered, figuring he had to agree. "She'll appreciate that." That was the truth. Betty was a lot like his mother.

"Would you like me to add that note to your other letter, too?"

"My mother would appreciate that, too." This was ridiculous. He didn't have anything to feel guilty about. Not when it came to Betty or to Nebraska. They had merely danced together, and now she was his nurse. One of his nurses.

"Is Betty who taught you to dance?" she asked.

"No, that was my mother. She loves to dance and every Saturday night, she'd turn the music up on the radio and everyone in the house, young and old, would dance in the living room."

"That sounds fun."

"It was, and they are probably still doing that. At least I hope they are. I hope nothing back there has changed." He didn't want anything to change.

The warmth of her hand as it touched the back of his seeped up his arm.

"But they have changed, Oklahoma. You aren't there, and I'm sure they are all missing you as much as you are missing them. It's hard being away from loved ones, but they know you are doing what you need to do, and therefore, they are doing what they need to do, too. Someday, which will eventually arrive, you'll be back there with them."

She was so uniquely different from others. At times, it was as if she had a wisdom that was beyond her years, yet at other times, she seemed as innocent and carefree as someone half her age. Then again, she was here, too, away from her family. "I guess we have that in common, too. Being away from loved ones."

"I guess so, and we are both in Hawaii."

"And in the hospital, except you work here and I'm a patient."

Her giggle was soft. "Do you know how to cook?"

"No," he answered.

"Sew?"

A chuckle bubbled in his throat at her unusual questions. "No."

"Then we have two more things in common."

The pressure of the chuckle increased and he let it out. "You don't say?"

"Oh, I say. So did my aunt. I'm afraid I was a disappointment to her when it came to cooking and sewing, however, I am very proficient at making fishing flies out of bird feathers. Uncle Sy taught me how to do that in the back room of the store when times were slow."

"Did you go fishing with him? Use those flies?"

"Yes, I did. Do you fish?"

"Yes. The Beaver River isn't far from our house and that's what we did on Sundays. It's my father's favorite habit."

"When you're feeling better, we'll go fishing," she said. "Sea fishing. Wouldn't that be a gas? My Uncle Sy would like to hear about that, and to see a picture of it. He bought me a camera before I left Nebraska. I'll take a picture of the fish you catch for you to send to your dad. I bet he'd like that."

"He would," K.T. admitted, even though he should say that he couldn't go fishing with her.

"Okay, then, we'll do that once you're better," she

said. "Right now, you need to get some rest. I'll be back later to check on you."

Guilt rose up in him again. "Sorry for keeping you from your other patients."

Wendy gave the back of his hand a final pat before removing her hand. She did have other patients to see to, but was more worried about him getting some rest. He didn't sound like himself, and she could understand that. He was worried about his family and his unit, and there wasn't much she could do about that for him. "You didn't," she said.

Over the next few hours, while seeing to other patients, and taking the time to check in on Anda and Pearl, Wendy told herself over and over again that she was happy that K.T. had a steady girl back home. That meant that they could just be friends. Her and K.T.

That's all they were, anyway.

Well, not really. They weren't really even friends. They'd danced one night and now she was his nurse.

Nothing more than that.

She'd never wanted anything more than that. Truth was, that had been part of the reason that she'd spent her spare time learning to make fishing flies with Uncle Sy rather than in the house with Aunt Ella. She'd never wanted to be someone that a man would want to marry. She'd never wanted a man to trick her into falling in love, either. That's what had happened to her mother. Her father had tricked her into falling in love with him, made her give up all her own dreams, then after she'd become pregnant, he'd left.

Abandoned her. Them. She would never let someone do that to her. Abandon her. Leave her on her own.

That's why becoming a Red Cross nurse's aide had been the perfect choice for her. She was fulfilling the promise to her mother, and the ones she'd made to herself. To never let any man have control over her life in any way.

The few times she'd asked her mother about her father, she'd simply say she didn't want to talk about him, about that time of her life, other than she was glad that she'd given birth to the most amazing daughter ever. Her mother never made her feel unloved or unwanted. Perhaps because she knew what that felt like.

Wendy had asked Aunt Ella about it one time, and had been told that her mother's heart had been broken, and no one wanted to talk about that. Wendy had figured there was nothing that could be done about it. Except for her to not ever follow in her mother's footsteps.

Aunt Ella and Uncle Sy had never made them feel unwelcome. Just the opposite was true, but her mother had never been truly happy there. That much Wendy clearly remembered.

She, on the other hand, had been happy. Aunt Ella and Uncle Sy had made her a part of their family, even before her mother had died. Her cousins, though older than her, had always treated her like a younger sister, and she adored all of Sid, Joe, and Ellen's children. All of them, her aunt, uncle, and cousins, had encouraged her choice of joining the Red Cross, and had assured her that she would always have a home to come back to with each and every one of them.

She loved them all, and appreciated knowing she'd always have her family, but would never want to have to live with any of them the way her mother had.

As she made her way back around to the workstation to mix up the solution for K.T., a keen sense of anticipation filled her. She wanted to know more about Betty. About the kind of woman that he had fallen in love with. Of course, that was none of her business, but she was curious. He was such a nice man. A good man, committed and honest, just a genuine good person.

At times, it was like he was two men in her mind. When she thought of him as a patient, he was K.T., a dedicated sailor, but when she crawled beneath the bed and saw his face, he was Oklahoma, a fun, happy guy. Her Fred Astaire.

Gloria was already at the station. "Congratulations on your first baby delivery! I heard you did an excellent job. I'm certainly not surprised. You are unflappable and most certainly excel at your job."

"Thank you," Wendy replied. "It truly was miraculous."

Gloria nodded, and her smile appeared to grow as she asked, "Want to know what else is almost nearly miraculous?"

"Yes. What?"

"Dr. Bloomberg declared that Lieutenant McCallister's burns are responding so well, that he's agreed to try the treatment on other patients."

"Oh, Gloria!" Wendy couldn't control her excitement and hugged Gloria. "That is so wonderful!"

"Yes, it is." Returning her hug, Gloria whispered, "Thank you, Wendy. Thank you so much for helping me. I know we still have a long way to go, but I truly believe that this treatment can help so many more."

"So do I," Wendy said as they parted. "And I will help you with any other patients that you need me to."

"Thank you. I've already mentioned that to Dr.

Bloomberg and he assured me that your dedication has not gone unnoticed." Gloria gestured to the table. "Let's get this mixed up. We'll help our patient sit up and eat some soup before putting on the new dressings. Then I'll go get some sleep and relieve you at midnight."

Chapter Five

That task, of helping K.T. sit up, eat some soup, and walk to the latrine and back again, was easier than it should have been, only because he was so intent on doing most of it himself, even though it clearly pained him. Wendy was glad when he was back in bed and the dressings all reapplied.

He was worn out and though he denied it, she was sure he was in pain. It was impossible to jump to the end of healing, but telling him that would be as useless as wishing there was more she could do for him.

After making sure he was as comfortable as possible, Wendy left the room, however, she'd barely entered the hallway when she encountered Seaman Scott Westman. A great sense of protectiveness rose up inside her.

"Good evening, Nurse Smith," he greeted. "I'm here to see Lieutenant McCallister again. Is he awake?"

Not only had K.T. requested to see him, the first time the tall, somewhat lanky seaman had come to the hospital she had recognized him as the man Oklahoma had been laughing with the night of the dance. She wanted to tell him to come back later, but knew that would only cause more frustration for both men. "Yes, he is," she answered. "But I can only allow you to stay for a few minutes. He needs his rest."

"Of course." The seaman turned worried green eyes to the door. "How is he doing? Is there any hope for him to return to duty?"

"Yes, there is, but it will take time." She gestured toward the room, then led the way for him to follow.

Arriving beside his bed, she touched K.T.'s arm. "You have company," she said quietly. "Seaman Westman."

He jolted slightly. "Scott?"

"Present," the seaman said. "I brought your mail. Letters from home. I can read them to you, if you'd like."

"Give them to Nurse Smith. She'll read them to me later. I need you to fill me in on what's going on out there. How's the unit? We lose anyone?"

Wendy took the three envelopes the seaman handed to her and slid them in her apron pocket, where the other two letters were that she still had to add notes to. "Five minutes," she mouthed, while holding up one hand, fingers spread.

The seaman nodded.

She stepped around the portable curtain wall to give them privacy, and spent the next five minutes trying to look busy all the while keeping a close eye on her wristwatch. The destruction and devastation covering the island was real, and though she had told K.T. about plenty of it, she didn't know about his specific unit, not the damage or loss of life. It was impossible to protect him from grief, to protect anyone from grief, no matter how deeply she wished that was possible.

Seaman Westman walked around the curtain just as the five-minute countdown struck on her watch. He gave her a slight nod. "I told him I'd be back tomorrow, if that's okay?"

"Yes, that will be fine," she replied.

Concern etched his face as he looked over his shoulder. "I had to tell him we had two men injured. They're on the *Solace*. From what I've learned, they are expected to make full recoveries."

"What are their names?" she asked, knowing K.T. would want more details. "I'll make inquiries."

"Nate Hardin and Gavin Perry."

"Nate Hardin and Gavin Perry," Wendy repeated so she'd remember the names until she could write them down.

"Yes, thank you. I'll stop by before dark tomorrow."

She nodded and waited until he'd exited the room before she walked around the curtain. Arriving near the head of the bed, she laid her hand over his. "Would you like a drink of water?"

"No, thanks, I'm fine."

He didn't sound fine. He sounded like a man heavy with worry. "Would you like me to read your letters from home now, while we still have some light?" Once night fell, the blackout orders didn't allow any lights except flashlights as needed.

His sigh seemed to echo off the walls. "Sure."

She reached in her pocket and pulled out the three envelopes. The return address on the top one was from Betty Nelson. She had been going to ask him which one he'd want to hear first, but assumed this might be the one to cheer him up the most. Quietly, she unsealed the envelope and pulled out a single, folded piece of paper.

Something slipped from the folds. A chain. Thin, and gold, like a necklace chain.

Unfolding the paper, she discovered it was a necklace. A dainty, very pretty one, with a teardrop pearl dangling off the gold chain. It seemed an odd thing for a woman to mail to a man, but who was she to judge? She'd never written to a man other than a family member. While licking her lips in preparation of reading the letter aloud, she scanned the first few lines just to familiarize herself with the handwriting, but what she read stopped her heart.

"On second thought, let's wait until tomorrow," K.T. said. "I'm tired, but I do have a favor to ask."

"Anything," Wendy replied while quickly shoving the letter, envelope, and necklace back in her pocket without putting the necklace or letter back in the envelope. Her insides were trembling because of what she'd read. So were her hands.

"A couple of my unit members are on the *Solace*," he said.

"Nate Hardin and Gavin Perry," she said. "I'll make inquiries and let you know everything as soon as I hear back."

"Thanks."

"Anything else?" she asked, trying to sound calm, even though her heart was still pounding over what she'd read.

"No, I'm just going to rest a bit."

She touched his hand briefly in parting, then left the room rapidly. In the hallway, she placed a trembling hand over her mouth in disbelief. Horrific disbelief. Maybe she hadn't read what she thought she read.

Dare she read it again? It wasn't any of her business, but there had been a necklace.

Digging a hand in her pocket, she felt the chain, the teardrop-shaped pearl. That was definitely there. What was she going to do? She couldn't tell him. Not while he was so sick.

He'd just heard bad news about others in his unit. She couldn't add to that. Tell him more bad news.

Several seconds ticked by as she stood there, contemplating what to do and if she'd truly read what she'd thought she'd read. It had just been a fast scan of the first paragraph. Maybe she'd misconstrued the words.

Glancing left and right, she pulled the letter out, to scan it again.

K.T. tried hard to get his mind off the pain. Getting up and sitting in a chair long enough to eat had hurt like hell, and walking to the latrine had made skin on the back of his calves sting like the dickens. If Nebraska had still been in the room, he might have asked her to go ahead and read the letters from home, just so he'd have had something else to focus on, but that would have only been a short-term fix. He needed to heal, get back to work. That's what was causing the real anguish inside him.

Nate and Gavin were good men. Good welders and divers. They'd been two of the first men he'd met after enlisting. Scott hadn't known much about their condition, just that they'd been injured by incoming fire and were receiving treatment on the *Solace*.

The rest of the unit had gone to work the day of the attack, salvaging. A daunting task. The USS *Nevada* was run aground just opposite from the hospital. The USS

Arizona and the USS *West Virginia* were in shambles, the USS *Oklahoma* was belly-up, and others complete wrecks. Scott claimed that at least seven battleships, three cruisers, three destroyers, a mine craft, and five auxiliaries were either destroyed, sunk, or damaged beyond use.

Thinking of the number of casualties was overwhelming. It was in the thousands and bodies were still being recovered.

Orders had been given that every ship needed to be repaired. Get back in service as soon as possible, or before.

Every available man had been assigned to the recovery effort, but it was still basically in the assessment stage. Scott had a good handle on the tasks, and K.T. had given advice and suggestions that could help. Lying here on his stomach was torturous. He should be out there, leading his unit under the water. It was his responsibility to make sure protocols were being followed. One gauge misread could cause the loss of a diver.

Every man in the unit knew that, and were well trained, the best at what they did. He appreciated that, but they shouldn't have to shoulder his duties.

He had no idea how long he mused over such things, but the room had gone dark. Pitch-black dark, thanks to the blackout curtains that didn't let any moonlight enter through the window. While sitting up earlier, he hadn't seen much of the room. Other than it was all white.

Everything was white. The walls, the floors, the beds, the blankets, the doors, the curtain separating him from the other patients. This was his first stay in a hospital. First visit, and he'd be glad if it was also his last.

Once he finally got out.

Snores coming from one or more of the other patients in the room weren't overly loud or irritating, they just confirmed that once the sun went down and darkness filled the rooms, there was nothing to do but sleep. Or think for those who couldn't fall to sleep.

That's the category he was in.

His mind was dragging up too many thoughts. Old and new ones.

The subtle creaking of wheels grew closer. A nurse pushing a cart. He'd heard it on and off all day. His heart quickened, but returned to normal as the creaking faded. It had simply been in the hallway, not his room. There was no denying that he'd been hoping it was Nebraska coming to see him. It probably wasn't time to change his bandages yet; he just wanted to talk to someone, get his mind off the things he couldn't do right now.

For the briefest of moments, he wondered if he was imagining the soft touch on the back of his hand, but the hitch inside him said he wasn't imagining it. This not seeing anything except the floor was for the birds. "That you, Nebraska?" he asked.

"Yes, it's me," she replied in a whisper. "How are you doing?"

"Not used to going to bed at six o'clock."

"It's almost seven if that helps."

He grinned, although he wasn't exactly sure why, other than she tended to make him smile. Had since the moment he'd first seen her on the dance floor.

"The blackout does have its inconveniences," she said.

Inconveniences wasn't the word he would use, but he also knew the reasons why the blackout had been issued. The entire island was under martial law and would continue to be for a long time. "How can you see to do your job? It's pitch-black in here." He was used to working in the dark. There was no light underwater and he'd been trained to use his senses, see with his hands, while working the welding torches.

"I have a flashlight," she said.

He scanned as much of the floor as possible, looking for a hint of light. "Is it on?"

"No, I have to save the batteries for when I need it."

As far as nurses, he'd only encountered her and Nurse Manning, and had no doubt that either of them let anything stop them from their duties. "You're walking around in the dark? From room to room?"

"Yes, I've gotten used to it. Hardly even stub a toe."

Stub a toe? Hell, she could fall down, trip over something, break a bone and end up in the hospital herself. "You need to be careful," he said. "And use the flashlight."

She giggled softly. "I do use it. Would you like a drink of water?"

"I don't want you to have to crawl on the floor, especially not in the dark."

"I'll be fine." Her hand patted the back of his softly. "I'll be right back."

The rush of heat throughout his system was shocking and unsettling. He had wanted someone to talk to, and had hoped it would be her. The only reason that made sense was because she was the only person he knew in this place.

Nothing more.

He swallowed against the dryness of his mouth.

A beam of light appeared and seconds later, her face

was directly below his. To say he was taken aback by her smile would be a lie, he was mesmerized by it, and did his best to quickly collect himself.

"I turned on the light so I don't poke you in the eye with the tube," she said, grinning.

Another sudden rush of heat had him questioning what had gotten into him. Earlier, he'd gotten a look at Nurse Manning. She wasn't homely, simply older, and had been as kind and efficient in seeing to his care as Nebraska, but he knew damn well, if Nurse Manning was the one lying beneath his bed, sliding the tube up through the springs for him to get a drink of water, his body wouldn't be reacting the way it was right now.

Nor would his heart.

The end of the tube touched his lips and he took a drink. Then another, just because she had to go to such lengths so he could drink. "That's enough," he said. "You can climb out."

She pulled the tube through the bed springs and lowered the glass to the floor. "Would you like me to read one of your letters from home?"

"No. I don't want you to waste your batteries on that."

A click sounded and the beam of light was gone. "Okay, then, what do you want to talk about?"

She was still lying on the floor. He could see a shadowy outline. Or maybe it was just his mind, recalling her image in the darkness. "Nothing. You can climb out."

"I don't have anywhere that I need to be until it's time to mix up the solution for your dressing changes." After a moment of silence, she continued, "I saw Pearl again. She's an adorable little baby, and Will said to say hello. He had to leave before curfew, which starts at sunset. Very few have actual night passes, where they can freely move about."

"What about you?" he asked. "You leave at midnight."

"I have a hospital pass. It allows me to walk from the hospital to my living quarters. The building is a short distance behind the hospital. There are machine gun stations on all corners of the roofs, manned at all times, and when I leave, the sentry outside has a flashlight, which is covered with blue paper with a tiny hole in it, and he flashes it at the men on the roofs so they know I'm walking between the buildings."

He wished he could touch her, comfort her, and searched for words to use instead. It was a far different world now than before. The tension and fear had to be so high that the men manning the guns might shoot at anything that moved in the dark. "Those men on the roofs will keep you safe," he said, unable to think of anything else.

"I'm not afraid of them."

She shouldn't have to be afraid of anything. That attack had changed everything. "We didn't have any carriers in port when we were attacked," he said. "They were out at sea, and still are. Loaded with planes ready to launch at the first sight of another attack." He and Scott had talked briefly about that earlier, and he hoped that would ease her fears.

"We are more prepared for them on land, too," she said. "Every roof has machine gun stations on them, and there are armed soldiers everywhere, at all times. We won't be surprised again."

They shouldn't have been surprised the first time,

but more than that, he didn't want her to become frightened by talking about the current situation. "Tell me about the fishing flies you made with your uncle. What was your favorite color?" It was the first topic that popped into his head.

"My favorite color doesn't matter," she replied. "That's up to the fish. But my favorite feather types, are pheasant feathers. They are plentiful, of the perfect form, and if you care about color, you have all bases covered. There's hardly a more colorful bird. I've had one fly that I made when I was ten or so, and it's still perfect. Dries out like new after every use. How about you?"

"I haven't fished with flies as much as worms," he admitted. "All I had to do was dig them up."

After a short silence, she asked, "Do you think sea bass are the same as the bass back home? I mean, do you think they go for flies? The bass back home sure do. Trout, too, at the right time of the year."

"I'm not sure. Why?"

"I'll have to find out," she said, "so we'll know what kind of bait we need when we go fishing."

That would never happen. Once he was out of here, he doubted he'd see her again. There would be no reason to. Be that as it may, it didn't settle well inside him. "What else did you do back in Nebraska?"

"I worked at my uncle and aunt's store, and every Sunday, I'd drive them over to Scottsbluff to see their son Sid. He's a lawyer, and he and his wife, Sarah, have two children. Sissy, whose real name is Cassandra, but we all call her Sissy. She's ten. And Sid junior, whom we all call Junior. He's seven. Aunt Ella and Uncle Sy's other son…"

She continued talking about her family, and he continued to listen, enjoying simply listening to her talk, right up until she proclaimed it was time for her to go get everything ready for his dressing changes.

Before leaving, she clicked on the flashlight and snaked the tube back up through the springs for him to have another drink of water.

He took a sip and as the light clicked off again, he closed his eyes, locking the image of her face in his mind.

There was not only a heaviness inside Wendy, there was a darkness that she'd never encountered before. She had no idea how to lighten it, either.

Well, she did, but she couldn't do it. Couldn't tell Oklahoma about Betty. He was strapped on his stomach with severe burns covering his back. The last thing he needed to hear right now was that the woman he loved, the woman he'd dated for years, had found another man.

Yes, she'd read the letter again. More than once, and that was exactly what Betty had said in the letter. That she was returning the necklace that K.T. had sent to her because she didn't feel right keeping it now that she was seeing someone else. A man named Jim Jackson that she said was someone who K.T. didn't know. Jim had come to town recently, and she hadn't been able to stop herself from falling in love with him.

Wendy didn't believe that. It was easy to not fall in love with someone. You just didn't. If she'd ever been worried about that happening, she would have simply stayed away from them. Of course, she never worried about that happening, because it wouldn't. She wouldn't fall in love with anyone.

An uneasiness made her stomach quiver. Was she like Betty, or actually, was Betty like her? Didn't want to be left behind? Is that why Betty fell in love with someone else? It wasn't the same thing! Oklahoma hadn't abandoned Betty. He was doing his job. Serving his country. That was completely different.

He was completely different.

Different than who? Her father? She'd never known her father. Or why he'd left. Why was she sticking her nose in where it didn't belong? That's what Aunt Ella would call it.

Keeping the news from him was wrong, but he was her patient and her job was to make sure he healed as quickly as possible. Grief of this sort could prolong his healing.

That was her justification, and she would stick to it.

Therefore, the next day, when it came time to read him his letters from home, she only read two of them. One from his mother that told him about how all of his family was doing, including that no one had heard from his cousin Ralph in North Dakota since he'd enlisted in the army and everyone was worried, and one from his brother, Jud, that told him all about a new dog they'd gotten, Buster, that was quickly learning how to behave from their old dog, Duke.

He expounded on both letters, telling her more about his family, including his cousins Ralph and Dale in North Dakota, and his dog, Duke, that he'd taught to round up the milk cows and herd them into the barn each night without even being told.

The conversation made her smile because it was

clear how proud he was of that dog. He spoke highly of all members of his family, but did question why his father had told surveyors to stay off their property. She had almost skipped over that part, because Betty had mentioned that Jim Jackson was one of the surveyors that had come to the area looking for natural gas.

Her stomach squirmed as she replied to his question, "It doesn't say why."

"I know why. He doesn't want to be swindled. A natural gas field that extends through the panhandle was discovered a few years ago and brought some jobs to the area, but the landowners felt they weren't being treated fairly, and the lawyers they hired to defend them ended up siding with the gas company when it came to mineral rights. It's caused a lot of contention. Our land was outside of the designated field area, but they could be looking to expand that. If gas was found, it could mean added income for my family and they need that, but it would depend upon the deal struck."

While he explained more about the discovery of the gas field, her mind went down another pathway. She knew nothing about gas fields or legal issues, but knew someone who did. Sid had discussed some of his cases with Uncle Sy during their Sunday dinners, and she recalled one discussion about mineral rights on farmland.

She didn't tell him that, because she was still thinking about Betty's letter, and the fact that she hadn't read it to him.

That thought plagued her over the next few days, and into the next week, where changes were implemented. Although the hospital was still filled with patients, discharges and transfers happened daily, and her hours were once again changed. Her shift was now twelve hours long, from eight in the morning to eight at night. So were Gloria's which meant another nurse was assigned to overseeing Oklahoma's cares during the night shift.

Although Gloria didn't always follow the schedule. She continued to be at the hospital day and night, leaving only long enough for a few hours of sleep. Her techniques were now being used on several patients. All nurses seeing to burn patients had been well trained, but Wendy still worried about K.T. and reviewed the notes in his chart every morning with intense scrutiny.

She was also provided with days off, as were all the staff. That was concerning to her, too, and during her first day off, staying away was impossible. Not only was guilt over Betty's letter eating at her, she was worried that he might receive another letter from her, or from a family member who mentioned Betty and the man she'd fallen in love with.

Wearing a blue-and-white-striped dress rather than her nurse's uniform, she entered K.T.'s room. By the way his feet were moving, she knew he was awake. Gathering a glass of water and his drinking tube, she walked to his bed, lay down and scooted beneath it without saying a word.

His smile sent her heart dancing.

"What are you doing here?" he asked. "It's your day off."

"I thought that I would put it to good use," she said. "I went to the *Solace* and visited with Nate and Gavin." Through her inquiries, she learned that they both had been hit by shrapnel. Nate had to have pieces of metal picked out throughout his torso, but was healing well, and Gavin had been hit so hard, his left leg had been broken. The trip had taken her the better part of the morning because the ship was on the other side of the harbor and she'd had to convince a boatman to take her there, for official hospital reasons, she'd assured the man.

"They both are doing very well and said to tell you hello," she continued, after telling him about their injuries. "Nate said he'll stop by to see you after he's released this coming week, and Gavin wants to know if you want to wager on who'll get out first between you and him."

"Me," Oklahoma replied, around the tube he'd been drinking from.

"I told him that's what you'd say. The bet is five bucks."

He took another drink before releasing the tube. "Sounds good to me, and thanks for the drink. I was getting thirsty."

A hint of irritation rose up inside her. "Did no one offer you a drink yet today?"

"Yes, they did. I had plenty to drink with breakfast and will have more with lunch."

Wendy remained silent for the next several moments, accepting the tangible sense of awareness she always felt in his presence. It went far deeper than she knew it should, because it was unique, different from anything she'd experienced. She wanted to believe it was because she was worried about his care, yet, couldn't quite convince herself that was the reason. She was also questioning if those unique feelings played a role in why she hadn't told him about Betty's letter.

She didn't want to believe that was true, because she

didn't want to contemplate what that might mean. "Well, that's good," she finally said, putting her thoughts back on his care. "You need to tell them when you're thirsty, though, at other times of the day."

"I'm not about to ask anyone else to climb beneath the bed. I wouldn't have asked that of you, either."

"It's all part of your care," she said, a bit defensive. Everything she did was a part of his care.

"Everything is part of your patient's care," he said, as if reading her mind. "To you, and that's why you are a very good nurse. The best nurse."

Warmth flooded her cheeks, because she knew that dancing with him hadn't had anything to do with nursing. Pushing that thought aside, she said, "Flattery will get you nowhere. You have to stay hydrated, or I'll request that another IV be stuck in your arm."

"You would, wouldn't you?"

The thinly veiled amusement in his eyes couldn't be missed. She gave him a mocking grin in return. "In a jiffy."

"Don't get too excited over that idea," he said. "Believe me, I don't want to be in this position any longer than I have to be."

She believed him, and it had become easier for him to get up to eat every day. A visceral stirring happened deep in the core of her being, one that said even though she wanted him to heal and return to duty for his sake, she would miss him when he was discharged. Miss him more than she should.

"What do you plan on doing the rest of your day off?" he asked.

Accepting his change of subject, she shrugged. "I'm not sure." In the past, her days off had been filled with plans for sightseeing long before the day had arrived. That had all changed. Traveling off the base was not allowed without permission, and only then for specific reasons. She had no reason; furthermore, she had no desire.

The memory of what she had planned for her last day off snuck in, that of going to see the palace. While dancing with him, she'd wondered if he'd want to see that, but now wasn't overly sure she'd ever see it. The memory was tarnished by the attack and by the fact that the entire band from the USS *Arizona* had perished that morning.

"Maybe you could find yourself a good book and sit in the sun, doing nothing but reading," he suggested.

"Is that what you would do?" she asked.

"Probably not. I was just trying to think of a way for you to relax."

His thoughtfulness made her smile. "What did you do to relax?" she asked. "On your days off?"

"Never really took a day off. There were always things that needed to be done. Paperwork, order forms, equipment repairs, blueprints to be studied, the list goes on."

She was sure it did, and she was sure lying here every day was getting harder not easier for him. "What did you do back home to relax?"

His gaze shifted away from her. It was noticeable because he couldn't turn his head, only move his eyes, and it dawned on her where his mind probably had gone. Any time off, he'd probably spent with Betty. Guilt struck again. Not only had she not told him about the letter, she hadn't mailed the letter he'd asked her to pen to Betty. She had mailed the one to his mother, and had added a note to it as promised.

She had also mailed letters to her family, assuring them of her well-being, small bits of information about the attack, and simply because of her own curiosity, she'd asked Sid if he knew of a respectable lawyer in the Guymon, Oklahoma, area who could help a family with a gas company wanting to survey their land.

Her nerves were getting the best of her over Betty's letter. Every day she wondered if another one had arrived for him from Betty, saying she'd changed her mind, or…just all sorts of things.

"I already told you that answer," he finally said. "Fishing with my dad."

She suddenly had something that she needed to do today. Something that would get her mind off other things. All she'd require were some fishhooks and feathers; her sewing kit would provide her with everything else, other than a good pair of pliers. Christmas was only a few days away and that would make the perfect gift for him.

"What are you smiling about?" he asked.

"Nothing, just thinking of my day off."

"Sure you are."

She let out an exaggerated sigh at his teasing. "Believe what you may, but that is what I'm thinking about." The very familiar sound of a cart being pushed along the hallway was her signal to leave. She didn't want the other nurses to think she didn't believe they were doing their jobs. "I better leave now."

"Don't want to get caught under my bed on your day off?"

Her cheeks burned and she did her best to ignore it,

and his grin, as she climbed out from beneath the bed. "Drink your fluids or else," she said before walking to the door, smiling at his chuckling.

Chapter Six

K.T. went ahead and let the grin remain on his face long after Nebraska had left the room. No one would know if he was smiling or not. Or why. That should be enough reason for him to not be happy that she'd stopped by to see him, but lying on his stomach day in and day out was beyond monotonous.

The other nurses were fine and did a good job. They just weren't her.

A guilt that had become far too familiar lately rose up inside him, and he once again told himself that Betty was the only woman he should be thinking about. He hadn't received a letter from her since arriving in Hawaii, but that wasn't unusual. There were always months between her letters. When a letter did arrive, she would apologize for her delay in writing and tell him about all the things she'd been doing. Everything from new recipes she'd tried and that he was sure to like, to the new dresses she'd sewn, and the preserves she'd put up at the end of the garden season.

Despite how hard he was trying to not think about Nebraska, his mind recalled when she'd asked if he knew how to sew or cook and how they had those two things in common because she didn't know how to sew or cook, either.

Most women probably wouldn't admit that, but she wasn't like most women. Leastwise, none that he'd known in the past. She wasn't the only woman to accept a calling in the armed forces, and he was amazed by all the women who willingly left home to support their country. That took courage. Real courage.

He was just more amazed by her, and couldn't put his finger directly on why.

"Are you ready for your lunch?" a voice asked.

"Yes," he replied. It was painful to move, to sit up, but each time that happened, it became easier. So did walking to the latrine. The backs of his calves no longer stung and he hoped that meant the burns there were close to healed.

Two nurses assisted him in the process. One was Nurse Manning, the other a young blonde, who seemed a bit unsure of herself, but did a fine job. He couldn't fault any that he'd met, and was grateful for all they did for him.

It took concentrated effort to eat and his burns stung fiercely by the time he was done, but he was happy that he was being given more to eat than soup.

He was exhausted by the time it was over and the cool, damp dressings draped over his back, shoulders, and neck felt like heaven, even though it meant he was once again held hostage on his bed.

Being confined to bed didn't get any easier as the hours rolled into days, and the days and nights rolled into weeks. During that time, he had to be perfectly honest at times and admit that the quiet conversations, some thoughtful, some playful, he had with Wendy had been the brightest parts of every long day.

Those dimples, that face and personality, brought joy where there was little.

By his count, it had now been eighteen days since the attack.

He had yet to see the changes at the base. The changes that Wendy, Scott, Will, and others from his unit and in the hospital had told him about. There were changes all around the world because of that attack. Things he'd heard about from those same people, and in letters from home he'd received yesterday. His mother, sisters, brother, had all sent him letters. Even his father had written one. K.T. was sure his mother had been behind that, since he'd never before received one from his father, but he appreciated it just the same. The words of encouragement that his father had penned had been sincere and reminded him of his younger years when he'd often gone to his father for advice.

He'd done that before leaving home, and had made his decision about not becoming engaged. His father had told him of the fear he'd experienced in the Great War that he wouldn't be able to keep his promise to return, and supported his decision not to ask Betty to marry him before leaving. K.T. knew that tying Betty to him before he left wouldn't have been fair to her. Four years was a long time and many things could happen.

Including exactly what *had* happened. The attack. It had taken lives. Changed lives.

Although he was able to sit up for longer stints, even walk around the room a small amount, Wendy had still read all of the letters to him yesterday afternoon when she didn't have anything pressing to see to. He'd forced himself to think about her only as Wendy days ago, and to call her that, hoping it would compartmentalize her in his mind as his nurse. Calling her Nurse Smith might be better and he did that at times, too.

Mainly when he referred to her while talking to others.

There was no longer a need for her to crawl beneath his bed. Each time they came in to change his dressings, he was able to get up and stay out of bed for longer stints, even in the middle of the night.

He'd hoped that would help him keep things straight in his mind. Her lying on the floor beneath his bed, no matter how innocent or necessary it had been at one time, had grown to feel too intimate. Even if Betty wasn't waiting on him back home, he wasn't here to do anything except complete his duty.

There still hadn't been a letter from Betty, and though it didn't surprise him, he wasn't sure he wanted one to arrive. It might help him keep his thoughts in line, but he also didn't want Betty to think that his injuries had changed anything. His ability to make a promise about the future was even more constrained than before. A war was no time to make promises to anyone.

Wendy had asked if he wanted to write return letters to his family, but he'd declined her offer. He would do that himself, in the privacy of his living quarters after being released. That would happen after the first of the year. That's what the doctor, Nurse Manning, and Wendy had all implied.

He was looking forward to that, for many reasons.

"Good morning, and Merry Christmas!"

That's all it took, the sound of her voice, and his

heart went wild. Once he was out of here, that would stop. There would be no reason for him to see her.

"Good morning, to you, too," he replied. "And Merry Christmas."

"How was your night?" Wendy asked.

"Fine. How was yours?" He could feel her already removing the strips of cloth from his back.

"Good. A band somewhere was playing 'Jingle Bells' as I walked to the hospital this morning. It made me smile, thinking about dashing through the snow when it's eighty degrees and sunny. It's not that way back home. Aunt Ella said they've already had a couple of snowstorms, and…"

As she went on talking about snow in Nebraska, he couldn't help but think about home. How his mother would already have a big goose in the oven, making the house smell wonderful while everyone gathered in the living room to open gifts from each other. He could almost see the images, smell the smells. Before leaving California, he'd sent his mother extra money, and asked her to buy a gift for each of his siblings, as well as herself and his father. She'd replied in a letter, told him what she'd purchased, including a new silk scarf for herself that she was going to enjoy after opening it on Christmas morning. He'd laughed back then, thinking of her wrapping her own present and putting it away until today to open it.

"Ready?"

The images in his mind cleared at the sound of Wendy's voice. "Yes," he replied.

Pushing himself upright was the hardest part, just because it made one particular spot in the center of his back sting like the dickens. Scott had brought him some of his uniform shorts and he wore them day in and day out. They beat the heck out of the flimsy shorts the hospital had been providing him, but he was mighty tried of feeling like an invalid instead of a man.

One look at her smiling face told him he wasn't a complete invalid. Certain areas worked just fine. The heat that rushed to his groin said that area was working more than fine. His attraction to her was dangerous to more than his peace of mind. It consumed his entire body and none of that was her fault. She was pretty, intelligent, filled with generosity, and a true ray of sunshine to all of her patients.

He was the one to blame. He was taking all of her amazing qualities too personally. Why? Because he'd been so lonely? If that was the reason, it sure had hit fast and hard. He'd been gone from home for over three years and hadn't had that problem before meeting her. Finding a way to make it disappear was what had to happen.

Doing so while she was near was difficult. Halfway through breakfast, as he sat in a chair with a rolling table before him, he wondered if there was another way. She had told him about her family, and a few other things, but had never mentioned anyone particularly special. "Besides family, are there others you miss back in Nebraska?"

"Oh, sure," she said, while tucking a clean sheet around his mattress. "There are neighbors and friends that I've known my entire life."

"Like who?" he asked, pressing further.

She tucked the sheet that had been cut to fit down into the hole for his face beneath the mattress and smoothed it flat while naming people who sounded like couples with Mr. and Mrs., until she said what he assumed was a single man's name, Seth Goldman.

"Who is that?" he asked, denying he felt any sense of jealousy. He'd wanted her to have someone special at home. Wanted her to be taken. "Seth Goldman?"

Her expression softened and she let out a soft sigh. "Seth Goldman is Uncle Sy's best friend. His wife, Gertrude, died before I was born, and he doesn't have any other family so always spent holidays with us. I worry about him now that Aunt Ella and Uncle Sy have moved to Scottsbluff."

That was not the explanation he'd been hoping to hear.

"I mailed a postcard wishing him a happy Christmas," she continued. "I mailed them to several people."

"People closer to your age?" he asked, sounding like a newspaper man digging to get a story. He knew what that was like. Reporters had always been hanging around the base in California, hoping to get the scoop on the first words of war.

"Yes." Standing before him, arms crossed, she stared at him with a look of insolence. "Are you wondering if I have someone back home waiting on me to return?"

"I guess I am."

"Well, there's not," she said, shaking her head. "I would never want to have someone waiting for me, nor would I want to be waiting on them."

"Why?"

"Because I wouldn't want to be disappointed when they didn't return, or vice versa." She shrugged. "In the blink of an eye, everything can change and people are no different. What they wanted today, isn't what they want tomorrow or the next day, or the next year."

There was that wisdom he'd seen her express before, giving him no choice but to agree. It was also no surprise that she didn't want anyone waiting on her. She would have been told the risks when she signed on with the Red Cross.

Wendy held her breath as she watched K.T.'s expressions change, from thoughtful, to, well, she wasn't sure what, and sincerely wished she knew what he was thinking. Actually, she did know. He was wondering why he hadn't heard from Betty. Why was because of her. Betty's letter and the necklace were still hidden in the bottom drawer of her dresser and not a day didn't go by when she didn't think about them, about telling him. Every time a letter arrived for him, she wondered if a family member would mention Betty, and half wished they would, so she would be forced to tell him.

That hadn't happened, and she assumed that his family was probably thinking of him, like she was, that he didn't need to talk about bad news right now.

His burns were healing remarkably well. Dr. Bloomberg had suggested a possible discharge next week. There were variables, of course, and he would return to limited duty.

She would tell him, soon, when the time was right. Even though that had to have been why he'd wanted to know if she'd had anyone waiting on her to return. He wanted to know if she knew what that felt like. She didn't, not really, but had seen her mother go through it and would never do it herself.

She didn't want him to feel abandoned by Betty, either.

This was truly a pickle and she had no one to blame

but herself, yet, if she had to do it over, she would do the very same thing. Protecting him from further injuries was part of her job. Heartbreak was an injury. One her mother had suffered from her entire life.

"I suspect you're waiting for me to crawl back into that bed," K.T. said.

She let out a quiet sigh, glad the topic had changed, and reached into her apron pocket. "Actually, I was waiting until you were done eating so I could give you this."

He looked at the small wrapped box she held out to him. "What's that?"

"Your Christmas present." She set it on the table and moved the tray holding his empty plate farther out of the way. "Go ahead, open it."

Though he was shaking his head, the smile that tilted up the corners of his lips chased away the heaviness of her earlier thoughts.

She bit down on her bottom lip as he folded back the paper and exposed the matchbox. "That's the only box I could find."

"It's a nice box," he said. "A man always needs a box of matches. Thank you."

"Matches are not in the box," she said, even though his grin said he was teasing. "It's just holding your present. Slide it open."

He slid open the outer box to reveal the four colorful fishing flies lying on the cotton batting. Unable to stop herself, she explained, "They are fishing flies."

"I see that." He carefully picked one up and examined it closely. "Very nice flies." Looking up at her, he asked, "You made these?"

"I did, for when we go fishing. I had help getting

the hooks and feathers. Nigel, a pharmacist assistant, helped me with that. He gave me the matchbox, too."

K.T. lifted one brow. "Nigel?"

"Yes, he works here and I get all the supplies for your solution from him," she explained. "He's quite helpful in finding anything we need at the hospital. Of course, my request for fishhooks and feathers was unusual, but he also told me where we'll be able to get fishing poles when the time comes. He knows many of the locals."

"Umm," he said, shaking his head.

A sudden urge to assure him that she wasn't trying to push him into performing tasks that he couldn't struck. "It'll be a while yet before you can cast a pole, but I wanted you to have the flies now."

"Thank you." He replaced the fly and looked at each of the others. "Thank you, very much."

"You're welcome."

"I feel bad that I don't have anything for you," he said while sliding the cover back on the box.

She hadn't thought about that, but knew how that felt. She'd once received a Christmas gift from a friend in school, a book that she had wanted, and hadn't had anything to give in return. Taking the pen out of her pocket, she flattened the wrapping paper on the table and quickly wrote a note on the paper.

Watching her, he read aloud, "'I K.T. will go fishing with Wendy when I'm able to cast.'"

She nodded. "That will be my present."

He looked at her for a stilled moment, then at the note, and chuckled. "Give me the pen. It's not official unless it's signed."

Very happy, she handed him the pen and watched as

he signed his name. "Thank you, very much," she replied, folding the paper and slipping it into her pocket along with the pen. Then, because it was time, she said, "Now, I do need you to climb back in that bed."

Wendy looked at that slip of paper a hundred times or more in the days that followed. She kept it beneath the little trophy that sat atop her dresser, next to the dish where she kept her hair pins and looked at the note each night and each morning. It was a bit ironic how happy that made her feel. Though it would be weeks before he could cast, when it happened, it would mean he was well on his way to being completely healed. That was the ultimate goal for his nurse to have, however, as his friend, she was going to miss seeing him every day.

She let out a long sigh.

Starting today.

Which also meant that she needed to give him Betty's letter.

Another sigh, a much deeper one, released as she felt her pocket where the envelope holding both the letter and the necklace was deep inside. After serious contemplation last night, she'd decided to just give him the letter when he was leaving the hospital, for him to read in private.

K.T. had received another Christmas gift the day he'd given her that note. Gloria had told him that he no longer would be strapped to the bed and could get up and move about at will. There had only been one large area on his back, between his shoulder blades that hadn't healed over, and rather than the solution-soaked dressings lying across his back, they'd started to use a soaked dressing pack and covered it with dry bandages that were wrapped around his chest and over his shoulders to hold the pack in place.

That had worked well, and though the wound was almost healed, even after he was discharged, he would need to return daily for dressing changes.

All of that made her wonder if she should wait to give him Betty's letter until he no longer needed to return for dressing changes. But ultimately, she knew she'd already waited too long.

She was nervous, very, and hoped that he'd understand why she'd waited to give it to him.

Right up until the moment she entered his room, to find his bed empty.

Then a profound emptiness filled her, one that instinctively told her he was gone. There were two other patients in the room, both sitting up and eating their breakfast. It was totally unlike her, but for a moment their names escaped her. Several patients had left and entered the room since he'd been admitted, but that was no excuse.

Forcing herself to act normal, she greeted the patients, one at a time and looked through their charts, refreshing her somewhat numb mind to their names and conditions. After checking their vitals and recording them, she stripped K.T.'s bed, feeling an even greater sense of loss as she looked at the hole in the mattress.

It was ridiculous. She should be rejoicing over his discharge, his recuperation. A part of her was; deep in her heart she was grateful. Would forever be grateful that he'd survived the attack and that she'd been his nurse.

Pulling up her resolve, she told herself that was all she'd ever been, his nurse, and set into her duties.

Near noon, she ran into Gloria. "Oh, Wendy, I apologize. There was an emergency this morning and Dr. Bloomberg asked me to assist him in surgery."

"I hope all went well," Wendy replied.

"Yes, thank you, it did." Gloria's expression softened. "I wanted to meet you when you arrived for your shift and let you know that K.T. was discharged early this morning, so you wouldn't be surprised."

Wendy merely nodded. She had known that January third had been set as his discharge date, and had known that was today. She simply should have prepared herself for the empty room.

"As you know," Gloria continued, "he will need to return each day to have his bandage changed, and we agreed that eight o'clock would be the best time. I figured you could do that for him when you arrive each morning. And of course, others will when you have a day off."

Wendy's heart skipped a beat. "Yes, of course I can do that."

"Wonderful. You can use one of the examination bays and report any changes in his chart. I left it at the main nurse's station for you to collect."

"Very well, thank you." Wendy knew she should be questioning the joy inside her. No one should want to see someone because they needed medical attention.

Gloria sighed. "I have to admit, I was sad to see him go, but also very happy. So happy."

"You made all the difference in his healing," Wendy said. "And because of you, more men are healing and leaving here, returning to duty, every day."

"We made the difference," Gloria said. "Come, let's

eat lunch together and talk about everything except our patients."

As it turned out, lunch with Gloria was exactly what Wendy needed. Other nurses joined their table, and for the first time since the attack, there seemed to be a more relaxed atmosphere. No one gobbled down their food to rush back to urgent duties.

Wendy was sure everyone was still apprehensive that another attack could happen at any moment, for that was the reality of the situation, but there was the knowledge that whatever came about, they could handle it, just as they already had.

That's what she'd do, too. Take care of whatever came about. K.T. had simply been one of the patients she'd taken care of. Nothing more.

The rest of her day went by relatively quickly and uneventfully, and she arrived back at her living quarters shortly after four that afternoon, because her shift lengths had been reduced back to eight hours a day at the start of the new year.

A stack of mail sat on her bed. Every letter and postcard was now censored and marked with ink stamps declaring it had been examined. Everyone had been informed that even telling a family member back home if your unit was being shipped elsewhere could be potentially dangerous if it landed in the wrong hands.

Therefore, any concerning comments were cut out of letters, and the process of all that meant letters could be delayed in reaching their destinations. Anxious to see who the letters were from, but also wanting to enjoy reading each one, she removed her nurse's hat and uniform, then quickly changed into a yellow and white dress.

After taking some change out of her dresser drawer, she carried the letters downstairs, purchased a soda pop from the machine, and walked outside onto the concrete lanai. Several housemates were seated in the sun, some reading and others clustered in groups visiting.

Helen waved. "Join us."

Wendy held up her letters. "I will, after I read these."

"I read mine earlier," Helen replied. "We can compare notes when you're done."

Stories from back home were often shared with each other. "Deal," Wendy said as she found a secluded chair. It wasn't just stories from back home they shared, it was things in their daily lives. Many things, yet, she hadn't told anyone that K.T. was the man she'd danced with and had become her number one patient. Her reason for not sharing was simple. Both events had made him special to her. So special, she wanted to keep it to herself, so no one could take it away.

She'd come to that through her own reasonings. Much like she had when it came to Betty's letter. Neither was like her, but things had changed. She'd changed.

Sitting down in the wooden chair, she admitted that it was as if the whole world had changed. Everything looked different compared to a month ago. The hospital itself was on what was called Hospital Point, a section of land that jutted out on three sides, facing the harbor on two sides and the channel that led out to sea on the third side. The navy base was inland, just to the west of the hospital, and Hickman Field, the army air base, was farther away to the south and ran the length of the ocean coast. The naval air base was on Ford Island, in the center of the harbor, and Pearl City was on another peninsula on the other side of the island. All of those sites had been targets, and now looked very different than before.

There were still tall palm trees, bushes, plants, and grass, but trenches had been dug everywhere, leaving long, twisting piles of dirt along the trench edges, and the once pristine white buildings no longer looked the same. Though any broken windows had been repaired, there were signs on nearly every structure from where bombs, bullets, or shrapnel had struck. Even the clothesline poles had bullet holes in them.

If she were to walk a short distance she'd be able to see the harbor, and the USS *Nevada* that had attempted to make it to the channel and out to open sea during the attack, but had been torpedoed and run aground on Waipio Peninsula, straight across the harbor from the hospital. The ship was still there, partially sunk, as were others.

So many others.

In time, things would all be repaired or replaced, forever hiding the carnage of the attack, but nothing would be able to hide all the scars. Some would remain forever.

So would the memories. The bad ones and the good ones.

Drawing her attention off the landscape, she slowly looked through the stack of mail, trying to decide which letter to read first.

That decision arrived quickly when the third letter in the stack was from Oklahoma. K.T.'s mother's name was on the return address.

Wendy quickly set the other letters on the table holding her bottle of soda, and lifted the folded piece of paper out of the envelope that had been opened during censorship. There was just one page, written with neat, slanted penmanship.

Dearest Nurse Smith,
It is with immense gratitude that I write this letter. Your note at the bottom of my son's letter provided us with the relief we'd been hoping for since hearing that dreadful bulletin on the radio. I was alone in the house that Sunday afternoon and my heart had dropped to my feet upon hearing there had been an attack on Pearl Harbor. I yelled for my husband to come inside and knowing K.T. was in the thick of it, we remained glued to the radio for hours that slowly had turned into days. Kent carried the radio upstairs to our bedroom each evening, so we didn't miss any updates, even in the middle of the night. I sought to tell myself that my greatest fear had not come to light, but do admit to shedding tears, fearing that very thing.

The day K.T.'s letter arrived, Jud ran all the way to the house from the mailbox, shouting so loud the cows ran along the fence line beside him, all the way to the barn. They must have thought he was Henny Penny and that the sky was falling.

For the world, it may seem as if that is exactly what is happening, for this war has just begun, but at that moment, it was just the opposite for our family. We were filled with joy.

Thank you for writing that letter for K.T., and for adding your own message about his burns and care. I wish I could thank you in person and hug you for your promise to take care of my son. I

hold you in my prayers and in my heart for the
part you are playing in K.T.'s life.

It is a mother's prerogative to carry worry for
her children, and I imagine that your time is consumed with caring for the injured and ill, but I
do hope this letter reaches you and that you understand how your message lightened that worry
for one sailor's mother.

With my sincerest regards,

Ruth McCallister.

Wendy blinked and wiped at the tears welling in her
eyes, then read the letter a second time. Never had a
letter touched her so deeply. Never had she wanted to
hug someone in return as much as she did K.T.'s mother
right now.

Other than him, that is.

Chapter Seven

K.T. was doing his best to avoid Wendy by going to the hospital early each morning, before her shift started, to have a new bandage put on his back. Nurse Manning, who always seemed to be there, had looked surprised that first morning, and had reminded him that Wendy didn't start her shift until eight.

He'd explained that he needed to be at the shipyard before eight, which had almost backfired when she'd reminded him that he hadn't been released for full duty.

That hadn't happened yet, but would soon, and in the interim, he was going to the shipyard by eight each morning and spending all day in meetings with others going over the current conditions and writing estimates for the ships that needed to be repaired.

The USS *Pennsylvania*, which had been in dry dock the day of the attack, had already been repaired and set sail for Portland, Oregon, in December. The USS *Helena* had been moved to dry dock, repaired, and had set sail earlier this week for San Francisco. The USS *Honolulu* was in dry dock now, as was the *Vestal*.

He would be glad when the time finally came for

him to suit up and do the job he'd been trained to do, because they were greatly limited on the number of underwater welders in comparison to the tasks that needed to be done. There was still a list of ships that needed underwater work in order for them to be hauled into dry dock.

Being back at work, even in the limited capacity, was good and kept him occupied for the greater parts of the day, but it didn't prevent him from thinking about Wendy. Didn't stop him from missing her smiling face, her cheery disposition, and her opinions on topics large and small.

With a disgusted shake of his head, he reached for another slip of paper and laid it on the desk in front of him. He missed her, damn it, and he shouldn't.

Better yet, he wouldn't.

As he had several times over the past week, he started a letter to Betty.

Another letter.

He'd started at least one a night since leaving the hospital.

Not a one had he finished or mailed.

That would not happen again tonight. He'd finish this one and mail it. To aid in his determination, he opened a drawer and pulled out the envelope that held several pictures of his family. One was of him and Betty when a carnival had been in Guymon nearly five years ago. It had cost ten cents to have their picture taken of her sitting on his lap in front of an elephant. You couldn't see anything of the elephant in the picture, because it had been behind a high wall, which had disappointed Betty after she'd waited the two hours for the photo to be developed.

He grinned at the remembrance of that. The missing elephant was the reason he'd ended up with the picture. She'd wanted the photo of the elephant as proof to having seen an elephant, but without the elephant in the picture, she'd said that no one would believe she'd seen an elephant. He'd offered to pay for another picture, but she'd declined, claiming she'd rather have another ride on the Ferris wheel, so that's what they'd done.

After leaving home, he'd kept the picture in his billfold, but it had started to wear and fade, so he now kept it in the envelope with others from home, protecting the image.

They were both looking at the camera, smiling, and he could remember having the picture taken with clarity, yet, couldn't remember how he felt having her sit on his lap. Had it made his heart pound? His breath lock in his lungs? His pulse echo in his ears?

In truth, he couldn't remember any of those things happening at any time.

Except for when Wendy would crawl underneath the bed and look up at him with those ocean-blue eyes. Or arrive next to his bed, touch his hand, or—

Disgusted all over again, he attempted to get his mind back on Betty by recalling that she had blue eyes, too. The picture didn't reveal that, because it was in black-and-white, and he couldn't remember if they were ocean blue, because he hadn't seen the ocean yet back then.

A knock rapped on his door, and it pushed open a crack before he had a chance to respond.

"Hey, Lieutenant," Chaz Martin, one of his welders said while sticking his head through the opening. "Someone wants to see you out front."

"Okay." K.T. dropped the picture into the envelope and put it back in the drawer while standing up. As he walked to the door, he made sure his white uniform shirt was tucked tightly into his uniform shorts. It wasn't yet dark, and the men who'd just gotten off work were most likely gathered on the chairs out front, enjoying a short reprieve before the sun went down. The nine o'clock curfew was strongly enforced island wide.

He walked down the hall to the main door, and out of the window saw several men seated in chairs. Divers were still assigned to underwater assessments and one of them probably had a question to do with that.

When he pushed open the door, and caught sight of all the occupants of the wooden chairs, his heart dang near beat its way out of his chest. It had been six days since he'd seen her.

Six days and six nights.

Barely a moment of that time had gone by when he'd hadn't wondered how he would react upon seeing her, merely by accident, because he was doing his best to not see her.

Now he knew how he'd react.

He'd stand there awestruck, just as he was doing right now.

With that endearing dimple-filled smile, she stood. "Good evening, Lieutenant McCallister, I hope I'm not disturbing you."

Damn if his mouth hadn't gone completely dry on him. His throat, too. He had to clear it in order to speak, and that was disturbing in front of all the other sets of eyes staring at him. "No, not at all," he replied.

"I was hoping I could speak with you for a moment," she said.

"Sure." He couldn't take her inside, but didn't need every man in his unit hearing her ask why he was avoiding her. She'd have figured that out by now. Pointing toward the edge of the building, where there were more chairs set up around the corner, he said, "This way."

She bade goodbye to the group of men sitting in the chairs grinning at her and him. Many of them had visited him in the hospital, and, knowing her, she'd probably remembered every one of their names. Whereas right now, he wasn't sure if he remembered his own name.

They walked in silence, side by side, until they'd rounded the corner, then he said, "Sorry, I've missed you at the hospital, I've needed to be at the shipyard early every day."

"Gloria, I mean Nurse Manning, told me that," she said. "And that your wound is continuing to close up. How does it feel? Sore? Itchy? Hot?"

"It feels fine, Nurse Smith." He gestured to two chairs. "Do you want to sit down?"

"Sure, thank you."

Not so surprisingly, he couldn't pull his eyes off her. He tried, but his eyes didn't listen any better than the rest of him. She was wearing a blue dress, light blue, with a white collar and thin belt around her waist, and her dark, thick hair was free, hanging down around her shoulders. Ignoring her, forgetting her, would be a lot easier if she wasn't unforgettably pretty. And nice, and caring, and delightful, and numerous other things.

He waited until she was seated, before sitting down in the chair next to her, still unable to look away.

"I have something I need to ask you," she said,

sounding nervous and clutching the handle of the white purse sitting on her lap. "Or tell you."

Concern rose quickly. "What's that? Is something wrong?"

"No." She grimaced. "I, well, I hope not. I don't think so, but I guess that's up to you to decide."

Perplexed by her nervous, yet earnest tone, he asked, "What is it?"

She looked down at her purse as she opened it. "I received a letter from my cousin Sid, Uncle Sy's son who is a lawyer, and I do need to respond to him, but I wanted you to read it first."

Growing concerned, he reached over and laid a hand on her arm. "Has something happened to your aunt or uncle?"

"No, nothing like that." She pulled an envelope out of her purse. "I wrote to Sid after I read the letter from your mother, the first one where your father had told those surveyors to stay off your property."

He recalled the letter, but had no idea what her cousin Sid had to do about it, and waited for her to say more.

"I asked Sid if he knew of a lawyer who might help your family," she said.

"There was no need for you to do that." His family didn't have the money to pay for a lawyer, not a Nebraska one or an Oklahoma one.

"I know I didn't need to, but I did, and I hope you aren't upset about that." She held out the letter. "I think you should read what Sid had to say."

He took the letter, but only because she'd made the point of walking all the way over here for him to see it. A lawyer was the last person who would change his father's mind, but for her and her efforts, he began to read. The first paragraph was full of how grateful they all were to hear from her and that she'd survived the attack. Then, her cousin went on to say he'd be interested in talking to the family she'd mentioned from Oklahoma. He was already working on a multistate land and mineral rights case, because natural gas was a principal source of helium, a gas that was in great demand to help with the war effort.

K.T. knew that. Helium was one of the gases used in diving and welding, but it was also used to fly the big barrage balloons used in the navy's anti-submarine efforts. His interest was spiked even higher as he continued to read.

Sid went on to explain how the production of liquefied natural gas was reaching unprecedented heights and how modernized seismographic equipment was able to detect gas fields with great accuracy. Ultimately, Sid made it sound like his family would greatly benefit from having the property surveyed, and the Oklahoma lawyers involved with him would make sure they were treated fairly by the oil company, who would pay all of the surveying costs.

From the way it was worded, it wouldn't cost his family anything if gas wasn't found, and if it was found, the gas company would pay for the equipment, and his family would receive dividends per barrel.

Cautious by nature, he read parts of the letter a second time, letting it sink in deeper. "This sounds too good to be true," he said aloud, half talking to himself.

"I know," Wendy replied. "That's why I wanted you to read it. Sid wouldn't say those things if they weren't true. I promise you that. But I didn't feel I could write to him, give him your family's name and address without your consent."

There was no reason for him to not believe her or her cousin. In fact, there were several reasons for him to believe her. She was as honest as the day was long, and truly cared about others. Cared so much about people she didn't even know that she'd written to her cousin about them.

A distinct stomach-churning realization came to him. She'd done that, had written to Sid about his family, because of him.

"I wrote to Sid," she said, as if reading his mind, "because I consider you my friend, K.T., besides your nurse, and I—I, well, I like helping my friends."

He nodded, while his mind searched for proof that he considered her as nothing more than a friend. Or perhaps, he was searching to figure out what he did consider her. She was more than an acquaintance. "We have been through a lot together," he said aloud, still working through his thoughts.

"We have." She grinned and shrugged one shoulder. "We have a trophy to prove it."

He chuckled. "We do, at that."

"Should I send Sid your father's name and address?"

Sometimes in life, there was only one choice. "Yes, and I'll write to my father, giving him Sid's name, and yours, so he's not caught off guard and doesn't say something he shouldn't."

She giggled. "Sid is used to Uncle Sy, who can say things he shouldn't more often than not, despite Aunt Ella's warnings."

"One more thing we have in common?"

Her smile grew even bigger. "I guess so."

He handed her back the letter. "Thank you, Wendy."

She tucked the letter back in her purse and clasped it shut. "All I did was write a letter, but I do hope for the best. I truly do."

For more than a moment he was transfixed by the glimmer in her eyes that was brighter than the noonday sun shining on blue ocean waters. An intense rush of desire was what made him pull his eyes off her, and bite his back teeth together. He let out a small cough, hoping to get his mind and body back in control. "I hope for the best, too."

"Well, I suppose I should get back," she said. "I don't want to be caught out after curfew."

"No, you don't." He stood and held out a hand, helped her stand. "And you aren't walking anywhere. I'll drive you."

"You shouldn't be driving," she argued. "Dr. Bloomberg hasn't given you permission to do that."

He gave her hand a squeeze. "I like friend Wendy better than Nurse Smith."

"Oh, really?" she asked.

Chuckling, he shook his head and gave her hand a little tug. "No, not really, but friend Wendy I can tell that I've been driving every day, all around the base, and she wouldn't tell Dr. Bloomberg."

Pinching her lips together as she looked up at him, she shook her head.

"Am I right?" he asked.

She sighed. "Yes, you are right."

"Good."

She gave him a sideways glance as they walked toward the parking lot. "As long as I witness that driving won't hamper your healing."

He laughed. "That will be easy to prove." The seat of the utility rig had a low seat that barely came up to the middle of his back, well below his bandaged area.

Wendy had seen the general-purpose vehicles called jeeps that were proclaimed to go anywhere and do anything, but had never ridden in one. There were no doors or a top on the shiny gray vehicle. Just one wide seat in the front, a windshield, and a small, flat cargo area behind the seat.

She climbed in on the passenger side, and wasn't sure if she was excited over the ride, Sid's offer that K.T. had agreed with, or seeing him. That alone was exciting. He'd been handsome while in the hospital, but seeing him in his white uniform, standing tall and straight as he'd walked out of the door of his living quarters earlier, had been like watching a sunrise. A sight that was indescribable to those who hadn't seen it.

It was more than his looks, though. His stance alone signified how upstanding, confident, and honorable he was. All things she knew to be fully true.

Memories of the last time she'd seen him dressed all in white had instantly flashed in her mind and her heart had fluttered as hard as it had while dancing with him that night. That feeling had remained with her, even while she'd been nervous to tell him about Sid's letter.

The nervousness wasn't so much about the letter or Sid's offer, it had been because she still had another letter to tell him about. She'd considered bringing it with her tonight, but figured one letter was enough.

"See," he said. "The back of the seat isn't high enough to come in contact with my bandage."

She did see that, and nodded.

"Want to know something else?" he asked as he started the engine.

"Yes," she answered.

He shifted the gear stick and backed up out of the parking space. "I drive this jeep to the hospital every morning."

She believed him, and to be honest, during her walk from her living quarters to his, she'd thought about him walking that far back and forth each day, and was glad that he wasn't doing that. It wasn't a long trek, but had been longer than she'd imagined.

"What else have you been doing every day?" she asked.

"Not much." He steered out of the parking lot and onto the road. "Mainly sitting in a chair, going over drawings of the damaged ships."

"Will you repair all of them?"

"That's yet to be determined, but we hope to," he replied. "The Bureau of Construction and Repair in Washington, DC, sent out Captain Jeffrey Heinz to oversee the Salvage Division. He arrived last week. I like him. He's committed and set a goal to assess every ship, and fix the ones we can well enough to get them to a shipyard on the West Coast for complete restoration as quickly as possible."

"That sounds daunting," she said.

He glanced at her and shook his head. "To me, it doesn't sound nearly as daunting as the job you and the others did at the hospital. We're just putting ships back together, you put people back together."

She appreciated his sentiment, and showed that in a smile. "I guess we all have our jobs to do."

"We do."

They were driving toward the entrance to the yard, and she glanced over her shoulder at the large buildings. "I didn't realize just how enormous the buildings here are. They look big from a distance, but not that big."

He slowed the jeep and made a complete turnabout, so they were headed back into the yard instead of out of it.

She tucked her hair that was flying about behind both ears. "Where are we going?"

"We have a few minutes to spare," he replied. "I'll give you a quick tour."

Always excited to see new things, she clutched onto the side of the vehicle as they drove closer to the buildings that were by far the largest she'd ever seen. Many places had big buildings, but those were often tall; these were long and wide. "Can a ship fit inside them?"

"Not the big ships, but a harbor craft up to twenty-five feet can easily fit inside. These shops have the capacity and equipment to fix or build just about anything. There's a gas plant here on the base, and right now the teams are using boundless amounts of acetylene and oxygen for the torches to cut through the metal on the hulls of the ships…"

He continued to tell her about a variety of things as he drove past the big buildings, ships in dry dock, and other points of interest. Some of the things he talked about she didn't quite understand, yet found interesting, and others she did understand and wondered about the work he did. "How do you see to use the torches and welders under water?"

"You don't really. It's kind of like you, working in the dark. You feel your way about, imagine what it looks like in your mind and try not to stub a toe." He grinned at her, then continued, "There's a man at the top of the water, talking through a phone wire, telling the diver where things are located and monitoring the oxygen as well as the gases for the torches and welders. I'll show you the suits we wear another day," he said, as they drove back toward the entrance again.

"I'd like that." He had told her about the suits while he'd been in the hospital and she'd seen pictures of diving gear, but never in person. She had to admit, he made it all sound so exciting. It was clear how much he enjoyed doing what he did.

"When's your next day off?"

"Sunday." She bit her lip, trying to ease her excitement before asking, "When's yours?"

He shook his head. "We'll be working seven days a week for months to come, but I'll be able to take time away to show you some things."

Her nurse's mind kicked in. "You are still healing and need your rest."

"Nurse Wendy is back," he said, flashing her another smile.

Her heart did a little loop-de-loop inside her chest. He had such an amazing smile. One that made her want to smile, too, even as she explained, "I just don't want you to have a setback."

"I won't. One hospital stay was more than enough, even though I had excellent care."

"I think I told you that flattery will get you nowhere once before," she said.

He laughed "I do think you did."

What had been a long walk, was a short drive, and as the hospital came into sight she was disappointed that their time together was at an end. Recalling the reason for her visit, she asked, "Does your family have a phone? I could give the number to Sid."

"No." He drove around the back side of the hospital and up to her barracks. "But he could call the feed store. Ed Tillis would gladly drive out and tell my dad to come into town and use the phone to call your cousin back. I've done that a couple of times."

She dug in her purse and pulled out a pen and Sid's letter. "What's the name of the feed store?"

"Tillis Feed Store. The operator will be able to connect him."

Having written the name, she dropped the envelope and pen in her purse. "I'll tell Sid, and thank you very much for the ride home."

He climbed out of his side of the jeep at the same time she climbed out of hers and they met in front of the vehicle. "I'll walk you to the door," he said.

"I walk to the door every night by myself," she said.

"I know, but I'll still do it," he insisted.

She gave a nod. This wasn't a date and there was no reason for her to think along those lines, but they were friends, and that made her happy. Happier than any friendship had ever made her in the past.

At the door, she said, "I'll write to Sid tonight."

"I will write to my father tonight."

His gaze floated across her face, and seemed to penetrate into her skin, making her cheeks grow warm and her breath stall in her chest. He couldn't possibly be thinking about kissing her, but that was where her mind went. She had to look away, hoping to make the thought disappear. Friends don't kiss. Well, maybe some do, on the cheek, but that wasn't the kind of kiss that had popped into her head.

He touched her arm. "Thank you, Wendy. This could be an amazing opportunity for my family, and I'm very grateful for that."

Pushing all other thoughts aside, she held up one hand and crossed her fingers. "I'll keep my fingers crossed that it all works out."

With a smile and a nod, he said, "Good night, Wendy."

"Good night, K.T."

He waited until she'd walked inside before he turned around, and she continued to watch through the window until he drove away, then she hurried up the steps to her room. Helen and Lois were both working the four to midnight shift, and she plopped down on her bed, still wearing her shoes, and closed her eyes, relishing the amazing feelings inside her. They were much like the ones she'd had the night of the dance. That was so nonsensical because she'd come home for over a month having seen him every day and never felt like this.

It could be because he was no longer her patient. She wasn't sure, and didn't spend time thinking about why. Instead, she lay there, just feeling happy for a moment, because that felt precious right now.

When her thoughts teetered on kissing again, she bolted upright and climbed off the bed to collect her stationery. There were only two sheets left in the box, and she wondered where she would be able to find more. She could use regular paper, but she really liked using stationery. The paper of this set had tiny daisy flowers printed on the corners and the envelope had one printed on the flap. Aunt Ella had given it to her when she'd left for California, along with a ballpoint pen.

Perhaps the supply depot would have some. She would check on her next day off.

A full-blown smile tugged at her lips. Her next day off would be spent with K.T. showing her more of the base. He hadn't mentioned when or where she should meet him, nor how long it would take.

Sitting down on the bed, she decided she would go to the hospital early tomorrow, to put on his new bandage and ask him. It would mean missing breakfast, but that wasn't a problem. She could eat at the hospital.

Satisfied with that plan, she crawled onto the bed and lay down on her stomach to write her letter to Sid. Responses to all the other letters she'd received with his had already been sent, including one to K.T.'s mother. She'd told her how K.T. had been discharged and was nearly as fit as before the attack.

Sid's letter didn't take long to write, for she kept it short, just the front and back of one piece of paper. She set the envelope atop her dresser, and after putting her stationery box in a drawer, she pulled out a nightgown and went down the hall to shower.

By seven thirty the next morning, when K.T. still hadn't arrived, she was wondering if he'd arrived before seven and whoever had put on a fresh dressing had forgotten to mark it down in his chart. That hadn't happened on days past, and each entry had listed a time of shortly after seven.

When seven forty-five rolled past, she wondered if he'd been caught out after dark last night and had been arrested. She'd never heard what happened to those caught out after curfew, but the orders had clearly stated that all violations would go before the provost court, where decisions would be made swiftly and penalties would be severe. It hadn't been dark when he'd dropped her off, but the sun had been setting and if he hadn't gone straight back to his barracks, he would have been out after curfew.

By eight o'clock, her heart was drumming as she imagined all sorts of things that could have happened to him. She didn't know what she could do to find out, either. Her shift was starting now and she wouldn't be off until four. Working all day, worrying about him—

"Good morning, Nurse Smith."

She spun around and wasn't sure if she should hug him or punch him in the arm for scaring her nearly half to death. Until his grin made her do neither. Squaring her shoulders, she smiled in return. "Good morning, Lieutenant McCallister."

"I figured I'd come over later this morning, so you could put on my bandage and find out what time you want me to pick you up on Sunday."

He was already unbuttoning his white shirt, and though she'd seen his bare skin a thousand times over, it felt different this morning. So different it was a moment before she understood what he'd said. "Pick me up?"

"Yes, for your longer tour of the base." He set his shirt on the table and then grasped the bottom of his T-shirt to pull it off. "Would nine o'clock work for you?"

A sudden wave of embarrassment washed over her and she spun around. Seeing the supplies she'd readied earlier gave her something to do, even though her hands were shaking so hard she had to ball them into fists for a moment.

"We could make it ten if nine is too early," he said.

"No," she answered without turning around. "Nine will be fine."

"Good enough."

She heard the wheels of the small stool squeak and assuming he'd sat down on it, she dared a glance over her shoulder. He was on the stool, with his back facing her. A back that was very familiar and her nerves calmed considerably.

Her nursing mind also kicked in. "You've already removed the bandage from yesterday?"

"Yes, I do each morning before taking my shower. Nurse Manning said I need to keep it clean and that's the routine we agreed on."

"Agreed on, or that's the one you suggested until she gave in?"

He chuckled. "Either way, it works."

It was working because his wound looked remarkably well. There was but a small slit where the skin hadn't yet grown back together. She'd read how well it was doing in his chart, but seeing it was still surprising. A wonderful surprise. The new skin was still red, and he had some scarring, but compared to what his back had looked like the first time she'd seen it, what she saw now was what she'd call a miracle. "Are you sleeping on your back?"

"Sometimes, but not for long, it's still tender," he replied.

She set the solution-soaked pack on his back and covered it with several large gauze pads. "That will last for a while yet, I'm sure, but all in all, it looks very good."

"It feels good," he said. "Compared to a month ago."

Still amazed by how quickly he'd healed, she said, "Nurse Manning had studied burns and was sure she could have yours healed in record time." Wendy collected a roll of gauze and began to run it over one shoulder, across his chest, under his arm, and across his back.

"She explained that to me," he said.

"She did?"

"Yes, she told me about her son, too," he said.

That was a surprise, yet at the same time not really. She could understand that Gloria would want him to know why she was so convinced her technique would work. "I'm glad she told you," Wendy said, while using a second roll of gauze to do the same on his opposite side so he had an X shape of gauze on his chest and back.

"It was the middle of the night, not long after I'd arrived and I'd asked her if she ever went home, got some sleep."

"She practically lives here," Wendy said, using bandage tape to secure the ends of the gauze, careful to make sure that none of the adhesive touched his skin.

"That's why," he said. "She's set upon turning tragedy into healing, and is doing one hell of a job at it."

"She is," Wendy agreed. "She truly is."

"Done?" he asked.

"Yes." Then curious, she asked, "Who helps you remove the bandage?"

"No one." He spun the stool around to face her. "I just cut the gauze right here." He pointed at his chest. "And it falls off." Grabbing his T-shirt, he pulled it over his head.

"Does the pack ever stick to your back?"

"Hasn't yet." He picked up his button-up shirt, hooked it with a thumb, and flipped it over his shoulder. "Same time tomorrow?"

She almost told him that she could be here earlier,

but then he might figure out that she'd been here for an hour, fretting over why he was late, and she didn't want him to know that. Didn't want him to feel bad about it, because he would. "I'll be here by eight."

"Me, too." He walked to the door. "Have a good day."

"You, too," she said. Then, as soon as he disappeared into the hallway, for no apparent reason, her knees wobbled and she sat down on the stool, told herself to breathe. Just breathe.

Closing her eyes, she pressed a hand to her forehead. It couldn't be. It just couldn't be. She opened her eyes and stared at the doorway. She couldn't be falling in love with him. That was impossible. She just wanted to be his friend. Nothing more. Yet, the things he made her feel were more. More than she'd ever felt before, and that could only mean one thing.

But he was in love with Betty.

Who was no longer in love with him.

Oh, this was all going so terribly wrong.

She had to fix it, and she had to make sure that she didn't fall in love with him. It couldn't be that hard.

Chapter Eight

K.T. had convinced himself to not have second
thoughts. He and Wendy were friends. After everything that she'd done for him, she deserved his friendship. Furthermore, he'd finally finished a letter to
Betty. He'd told her about Wendy. Nurse Smith, who
had worked diligently to see he was healed and back
on duty, and had contacted a lawyer to help his parents with the oil company wanting to survey their land.

He'd skimmed over his burns and treatment, and
the attack, in the letter saying as little as possible, because he didn't want her to worry. Nor did he mention
the necklace he'd mailed her a couple of months ago,
because he didn't want her to feel bad about not writing to let him know that she'd received it. Or maybe
she hadn't received it. Maybe he should have put it in
a box, instead of just an envelope.

Betty hadn't written him after the letter that Wendy
had penned for him, and he wondered if their time apart
had finally gotten to her. His father had said that could
happen. To both or either one of them, and that no one
would be to blame. If they loved each other, that love
would last four years, and many more after that.

K.T. looked at the letter. He'd planned on dropping it in the outgoing mail this morning, on his way to the hospital for his bandage change. Wendy had changed it for him the past two days and had offered to meet him there at eight this morning, but he'd declined. It was her day off and he wasn't going to make her go into work just for him.

He opened his desk drawer and dropped the letter inside, deciding to mail it later, then left for the hospital.

The nurse who put on the dressing was one he'd had while in the hospital, and he thanked her for doing a fine job before leaving the hospital. Although he'd be glad when he no longer needed any bandages, he would never forget the pain of those first days. He'd never forget the care he'd received, either.

A few moments later, the hitch inside his chest was caused by two things. Knowing who had provided that care, and seeing her standing outside of her barracks as he turned the corner around the back side of the hospital. She was wearing the same red polka dot dress as the night of the dance, and looked just as pretty as she had that night.

Prettier, because he now knew more about her. So much more. She was far more than a pretty face.

She walked to the edge of the sidewalk and waited for him to stop the jeep.

"Good morning," he greeted while turning off the engine.

"Good morning."

There was no door for him to open or close, but he still got out and walked her to the passenger side of the jeep. He waited for her to climb inside, before he walked around and climbed in the driver's side. "Ready?"

"I am."

He started the engine and shifted into Reverse. Turned out, he had the day off, too. There were others working today, but because of his limited capacity duty, there was nothing he could participate in. Unaccustomed to ever having idle time on his hands, he would have been as utterly restless today as he had been in the hospital. He also had a surprise for her, but would wait until later to mention that. She'd said that she had the entire day free, and he'd decided to make the most of it.

"I haven't seen much of the island since the attack," he said. "Would you mind if we took a drive around?"

"Not at all," she said. "I haven't seen much, either, and have wanted to." She grimaced slightly. "I don't need reminders of the damage, but I do want to know what we survived, because that will make us stronger."

He nodded, fully understanding. It was natural curiosity to want to see how things had changed, and he, too, felt that it was necessary. "I agree. You surprise me sometimes with the things you say."

"I do? Why?"

"Because you seem to be so wise for someone so young."

She sighed. "Wisdom doesn't only come from years."

"You are right about that, too." He followed the road around the hospital, and inland, toward the road that went to Honolulu. Sandbags and boxes surrounded every building, and manned machine gun nests were stationed at all corners atop the buildings, but as they drove off the base, it was evident that was the case everywhere, as were antiaircraft stations. The long guns with their big heavy metal stands and wheels were visible in all directions. There were also numerous signs indicating the way to first aid stations and reminding travelers of the martial laws in effect.

Although the two of them discussed what they saw now and again, for most of the time, they were silent, merely taking in the sights. Hickman Airfield had practically been destroyed. Complete hangers had been bombed, destroyed, along with the planes that had been inside them.

K.T. knew the army was just as set on repair and rebuild as the navy, and silently wished them well. Every military man knew no one fought for only one unit or branch, they all fought together, for the men at their sides and the people back home.

"Look at the beaches," she said, as the road curved and then followed along the coastline. "What is that?"

"Rolls of barbed wire," he replied. "And trenches." The deepest ones he'd seen yet. The entire jeep could drive down into them and not be seen.

"How did those people get on the other side of it?" she asked.

There were people on the other side of the wire, some fishing, some swimming, and some simply playing in the sand. "Where there is a will, there is a way," he replied.

"Will they be arrested?" she asked.

Considering the armed guards stationed along the trenches, he said, "If they are still there at curfew, yes, but during the day, people are allowed to go about their business."

"That's good, don't you think?" she replied. "Everyone is on high alert, but they still need to live."

"I agree." Following the road to Downtown Honolulu, he asked, "Is there anything you want to see?"

She looked his way, but didn't say anything.

"What is it?" he asked, reading her thoughtful expression. "What do you want to see?"

"Well, we don't have to, but the day of the attack, I had planned on taking a jitney into town to see the palace."

"The palace?"

"Yes, the Iolani Palace, it's being used as the capitol building for the territory."

He was aware of that, but hadn't given it a lot of thought. His duty came first.

"When King Kalākaua died," she continued, "his sister succeeded him. Queen Lili'uokalani. That was in 1889. She was vastly opposed, and eventually the monarchy was overthrown, but before then the royal family hosted lavish balls and parties for people from around the world. The palace had amenities that were practically unheard of at the time, including indoor plumbing, electricity, and a telephone."

"I didn't know any of that," he said.

"I like learning about new things."

He glanced her way quickly. "And seeing things." There was little that he'd ever forget about her or the things she'd told him. "Seeing the world."

"Yes, seeing the world."

"Well, then, it's a palace you shall see today."

It was easy to find, and an impressive structure of stone masonry. Two stories aboveground, with a row of windows indicating it had a full basement, the building was sandstone in color, and had square turrets on each corner of the roof, and a larger turret in the center. It was surrounded by rows of palm trees, and guards, including atop the building and blocking the entranceway.

He brought the jeep to a stop, so she could look at it from the distance of the long driveway. "Sorry, looks like this is as close as we can get."

"That's fine, I just wanted to be able to say that I've seen a palace." She let out a long, soft sigh. "And now I have."

He looked at the palace again, wondering what she saw, because there was a certain glow on her face and in her eyes, which to him, was more enticing than the building. He'd never been enticed by someone before, and wasn't comfortable thinking about why he was this time.

She sighed and started talking about Queen Lili'uokalani being arrested and confined to a bedroom on the second story of the palace, and though he heard every word, his mind was still on her, and the situation he found himself in, and what he should do about it.

"I think we should leave now," she said. "Before a guard comes and questions us."

Noticing the guard looking at them, he shifted the jeep into first gear. "Where to now?"

"Wherever you want," she said, opening the purse sitting on her lap.

K.T. had to force himself to pull his eyes off her and onto the road as she pulled a pair of sunglasses out of her purse and slid them on her face. Although he'd been issued sunglasses back in California, and wore them regularly when on the water, up until this moment, the only women he'd seen wear a pair of sunglasses were movie stars in magazines. Round, with thick wire frames, they looked adorable on her. "Where did you get those?" he asked.

"Uncle Sy. He saw them in a catalog and gave them to me before I left. He said, *'Now, Wendy—'* That's what he always said, 'Now, Wendy,' like now was my first name and Wendy my last. *'Now, Wendy, all the women in California are wearing them, so you best have a pair, too. The sun must be brighter out there.'"*

K.T. figured her uncle Sy must have been looking at the same movie star magazines as he had.

"I would have brought along a hat, had I known the sun would be this bright." Then, with a laugh, she added, "No, I wouldn't have. The only hat I have is tan colored and wouldn't go with this dress."

Her honesty made him laugh. He hadn't expected her to not be honest, because she never had been; it was just the way she said things that tickled him. That, too, was unusual. "Well, the glasses look very nice."

"Thank you. I like them, too. I would have brought along the camera he gave me, but I thought were we just going to the base, and I know that no one is supposed to take pictures of anything that the enemy could use to gather intelligence."

That was the standing order, and he wasn't surprised that she'd follow all orders to a T. "We can come to the palace another day for you to take a picture."

"That's okay, I already bought a postcard with a picture of the palace. It's much nicer than one I would have taken."

They ended up driving around Honolulu, seeing some interesting sights, including Diamond Head, the Aloha Tower, and the Royal Hawaiian Hotel, and many not so pleasant things. Buildings that had been damaged, windows that had been painted black, parks and school yards that now hosted long trenches and gun stations.

Their conversations were just as varied. She was full of information about the island, things he would never have known.

As they drove past an area where several children were playing, she asked, "Do you think everyone on the mainland has been issued a gas mask?"

He'd seen the pile of them near the children, and his, as well as her box, were on the seat between them. "I'm not sure."

"That would be a lot of masks."

"Yes, it would," he agreed.

Still watching the children, she giggled and shook her head.

Curious, he asked, "What are you giggling about?"

"A memory," she said, and twisted slightly to look at him as she spoke. "There was this little boy, Todd, who lived about three blocks from the store, and a few years ago, he came in one morning with what I thought was a list of things that his mother needed. He asked if we had any eggs, and I said yes, then he asked if we had any yield."

"Yield?" he asked, questioning if he'd heard her.

"Yes." She laughed. "I questioned him, and he showed me the list. It was actually a recipe. He wanted his mother to make him some cookies, and she said she couldn't because they didn't have all the ingredients. He said he'd checked and the only things they didn't have were the eggs and the yield." Fully animated with laughter, she added, "The bottom of the recipe said yield two dozen."

He laughed, too. It felt good, and reminded him again of how right she was that even amidst a war, people needed to live. To laugh. Have fun. He was going to do just that today. There would be time for him to contemplate everything else later. "What did you do?"

"I gave him two eggs and explained that yield meant how many cookies his mother could then bake." With a smile still filling her face, she sighed. "Later that day, he brought me a cookie."

"That was nice of him, and nice of you to give him the eggs."

"It was nice of him, but a week later, when his mother came in, I discovered that she'd sent a plate of cookies to us, not just one." Laughing again, she said, "Todd had hidden the rest of the ones he was supposed to deliver, for himself."

"He sounds like he was quite a kid."

She nodded. "Did you ever hide something from your mother?"

"Yes. All kids do."

"Tell me one."

"There was the time I got bucked off a horse and knocked my shoulder blade out of place. I was eight. As luck would have it, I had to use both hands to climb back in the saddle, and doing that popped it back in place. Which hurt worse than falling off had, but by supper time, it was feeling good enough that I never told anyone."

"You didn't? Why not?"

"Because I wasn't supposed to be riding that horse." He didn't explain that the stallion had belonged to neighbors and had made its way to their house looking for a mare. Another memory formed. "There was also the time I tore my shirt on purpose, but claimed it was an accident."

"Why would you do that?"

"Because it had flowers on it. Tiny blue ones. My mother had said no one would notice the flowers. She had sewn it for me out of one of her old dresses, claiming I'd been growing so fast she couldn't keep me in clothes. I'd rather have gone shirtless. I knew the exact nail to let it catch on in the barn and ripped it from the collar to the hem, then ran to the house, convinced it wouldn't be repairable. It was. She stitched it up and I had to wear that flowered shirt for dang near a year."

Wendy was laughing so hard, she'd pulled a handkerchief out of her purse and wiped her eyes. "I'm sorry, but that's too funny."

"It wasn't to a ten-year-old boy."

They continued sharing stories, and he took the longer inland route back to the base. Along the way, he pulled over once in a while to get a better look at the mountain range, some umbrella-shaped Hitachi trees, and the bark of the colorful eucalyptus trees. He could have wondered why he took the longer route, but already knew. These were all things she would like to see, and he wanted to be the one to show them to her.

Once they arrived back at the base, he took her inside one of the buildings, where his unit's supplies and equipment were stored. Half his unit was working today, under Scott's command, and the other half had the day off.

She was full of questions about the rubberized coveralls, complete with gloves, and the heavy, lead-weighted belts and shoes, and the big copper helmet and breastplate they wore while diving. He didn't mind answering all of her questions. For years, he'd explained in letters and during his two trips home, what he did and about his equipment, but this was the first time he'd shown it to anyone.

"Good heavens," she said, attempting to pick up the eighty-five-pound belt. "How can you move with this on?"

"It's hard on land, but under the water, the weight counterbalances the buoyancy of the suit and we can move easily. Without the belt and the weighted shoes, we'd be constantly floating upward and never get any work done."

"I see it all, but I still can't imagine wearing any of this." She touched the air hose that connected to the helmet. "I can't imagine depending on someone else to make sure I have the air I need to breathe, either."

"The men on the surface provide us with everything we need, air, sight, direction. We couldn't do any of it without them."

Wendy's heart was thudding in her throat at the idea of him wearing all this heavy equipment and counting on someone else to make sure he could breathe. To her, it was as frightening as it was unbelievable, yet, she could hear the pride in his voice, and the passion. He enjoyed being a diver. Immensely. From her conversations with the members in his unit who had come to see him at the hospital, she knew he was one of the best, too.

"Thank you for showing me all of this," she said. "It's so very interesting, and I'm totally in disbelief at what you do. At how you do it."

"I'm just one of many."

She shook her head at how he was normalizing how specific and specialized his job was, and him. A swell of emotion filled her from head to toe as she looked up at him. He was such a remarkable man. Truly remarkable. "I am honored to know you, Oklahoma." Then, she might never know what prompted her to do it, but she stretched up on her toes and kissed his cheek. "Very honored."

He went as stiff as a board, and for the next second or more, she questioned her own sanity.

Until he laughed and gave her a quick, but solid hug. "I'm honored to know you, too, Nebraska," he said as his arms slipped away.

She used the time to get her breathing and nerves back under control while he made sure the equipment that he'd shown her was all back in its proper place. It wasn't easy, and she hadn't quite accomplished gaining control, when he turned about, with a full-blown smile on his face.

"It's time for your surprise," he said.

She blinked, now working on understanding his comment. "Surprise? What surprise?"

He clasped her hand and started walking toward the door of the building. "Didn't I tell you that I have a surprise for you?"

"No, you did not, and you know you didn't," she said, heart pounding hard enough that it could easily explode at any given moment. His hand holding hers was the culprit, yet she didn't want him to release it, either.

"I guess I forgot."

"Forgot?" She shook her head, because she didn't believe that. "What is it?"

"A surprise."

He was enjoying this way too much. So was she, and just like holding his hand, didn't want it to end. She should, and she should be thinking about the consequences, but not today. He deserved a day of fun after all he'd been through, and that's all this was. A day of friends having fun together. "I demand you tell me this instant."

His laughter echoed inside the building. "Demand all you want. This is a wait and see kind of deal."

They arrived at the door to the building, and as he opened it and gestured for her to walk outside, she said, "I don't want to wait and see."

"You don't have a choice." He stepped outside beside her and after he'd shut the door, continued to hold her hand all the way to the jeep.

She climbed in and once again took her glasses out of her purse, merely for something to do because her hand was still tingling and sending little shoots of happiness right to her heart.

He climbed in the driver's side and winked at her before he started the engine.

Good heavens, but her insides were leaping for joy, and she once again told herself that it was only because they were friends, having fun. Just like the night of the dance. "What are you going to do after the war?" she asked, practically out of the blue because she hadn't planned on asking that. "Will you keep diving and welding?"

He shifted the jeep into Reverse and backed up. "I don't think there will be a lot of need for that in Oklahoma."

"No, I suppose not." She wasn't sure what she'd expected as an answer, nor what she'd wanted to hear.

"What will you do? Keep nursing?"

That was easy to answer. "Keep seeing the world.

I'll find another way once my time with the Red Cross is over."

He looked at her with a slight shake of his head. "I believe you will."

She contemplated telling him about Betty's letter, but quickly decided that would ruin the day, and she didn't want to do that. She did need to do it soon. He needed to know, and not just because someone else might tell him in a letter, even Betty herself if he was to write to her. All of that was on her mind continuously, but even more concerning was why she hadn't told him yet. She'd never done anything so deceiving, and was beginning to understand why she was doing it. She didn't want their friendship to end.

Turning her head so he wouldn't hear her release a heavy sigh, she decided that she'd tell him about the letter tomorrow.

He drove past all the buildings and then along a short road that led to several blocks of military housing. Some were single homes, but more were duplexes, two houses built in one, and the road he turned on hosted at least a half a dozen identical dual homes side by side, separated by small yards.

"Where are we going?" she asked.

"It's a surprise," he replied, while turning into a driveway of one of the duplex homes. It was white stucco, as they all were, and one story tall with dual front porches opposite each other.

She removed her sunglasses and glanced from the house to him. "Who lives here?"

"Let's go see." He climbed out and met her at her side of the vehicle.

Clasping her purse, after having dropped her glasses

inside, she climbed out and walked beside him to the door. The one on the left. The other half of the house's front door was on the right.

Her joy of the day and the surprise had waned due to her own thoughts, until the door opened. Completely surprised and thrilled, she gasped. "Anda!"

Anda stepped onto the porch and they hugged. Tightly. As the hug ended, Anda said, "When Will said that K.T. was showing you the base today, I told him to tell K.T. if he didn't bring you around to see me that I'd never forgive him."

Wendy looked at K.T.

He grinned. "Surprise!"

She gave him a soft slap on the chest and told Anda, "He didn't tell me a word about it. I had no idea. How are you? How is Pearl?"

"We are both wonderful," Anda said. "Come in. Come in. Lunch is ready and staying warm in the oven. You can see her before we eat."

Wendy shot a look over her shoulder while following Anda inside the house, and shook her head at K.T.

He merely grinned.

"She's sleeping," Anda said. "But no one knows for how long. Could be an hour, could be three." She waved an arm toward the living room. "Will's in the kitchen, K.T., setting the table. That's what I was doing when he said you'd pulled in the driveway."

"I'll go see if I can help him," K.T. said.

"Oh, I'm so happy to see you," Anda said, hooking an arm with Wendy's. "I've thought of you so many times since leaving the hospital."

"As I have you," Wendy said. "Every time I walk past your room, I think of you and Pearl. Especially after K.T. was discharged, before that, he'd give me up-dates from when Will or Scott stopped in to see him."

"So many families have evacuated back to the States," Anda said as they walked down a short hallway and stopped near a door. "There are only three wives left in the entire neighborhood, and it's been so lonely."

So many things had changed. Wendy laid a hand on Anda's arm. "Now that I know where you live, I can come visit on my days off."

"That would be so wonderful." Anda opened the door and they walked into the room to gaze at the baby sleeping in the wooden cradle.

"She's grown," Wendy whispered, gently touching Pearl's downy soft dark hair. "And even more beautiful than the last time I saw her."

After a few moments of whispering and adoring the baby, they left the room and met the men in the kitchen, where the table was set. A delicious aroma filled the room, reminding Wendy that she hadn't eaten a home-cooked meal since leaving Nebraska.

"Let's eat while we can," Will said. "Pearl has been known to interrupt more than one meal."

His statement was said jokingly, and the look that he and Anda shared made Wendy wonder what it would feel to have a love like that. For a moment, she questioned why she wondered that now. Her aunt and uncle loved each other, and her cousins loved their spouses, and she'd never given it a second thought.

Perhaps because she'd known that it wasn't something she'd ever want. She didn't want that to change. She didn't want to love someone and didn't want them to love her. She'd promised herself that she wouldn't depend on any man. So she refused to let it happen.

The four of them sat at the table, and she joined the conversation, yet couldn't stop herself from noting the way Will and Anda smiled at each other, laughed at what the other was saying, or how their love for one another was reflected in their eyes.

After the meal, she insisted upon helping Anda wash the dishes, something she hadn't done in ages. It was a silly thing to miss, and she hadn't realized that she had until now.

Or maybe it was the companionship she felt with Anda as they worked together that she'd missed. It was different than working at the hospital. There was a normalcy in doing dishes. There was nothing to think about, just wash, dry, and put away, all the while visiting.

That's what she wanted. Things to just be normal, and to not think about who loved each other and who didn't.

There was also a normalcy in the events that happened afterward, how she and K.T. spent a large portion of the afternoon with Will and Anda, and Pearl after her feeding and before she fell asleep again. She enjoyed every minute, especially listening to K.T. and Will share comical stories about their work.

When they took their leave, Wendy promised to visit on her next day off. "It's not that far of a walk," she told Anda.

Anda laughed. "I thought that once."

Wendy covered her mouth with her hand. "Oh, I'm sorry! I had forgotten about how you walked to the hospital while in labor."

"I'd suggest you have K.T. give you a ride instead," Anda said.

"I'm sure we can work something out," K.T. said.

For a heart-stopping moment, Wendy imagined spending other days off with him. Then, she told herself to settle down, because that would not happen. After she told him about Betty's letter, he might not want to be her friend. Not want to give her a ride anywhere. "Thank you again for lunch. It was delicious," she said as she stepped off the porch. Despite her self-talk, her heart was still thudding, because K.T. was right beside her.

They walked to the jeep, and climbed in. Wendy tried her hardest to not look at him, because there was still enough commotion going on inside her, yet lost her battle when he didn't start the engine.

He was looking her way and grinning.

Her heart flipped and she shook her head, giving up on herself. "Thank you for the surprise. It was wonderful to see Anda and Pearl."

"You're welcome." He started the engine. "Where to now? We still have a few hours before sunset," he said. "Unless you have something to do?"

"No," she replied, "but...do you?"

"No."

He backed the jeep out of the driveway. "Let's drive over to Pearl City, see if the Monkey Bar is open."

Wendy had heard of the Pearl City Tavern, which people called the Monkey Bar, but had not visited it. "We are still under prohibition," she said. "That's what the last notice said. Until stores can be replenished from the mainland."

"I know, we'll just have a soda pop, or even coffee. Surely, they'll have that." His brows creased together as he glanced her way. "Sorry. I can just take you home."

"No," she said, too fast and quick, because the idea of disappointing him had made her stomach sink. "I'd like to see the Monkey Bar, and soda or coffee would be fine."

"We don't have to. I've already taken up enough of your day."

"No, really. I don't have anything to do." She laid a hand on his arm, and the same tingles as when he held her hand shot up her arm. Why was it that she could touch him as a patient day in and day out, yet now, as a friend, as a man, her insides went into chaos at the slightest touch, or look? Maybe it was a warning sign, like the alert sirens, telling her that she cared too much about him and had to stop. She'd already told herself that much, yet, even knowing that, she said, "I've wanted to see Pearl City."

"You're sure?" he asked.

She swallowed the lump in her throat. It was as if he had some kind of magnetism inside him that her insides were attracted to and it took a defined force to pull them apart. She removed her hand from his forearm and ran it over the skirt of her dress to ease the heat pooled in her palm. "Yes, I'm sure."

Maybe not falling in love wasn't as easy as she thought. Not when it came to him.

Chapter Nine

K.T. was regretting the suggestion of driving to
Pearl City. He sure as hell didn't need a beer, spending the day with Wendy was intoxicating enough. Why
hadn't he realized that and taken her straight home?
That would have been the smart thing to do. He'd gotten so hung up in not being alone, not being the odd
man out, that he hadn't wanted the day to end yet.

Which was absurd. He'd never minded any of that
before.

The deluge of anger he'd summoned at himself,
stayed with him as he drove around the east loch of
the harbor. The red dirt road was rough, and the noise
from the engine and the gravel was too loud to talk
over. That could be considered a blessing or a curse.
The silence gave way to thinking that went in two directions. She wanted to see new things and places, but
he didn't need to be the one to show them to her.

More specifically, he didn't need to complicate his
life. That's what he was doing. Before meeting her,
things were all in order. Now there was chaos everywhere, all around and inside him.

He didn't blame her. None of it was her fault. The

attack wasn't to blame for the chaos inside him, either. He'd managed to create that all on his own. Just like he'd created this—bringing her to the bar because he thought it would be a place she'd like to see.

Pearl City wasn't very big. The main attraction was the tavern, inside a large tent, that had been labeled the Monkey Bar because of the monkeys that amused the guests in a large habitat area that was built behind the bar. Inside their screened cage, the monkeys swung from branch to branch and screeched at the guests. The place had become one that military men from all branches gravitated to. He couldn't recall many women visiting the bar. Then again, he'd never looked for any, either. Had never looked at any before her that night of the dance.

What the hell was he doing?

He was supposed to be thanking her for all she'd done for him, and figured he'd make a day of doing that. Nothing more. There would have been nothing wrong with ending it as soon as they'd walked out of Will's house.

He was still silently badgering himself when he pulled into the parking lot that held a variety of vehicles. Music filled the air, and as he turned, caught sight of the grin on Wendy's face, all of his regrets vanished.

"They have music here?" she asked.

"Yes," he answered. On the few times he'd patronized the tavern, he'd spent most of his time talking with the bartender, George, who was also the owner, but knew there was a jukebox and a dance floor near the back wall where the canvas was often pulled up, exposing a large lanai.

"Are there really live monkeys?" she asked.

"Yes. Still want to go inside?"

"More than ever," she replied.

She was already out of the jeep by the time he walked to her side. Looking at the variety of automobiles, from jitneys to passenger cars, and a variety of military vehicles, she said, "This must be the happening place."

"Looks that way."

"Is that because all the events at the Bloch Arena have been canceled?" she asked as they walked toward the large sun-faded canvas tent.

The outside was a bit deceiving, because the inside looked like any other building, with wooden floors and walls, tables, chairs, and a bamboo bar complete with stools. "Could be," he answered.

They entered through a wooden screen door attached to the canvas with a wooden frame. Tables were full of occupants, as was the bar, and nearly every one of them had a bottle in their hands.

Wendy glanced up at him with a grin. "Looks like prohibition hasn't struck here, yet."

He nodded. "That explains the crowd." Spying two stools near the corner of the bar, he asked, "That okay?"

"It is. It also looks like the only seats in the joint." Glancing about, she added, "This place is amazing. The outside doesn't do the inside any justice."

Before they'd even settled on the seats, the bartender, who had to be at least six and a half feet and made up of all muscle, shouted, "Lieutenant! Aloha! Good to see you!"

"Good to see you, too, George," K.T. replied.

"I heard you were in the hospital," George said. "Glad to see that's no longer the case."

"Me, too," K.T. replied and waited until Wendy sat

on a stool before sitting down beside her. "Meet the reason I'm out of the hospital. This is Nurse Smith." Calling her that hadn't helped him compartmentalize her in his mind as he'd hoped, and he'd have to think of something else that would.

"I'm honored to meet you," George said to her. "You gals have done a hell of a job for our boys. That's for sure."

K.T. fully agreed with that statement.

"Nice to meet you, too," she replied.

"Looks like you have a full house today," K.T. said.

George laughed and winked at Wendy. "This is the good old US of A! A few bullets and bombs may have knocked us down, but nothing will keep us down. For you, Lieutenant, I will get a beer, and how about some torpedo juice for the young lady?"

The expression on Wendy's face said she'd never heard of torpedo juice. K.T. nodded to her and told George, "Sounds good."

George slapped the bar as he turned about. "Be right back."

"What is torpedo juice?" Wendy asked.

"Pineapple juice with rum." He pulled his billfold out of his back pocket. "Do you like pineapple juice?"

"Yes, I do. I'd never had it before coming to Hawaii."

"Me, neither, but it's good." He took money out of his billfold, laid it on the bar, and returned the billfold to his pocket. "I hadn't had coconut syrup on pancakes, either, but that too is good."

"I love coconut syrup," she said, but her eyes were locked on the monkey cage behind the bar. "Those are real monkeys in there."

"Did you think I was lying?"

With a soft giggle, she shrugged. "I wasn't sure."

George arrived with their drinks and laid his hand on the money K.T. had set on the bar top. "This one's on me. It's my honor."

Both he and Wendy thanked George, and watched the monkeys frolicking from branch to branch for a few minutes while sipping their drinks. She appeared enthralled with the animals, but his gaze went from the monkeys to her profile. From the first time he'd seen her, he'd been amazed, and that had continued to grow while he'd been in the hospital, and again today. He was glad that Will had suggested it, or actually it had been Anda who told Will to tell him to bring Wendy to their house for lunch. Her joy over seeing Anda and Pearl had been genuine and it had been fun to watch her tell Will and Anda things about her home life back in Nebraska.

He'd known most of the things she'd shared, and that had produced a rather unique satisfaction for him. She was creating so many unusual and unique sensations inside him. Some familiar ones, too. It had taken all of his willpower to not turn his face and catch her lips with his when she'd kissed his cheek, and a full minute of freezing every muscle in his body to make sure he didn't even after her fast kiss had ended.

Then he'd remembered that she'd only done that, kissed his cheek, because they were friends. He'd never felt the things he felt for her, for a friend.

He'd done his best to act like her kiss was as normal as the sun coming up. Had hugged her just to reinforce that her kiss hadn't affected him, which had been another mistake. She'd felt too right in his arms.

Taking a sip of beer, he used it to swallow the sigh

that was stuck in his throat, because that had been like the sun coming up, but not in a normal way. It had been more reminiscent of watching a sunrise. One so glorious that a person felt it deep inside.

He'd never felt that before and that worried him. Even if Betty wasn't waiting on him back home, expecting them to get married, he could never pursue anything with Wendy. She wanted to see the world, and he believed she would. He, on the other hand, would return to Oklahoma where there wasn't a whole lot to see.

All he could do was accept her as a friend, and be happy about it. Happy that because of her, he would be able to return home.

"Hey, K.T.!"

The voice and the slap on the counter had him turning on his stool, and dang near choking on the beer he was trying to get past his throat.

"And Nurse Smith! What are the odds?" the man asked. "Remember me? Wes Henderson, we shared a room at the hospital for a while. Glad to see they set you free."

"It's good to be free," K.T. replied, finding his ability to speak. He hadn't seen the man as much as he'd talked to him, while face down on the bed, and definitely recognized the voice. "How are you doing, Wes?"

"Good. Real good, thanks in part to Nurse Smith here. Why don't you two join us? Faye and I, and some others, are over in the corner. There's room for two more chairs."

K.T. looked at Wendy, letting her know it was her call.

She shrugged, but in the next instant nodded.

"Sounds good," K.T. replied to Wes.

"Great!" Wes said before turning to the bartender. "George, I need two more beers!"

"Coming right up!"

As soon as Wes had been handed the bottles of beer, he led the way through the tables to one in the corner near the open flap of the canvas and surrounded by six people, men and women.

Faye, whom K.T. also knew from the hospital jumped to her feet. "Wendy! Lieutenant McCallister!"

Wendy and Faye embraced. K.T. said hello, and while introductions were being made, two more chairs were pulled up to the table for him and Wendy.

He'd half expected an awkward moment or two, because he normally wasn't one to join a group of people he barely knew, but that wasn't possible with Wendy. She could befriend someone in a heartbeat. He was proof of that.

They were instantly included into the group and the conversation.

Still, K.T. was prepared to just sit back and listen to the idle chitchat, but there, too, Wendy had something else in mind, because the first thing she did was tell everyone about his diving gear, which brought on a round of questions.

The shine in her eyes held his attention more than the questions. He liked watching her. Liked seeing her free spirit rise and shine. He also liked the way she would slap his arm or lean closer while laughing. Especially at Alan, a big, barrel-chested, bald sailor, who had to be the best storyteller in the navy. Between his jokes and fables, for they couldn't possibly be true, Alan kept the entire table laughing for the next several hours, even as they ate the evening special of sausage and rice.

Right up until a bell rang.

"What's that?" Wendy asked him.

"I'm not sure," he answered.

Everyone else at the table was downing the last bits of their drinks as if they'd been dying of thirst.

"Drink up!" Wes said, between swallows. "That bell means we have half an hour until curfew!"

K.T. stood, and held a hand out to assist Wendy. His beer had long ago been finished, as had her drink, as well as the soda pops they'd ordered to drink with their meals. No one really took time to say goodbye, except for George, who shouted, "Aloha! See you soon!" as the entire crowd rushed for the door.

Outside, people were running toward the variety of vehicles, including those from their table, with waves and shouts of aloha and goodbye.

K.T. grabbed Wendy's hand to lead her on the shortest route to their jeep. It was only ten miles to the base, but the dirt road was rough and narrow. "We have to run," he told her. "If we get stuck behind one of those trucks, we'll be eating dirt the entire way!"

Nothing about her should surprise him, but discovering that she ran like a deer, did. She had no trouble keeping up with him as they raced across the parking lot.

They were in the jeep and pulling away, while others were still running to their vehicles.

"Go, go!" she shouted.

He laid his foot on the gas pedal, and maneuvered around the parked vehicles quickly, but cautiously, because he didn't want to scare her by driving too fast.

Another jeep cut them off just as he was nearing the road. Had he been alone, that wouldn't have happened.

"Oklahoma!" she shouted. "If you can't drive any faster than this, move over and let me drive!"

"I can drive faster," he said.

"Then do it! Now!" Her hair was flapping in the wind as she twisted about to look behind them. "Or we're going to get passed like we're sitting still!"

He laid his foot on the pedal and caught up with the jeep that had cut them off. It was Alan, who was grinning from ear to ear as he hit the next gear and bolted forward.

K.T. shifted the jeep into a higher gear and put the gas pedal all the way to the floor.

Wendy's laughter could be heard above the engine, as could her shouts, "Yes! Go! Go! Faster! Faster!"

As they zoomed past Alan, she waved. "Bye, Alan!"

Alan honked his horn at them, and without missing a beat, she reached over and pushed the horn button on the flat dashboard, giving it two solid blasts.

K.T. laughed, but felt he needed to warn her. "You know what this means? Us being in front of everyone?"

Her glee literally filled the air as she shouted, "Yes! It means you better not slow down, because we are going to win another contest!" She spun her head around, looking at the vehicles behind them. "Someone's passing Alan! Another gray jeep!"

"Turn around and hang on!" he shouted. "We'll lose if you fall out!"

She laughed. "Are you worried about me falling out, or us losing?"

"Both!"

She patted his arm. "You focus on driving, and I'll make sure I don't fall out. Deal?"

He laughed. "You just don't stop, do you?"

"Stop what?"

Chancing a quick glance her way, he shook his head at the grin on her face. He had never met someone who enjoyed life like she did. "Having fun!"

"No one wants to stop having fun!" She spun around again. "They passed Alan and are gaining on us! Faster! Go faster!"

His hands were tight on the wheel and his foot hard on the pedal as he steered from one side of the road to the other, dodging ruts as they sped forward. "Who is it?"

"It's Wes and Faye!" She waved at those behind them. "Catch us if you can!" Spinning about, she pushed on the horn again.

A matching sound came from behind them, and she honked their horn again.

The recklessness of this was playing havoc inside him. He was always the first to point out acting responsible and sensible in all situations. A trait he inherited from his mother and her signature line of being a Mc-Callister. Driving at this speed, on this road, was not sensible, yet Wendy was enjoying every moment. So was he. However, he felt the need to warn her. "You do know that they are going to get to the base first, don't you?" he asked.

"No, they aren't. We are."

"The road to the base is before the road to the hospital," he said.

"Awe, shucks!" A second later, she rebounded. "We'll still be the first one to pass the road!"

He reached over and honked the horn, and laughed along with her.

* * *

Time had a way of speeding by when a person was having fun, and that's exactly what had happened today. Wendy's heart was singing with happiness as they sped along the road with a line of jeeps, trucks, jitneys, and cars behind them. The race was on, not only with the other vehicles, but with the sun that was slowly lowering toward the horizon.

The entire day had been wonderful and she didn't want it to end, but the consequences of being out after curfew were not something she wanted to face. Moreover she didn't want K.T. to face them. Although people could be outside until nine at night, all cars had to be off the streets by seven forty-five.

Combining that with her eagerness to win the race, an idea formed. "You can pull into the base," she said. "I'll walk from there."

He shook his head. "Just hold on!"

He swerved around a rut in the road, and she laughed at the way she swayed in her seat. "This reminds me of riding with Uncle Sy!"

"He drove fast?"

Holding on to the edge of the seat with one hand, she used the other to keep her hair from whipping around her face. "Yes! Not when Aunt Ella was with us, but when it was just him and I, he never drove slowly. Not even when he was teaching me how to drive. He claimed driving faster made the road smoother."

"I'm not sure that is true!"

"Me, either!" She twisted, glanced behind them at the line of vehicles still coming. There was a huge cloud of dust as far back as she could see and she was glad they were first in line. "I think it was because he wanted to stay ahead of the dust!"

"That I do believe."

She turned back toward the front. "He would love this, and would be shouting for you to go faster!"

"Just like you!"

"Yes!" She'd learned a lot about K.T. since that night of the dance, and one of those things was just how reserved and in control he needed to be in practically all situations. However, it wasn't surprising that he was enjoying himself, because he'd enjoyed dancing, too, once he'd been challenged into it. She hadn't verbally challenged him into anything today, but had known at the bar that they would have left if she hadn't agreed to join Wes and Faye at their table.

She'd been being selfish, because she hadn't wanted the day to end, but didn't regret it. Seeing him laughing as he had at the table, and again now, was worth it. After all he'd been through, he deserved some happiness.

They both had jobs to do here, and those jobs weren't all roses and sunshine. Some parts were devastating and a person has to balance that with good things. That, too, was something Uncle Sy had instilled in her.

Horns behind them began honking as they neared the base, and she pressed the button on the dash, honking in return as K.T. slowed enough to make the corner onto the road that led to the base.

The entire caravan had slowed, but Wendy was still bubbling with happiness over the fast ride. She honked again when K.T. didn't turn into the base and she spun around, waved at the vehicles behind them.

"That was amazing," she said, smiling half to herself and half at him.

He nodded as he turned the corner toward the hospital. "Yes, it was."

Her happiness could easily have slipped away as her barracks came into sight, but she wasn't going to let it. Not even as she collected her purse and gas mask box off the seat between them. "Just slow down long enough for me to jump out," she said. "It's almost curfew time."

He didn't say anything, just drove all the way up to the front of her building before he stopped the jeep, and climbed out of his side the same time she climbed out of hers.

Meeting him near the front of the jeep, she grinned and shook her head.

He took her elbow. "Walking you to the door won't cause me to break curfew."

She knew that, but had known that having him walk her to the door was going to make her think about things that weren't true. This hadn't been a date, and she should be happy about that. "Thank you for a wonderful day," she said as they walked along the walkway. "It was so nice to see Anda and Pearl, and, well, it was just all very nice."

"It was." They arrived at the door and after a long moment of silence, he gave a slight nod. "Have a nice evening."

"You, too. I'll see you in the morning."

He looked confused for a moment, then nodded again and opened the door, held it for her to cross the threshold. "Good night."

She stepped inside. "Good night." A heavy sigh

seeped out of her lungs as he closed the door and she watched him walk toward the jeep. The day had been fun and exciting, so why did she suddenly feel disappointed? Like she'd wanted more.

The answer was easy.

She had wanted more and was finding it hard to remember that there never would be more between them than friendship. Which was exactly what she wanted, so why wasn't she happy about that? He had a life to return to, and she had a world to see.

"Why didn't you tell me?"

Wendy spun around, saw Helen behind her. "Tell you what?"

Helen walked to the door and pointed out the window. "That's the sailor you danced with at the dance."

There was no sense in trying to keep it hidden any longer. "Yes, it was."

"Ooh, la, la." Helen twirled a clump of her hair with one finger as she continued to stare out the window. "Can't say I blame you. I'd want to keep that all to myself, too."

"He took me to see Anda and Pearl," Wendy said, seriously wanting to change the subject. Helen had just pointed out a clear fact. She did want to keep K.T. to herself, even though she knew he wasn't hers to keep. "They are both doing wonderful. Pearl has grown and is as adorable as ever. She has the prettiest blue eyes."

Helen turned around and her brown eyes were even bigger than usual. "Wait a minute. Is he the dance sailor and your burn patient, one and the same?"

Wendy combated the frustration at herself by holding her breath for a moment. She should have realized by saying that about Anda and Pearl, that Helen would have put two and two together. "Yes, he is."

Helen stared at her for several seconds, with a big grin, before she sighed. "Well, I'm happy for you, and now I'm wondering if you'll be excited about the news I wanted to tell you."

Fully willing to change the subject, Wendy asked, "What news?"

Helen hooked their arms. "I'll tell you in our room. I heard it today while on my shift, but the announcement won't be made for a few weeks."

More than curious, Wendy whispered, "Give me a hint."

"The South Pacific!" Helen whispered with excitement.

"What about it?"

"Hurry, and I'll tell you."

They rushed up the steps to the second floor, and down the hallway. Once in their room, with the door closed, Wendy asked, "What about the South Pacific?"

"Pago Pago," Helen said. "The capitol of Samoa. The Tutuila island. That's where the *Solace* will be sent in six weeks. From there she'll sail to the Tonga islands, then New Zealand and Australia, the Fiji islands. All over the South Pacific!" Helen twirled around and plopped down on her bed. "It's our opportunity to see that entire part of the world."

Wendy froze, midway to her bed. Helen was from Iowa, but they'd met in California and had formed an instant friendship over the desire they shared about volunteering for the Red Cross because they both wanted to see amazing places and people, and everything. For

Helen, it had been for herself, not a promise she'd made to anyone, but the goal was the same.

Rubbing her arms at the chill still rippling over them, Wendy slowly, almost as if she didn't have full control of her body, or her thoughts, finished crossing the room and sat down on the bed.

The movement helped because her brain started working. "We aren't assigned to the *Solace*."

"Not right now, but we could be," Helen said.

"How?"

"I was eavesdropping." Helen held up a hand. "Not really, and not on purpose, I was getting things from the supply closet and the door was open across the hall. I just overheard what was being said. A medical officer from the *Solace* was talking to hospital officers and said that according to Fleet Medical Headquarters, orders were in the pipeline for the *Solace* to set sail for Pago Pago by the beginning of March. Current patients aboard the ship who would still need care beyond that time would be transferred to the hospital, and that there would be a call out for more nurses to be assigned to the ship. He stated more nurses would be shipped over from the mainland within the next few months, and asked for nurses from the hospital to transfer to the ship, as well as Red Cross volunteers."

Wendy waited for her mind to do something besides conjure up the image of K.T.

"Did you hear that?" Helen asked. "We can volunteer for a transfer from the hospital to the ship. They are the safest. No one attacks them. Wouldn't that be amazing? Sailing around the world? Seeing ports and cities across the South Pacific?"

"It would be," Wendy admitted, feeling the need to

answer. There was also a hint of excitement inside her. One that should have been bigger. This was her dream. "You said by the first of March?"

"Around then is what he said," Helen said. "We'll have to wait until the official order comes through, but it wouldn't hurt to hint that we'd be interested in having our assignments transferred. Especially to Nurse Manning. She's the one who would have to approve it, and we both know she'd do anything you asked. You could teach others her burn therapies throughout our travels."

It might be conceited, but Wendy was sure that Gloria would approve a transfer. All she'd have to do was ask and her dream would come true.

Chapter Ten

K.T. wasn't impressed with the direction of his thoughts. Every route led to Wendy. It had been that way for a while, but after spending the entire day with her yesterday, he couldn't make another thought form. She was pretty, fun, and he enjoyed spending time with her, but...

There was a very big but, because there was more. So much more.

He knew what he felt for Wendy went beyond what it should.

That had been confirmed again this morning when he'd gone in for his bandage change. It was unreal how just seeing her made him feel different. Whole. Like something had always been missing inside him and she'd brought it to life.

Dr. Bloomberg had been there this morning, too, and had given him the okay to return to doing more than just sitting in meetings and reading blueprints. He still couldn't dive or weld, but the tasks of getting the ships repaired were endless and he was excited to get back to work.

Being busy, staying busy, would be his answer to

getting Wendy off his mind. He wasn't fool enough to believe that would solve his problems. What he felt for her was special. More special than what he'd felt for Betty. He was severely disappointed in himself. It wasn't something he'd ever have expected to happen, but now that it had he needed to do the right thing.

He'd been up half the night thinking about it, and knew he had to break things off with Betty. She deserved a man who loved her, fully. Completely. That wasn't him. Would never be him. He also knew that he couldn't marry Wendy. Couldn't even tell her how he felt. Not with a war going on. She wanted to see the world; she didn't want anyone waiting on her, and didn't want to be waiting on anyone to return to her.

The only thing he could do was to stay away from her, try to get over these feelings, and work would help him do that.

Upon hearing he had limited clearance for work, Captain Heinz assigned him to oversee a crew working on getting the USS *Nevada* from where she'd run aground to a dry dock. K.T. gladly took the assignment. He'd been in meetings about the ship, knew the blueprints by heart, as well as her current condition. Although other ships had been repaired and sent to California, and others were in dry dock, their damages hadn't compared to the *Nevada*. She was one of the first major salvage projects. Though she was in shallow water, the ship was in rough shape. The attack had twisted her about and she'd been run aground backward, stern first. Her bow had settled into deeper water, leaving her deck awash with seawater. She'd been bombed and torpedoed, ended up with a twenty-five-foot hole in her port side. A patch had been constructed to cover the hole in order to raise her, and though divers had worked endlessly to secure the patch, that couldn't be done. The hull had been warped by the bomb explosions. The alternate plan had been to patch the smaller holes and secure every door and hatch in the ruptured compartments and hope that would be enough to raise her once they got the seawater out of her.

Using every available pump, they were removing the water from her lower sections into the upper sections, then more pumps were moving that water over her sides. As luck would have it, the pumps were working faster than the unrepairable holes were letting water in, however, if any one section was drained too fast, the ship could list or capsize.

To get her afloat and to dry dock, they had to lighten her load. That was K.T.'s job.

Every sailor loved their ship, and the *Nevada*'s crew were committed to getting her back in the water, back in the fight, despite her current condition. They were good men, quickly agreed with the plan K.T. laid out, and instantly went to work.

The entire ship has been coated with filth. Oil and mud were mixed in with supplies that had been on the ship when she went down; papers, clothes, rotting food was everywhere, and feet deep as the water was pumped out of every compartment.

After shoveling out the filth in any one section, hoses were brought in and everything was hosed down with seawater. Oil stores and fuel would need to be transferred out of tanks, and guns, ammunitions, motors, engines, and anything else salvageable needed to be removed and transferred to a building in the yard to be cleaned, repaired, and prepped for reinstallation.

It was hard, consuming work, and K.T. appreciated how it kept his mind busy. His evenings were taken up writing reports and creating plans for additional holes to patch.

Tired, he slept at night, but there was that time between lying down and falling to sleep where his mind reverted to Wendy. His plan of staying away from her had one major flaw. She changed his bandage each morning, and while doing so, was full of questions about his work on the ship. Before falling to sleep, he'd go over things that he'd tell her in the morning.

Talking to her about his work reminded him of home, of sitting around the dinner table at night, listening to everyone talk about their day. He'd missed that.

His fifth day on the ship, Friday, the crew were in high spirits. Their hard work was paying off. Although parts were blackened from the fires her crew had fought during the attack, with her deck free of water and clean, that part of the ship looked more like her old self.

"When you came aboard on Monday and told us that we'd have her in dry dock in two weeks, I didn't believe that was possible," Brock Hanson, one of the ship's crewmen who was overseeing one of the pumps, said to K.T. "But now, I think it's possible. More than possible."

The ship had lost over fifty of their assigned crew that had totaled nearly fifteen hundred in the raid, and K.T. knew every crew member was committed to seeing her back on the water in honor of their lost companions. He was, too. "A week from today, we'll be tugging her toward dry dock," K.T. replied.

Brock, who had curly red hair and was built like a brick outhouse, laughed. "Is that a goal or a challenge?"

"A promise," K.T. said, slapping Brock's shoulder. He'd been in the navy for over three years, working on a large variety of ships and watercrafts, but there was something about being here, on this ship, with her shipmates, that told him he was exactly where he belonged. Doing exactly what he needed to be doing.

Brock nodded, and glanced around the ship with a thoughtful gaze. "We were the only ship to get underway and to shoot down an aircraft that day," he said. "It's fitting that she gets a second chance in this war."

"It is," K.T. said. "Let's get it done."

"Aye, aye."

Brock turned back to his pump, and K.T. proceeded along the deck.

Although the pumps were running around the clock, there was still water everywhere, because the ship was still sitting on the ocean floor, and would be until they could unload her completely in order to give her some buoyancy. A tanker had anchored next to the ship last evening and this morning, they'd start unloading her stored oil and fuel.

K.T. made his way to where that was set to happen, and once satisfied the transfer was proceeding without a hitch, he made his way below deck, to check in with his unit. The lower he went into the hull of the ship, the stronger the stench grew. Crew members were still hauling out trash, muck, and equipment to be refurbished.

The hull was a labyrinth of compartments, rooms, and walkways, and the men working were like ants—a steady trail of movement with each man focused on their job at hand. Some might see it as chaos with so many moving about, but K.T. saw it as precision progress.

He found his unit in the engine room, where everything was being dismantled and removed. Despite the portable lighting the room was dark, and K.T. clicked on the headlamp attached to his hat as he walked through the ankle-deep water.

Will, along with another member of his crew, Adam Foss, were bolting patches over smaller holes discovered as equipment was removed by sailors.

K.T. had thought a lot about Will lately, how he was married, had Anda and the baby living here with him. It all seemed to be working out fine for them, and other married men. Back in California, when he'd requested living quarters for the married men in his unit, he'd thought he understood why those men had wanted their families with them, now he wondered if he had. Wondered if he'd known what those men had felt for their wives and why they'd wanted them with them, through thick and thin.

As he crossed the room, toward Will and Adam, K.T. scanned the area, the crewmen carrying out the heavy equipment, scraping aside muck, and wiping down the heavy vaulted door. His gut tightened into a hard knot of warning at the sight of one sailor grasping the handle of a door. "Don't open that!" he shouted. The oil reserves were behind that door and if any seawater had leaked into it, sewage gases could have built up in the compartment. He'd ordered that no sealed doors were to be opened until all the fuel had been drained.

"Don't open that!" he repeated, but the noise of the water pump drowned out his shouts. K.T. ran to the pump and hit the kill switch, but the silence hit at the same time the sailor pulled open the door and was instantly hit by a flood of oil-filled seawater. The man didn't even wobble, just collapsed into the water.

"Evacuate!" K.T. shouted. "Evacuate!"

Two other crewmen near the opened door wobbled, then fell to their knees.

"Gas!" K.T. shouted. "Get out! Now!" Turning to Will and Adam, he shouted, "We have to get these three out of here! Don't breathe! Don't breathe!"

Holding his breath, K.T. ran to the first man who'd gone down, while Will and Adam each grabbed one of the men on their knees.

K.T.'s lungs were burning from the air he held in as he dragged the man away from the door and slammed it shut. The muck made everything harder, but he didn't dare breathe, knowing it could be deadly. Grasping the man beneath the arms, he dragged him toward the exit, following Adam and Will, who were each dragging a man.

He didn't take a breath until they were out of the room.

The hallway was full of running men, repeating his evacuation order. Another sailor grasped the legs of the man K.T. was dragging, helping him as they ran along the hall to the stairwell.

Once on deck, K.T. ordered a boat to transport the fallen men across the harbor to the hospital, along with Will whose left leg was bleeding from something he'd encountered during the evacuation.

Thinking only of rescuing others, K.T. ordered everyone to put on their gas masks, wishing he'd made that request earlier, then led a group of men into the hull, to search for anyone who may not have heard the evacuation orders, or had succumbed to the gas.

* * *

Wendy was on the second floor of the hospital, restocking a closet with supplies, when she heard that men working on the USS *Nevada* had been brought in due to exposure to a deadly gas. Her heart dropped to the floor with fear. She left the task half done and ran downstairs.

She could have attempted to tell herself it was in order to offer help, but didn't even try. She had to know if K.T. was amongst the men.

With her heart pounding and her hands shaking, she rushed toward the examination rooms. A familiar voice caused even more turmoil inside her. It wasn't K.T.'s voice, but it was Will's.

She entered the room and nodded at Gloria who was examining Will's leg as he lay flat on his back on a gurney. "What happened?" she asked Will.

"I bumped into something during the evacuation," he said. "It's just a scratch."

The gash on his shin was more than a scratch and would need stitches. Understanding that, and the dangers of his work environment, she locked eyes with Gloria, who nodded.

Wendy crossed the room to prepare a tetanus shot, and still concerned about K.T., asked, "Why were you being evacuated?"

"A crewmember opened a door to a compartment that wasn't supposed to be opened."

Wendy carried the prepared shot back to the exam table. She wanted to ask if K.T. was one of them, but stopped herself short of her question being that specific. "How many were injured?"

"Three that I know of," Will answered. "K.T. was

going to look for more when I climbed in the boat to come here." Pointing at her hand, he asked, "What's that?"

"A tetanus shot," she answered. "K.T. was going back into a gas-filled chamber?"

"They poked me when I first enlisted," Will said, leaning away from her.

"Not for tetanus," Gloria replied.

He wasn't the first man to shy away from needles, and Wendy felt compassion for that, but was more worried about K.T., and asked again, "K.T. was going back into the gas-filled chamber?"

Will nodded, but his eyes were on Gloria as he asked, "Are you sure about that?"

Wendy had to bite her back teeth together to keep a growl of frustration from escaping.

"Yes, I'm sure," Gloria replied. "It won't hurt. Nurse Smith is very good at giving shots."

Will shifted his gaze, but it wasn't to her, it was to the needle she was flicking to remove the air bubble. A second later, his eyes rolled back and he fainted.

He wasn't the first man to pass out at seeing a needle, nor would he be the last. How men who were so big and brave on so many occasions, yet couldn't stand the sight of a needle, had amazed Wendy at first, but it no longer did. It was just proof that everyone was afraid of something. She rolled up his sleeve and gave him the shot, while saying, "I'll get the smelling salts."

"Let's get this leg stitched up first," Gloria said. "It's only a few stitches and will all be over when he comes to."

Wendy checked Will's pulse and respiration as Gloria stitched the gash together with a perfect line of small stitches.

"I know you're worried about K.T.," Gloria said, "but Will doesn't know any more than we do right now. It's a wait and see moment."

Wendy knew that, and had no choice but to nod.

"Staying busy will make the time go faster," Gloria said.

Wendy nodded again, but knowing all of that didn't lesson her fears over something happening to K.T. The quandary she found herself in over him increased daily. She liked him, cared about him, enjoyed being his friend, but could no longer say that all she felt for him was friendship. She had to admit that not falling in love with someone was not easy. In fact, it was impossible to stop it.

The idea of leaving the island, boarding the *Solace*, sailing away and never seeing him again was playing havoc with her dream of seeing the world. She had other friends here, people she cared about, but none of them instilled the same fear of never seeing them again as he did. Nor did what she felt now compare to how she'd felt about leaving Uncle Sy and Aunt Ella. She loved them, too.

Too was the word that scared her. Was she letting her mother down? Putting herself in a situation where a man could disappoint her? K.T. hadn't tricked her into falling in love with him. She'd managed to do that all on her own. She hadn't found a way to stop it.

Will let out a moan, and opened his eyes, blinking a couple of times before it became clear that he remembered what had happened. "You won't tell anyone, will you?"

Wendy smiled. "About what?"

He sighed and nodded. "Anda's wondering when you'll be able to visit her again."

"Soon," Wendy replied, not wanting to make a promise that she couldn't keep. "I'll go see about finding you a way to get home."

"I need to get back to the ship," he said.

"Not today," Gloria answered as she finished applying the bandage on his leg. "This needs to stay dry and clean for a few days."

While Gloria went over more instructions for Will about his injury, Wendy left the room to procure him a ride home, and to see if any other men working on the *Nevada* had been brought in.

Learning that besides Will and the three others brought in at the same time, there had been no others, didn't fill her with relief. It could merely mean they were still attempting to rescue others. Men had been rescued for days following the attack back in December.

She did her best to hide the anxiety growing inside her as the hours slowly ticked past. No other men were brought in from the ship. That still didn't ease her worries. The other three men who had been brought in with Will were receiving breathing treatments for the gas they'd been exposed to. If not for how quickly they had been hauled out of the room, they would have died from the deadly toxic gases. They couldn't remember being hauled up to the deck and transported by boat to the hospital. They still had terrible headaches, even with the oxygen treatments.

No matter what she tried to tell herself, Wendy's worries increased throughout the day. By the time her

194 A Dance with Her Forbidden Officer

shift ended, she'd imagined one scenario after the next, until she wasn't sure which one scared her the most.

She hurried to her barracks and changed out of her nurse's uniform and into a blue dress. Due to her hands trembling so hard, it took far longer than she wanted. Her mind was just as shaky. Images of K.T. overcome by gas kept forming in her mind. He could have gotten trapped in an area and no one was able to find him. Or, oh, goodness, there were so many possibilities of what could have happened, she couldn't keep them straight.

She didn't take the time to brush out her hair, merely left it pinned up after taking off her nurse's cap, and hurried out of the building to go to the dock at the shipyard.

Someone had to know something. It had been all day.

If no one there could tell her anything, she'd find a boat to take her to the ship. She wasn't sure that was possible, but would find a way.

Wendy was barely across the lanai when she saw a gray jeep on the road to the hospital and something far deeper than relief or excitement filled her as she recognized the driver.

Focused only on making sure he was okay, she shouted, "Oklahoma!" and ran, waving her arms. "Oklahoma!"

The jeep stopped, backed up, and turned on the road to her barracks.

She ran faster.

K.T. stopped the jeep as they met on the road and jumped out. "What's wrong?"

Without taking a moment to think, she wrapped her arms around his waist, hugged him tight. "Thank heavens you're okay!"

His arms went around her, held her tight. "I'm fine. I was coming to check on Will and the others."

"Will was sent home with stitches in his leg, and the others are doing well," she answered without loosening her hold or lifting her head. She couldn't let go of him, not yet. "I was so worried about you."

His arms tightened around her, as if he too needed to hang on to her as much as she did him. Or maybe he just knew what she needed right now. Her entire body needed to be pressed up against him. Not only to confirm he was okay, but because nothing had ever felt so right or so comforting.

"I'm fine," he whispered.

"I was afraid you'd gotten trapped while rescuing others," she said.

He softly rocked her sideways while still holding her close. "There were no others. Every man was accounted for and evacuated from the ship."

The relief inside her was immense, and that brought about her own sensibilities, for she was gradually able to think about things other than him and herself. That had been where her thoughts had been all day. On him, and her fears over his safety.

Drawing in a deep breath, she said, "That's good. I'm glad everyone was accounted for."

He leaned back and knowing he was looking at her, she lifted her head to meet his gaze. "I'm sorry you were worried."

The gentleness of how he touched her cheek with one hand and the sincerity in his eyes shattered something inside her. Some sort of barrier that she couldn't explain, but suddenly, she wanted to wrap her arms around his neck and kiss him. Really kiss him, on the lips. She knew why it was impossible to not love him. He made it too easy. He was so good and kind and caring and honorable.

He was still looking at her, and the way his gaze lingered on her lips made something else explode inside her. She jumped back, out of his arms. He was honorable. Very. And she wasn't. She still hadn't told him about Betty's letter, and she was afraid that she knew why.

"There was no need to worry," he said. "Once everyone was accounted for, we took extra precautions as the gas was released."

"That's good," she said, even though her thoughts were still on herself. She may have started out wanting to protect him by not giving him Betty's letter, but at some point it had changed to protecting herself. She'd never have imagined that she could be so selfish, but she was. Letting him believe Betty was still his girl had given her a reason they could only be friends.

"From now on, everyone will be required to wear a gas mask when going into the hull," he said, "and have a litmus paper badge that will detect if gasses are present."

He was still attempting to ease her fears, but the ones she felt now had nothing to do with today's accident. Having no idea what she was going to do about the situation she'd brought on herself, she let the air seep out of her lungs. "That's good," she repeated. Her heart thudded as she met his gaze. His smiles had affected her since the night she'd met him. Was that when it had happened?

Surely not. A person can't fall in love that fast, but it might have been a teetering point, and she'd been stumbling downhill ever since. If she'd known that, she might have been able to save herself. It was too late for that now. For her, but not for him. She had to find a way to fix what she'd done.

"I—" She searched for something appropriate to say. "Will. Will's leg needs a few days to heal. It needs to stay clean and dry." It was a completely different topic, but that's what she needed. Something else to think about until she… What? She wasn't sure, but had to figure this out. "The others will remain in the hospital for a day or two, but they should be fine. Dr. Carson is overseeing their care. He can tell you more."

K.T. nodded. "Do you know where I can find him? Is he still at the hospital?"

"Probably." Drawing in a fortifying breath, she added, "I can go with you to the hospital and help you find him."

"Thanks, I'd appreciate that."

Chapter Eleven

The gas incident had been a precarious one, and K.T. was grateful the injuries hadn't been any worse. Per the doctor, Will and the three crewmen would recover with no lasting effects.

He wasn't so lucky. The lasting effects on him were from Wendy. He'd never forget how she'd been trembling from head to toe when she'd wrapped her arms around him. That had confirmed what he'd already known. He'd let this go on too long. Let it go too far.

Yet, what had his reaction to that been? He'd hugged her, then asked her to accompany him, not only to the hospital, but to Will's house afterward. He'd told himself it was because he hadn't known what else to do. She wasn't one to indulge in theatrics. Her actions, her worry about him, and her trembling, had been authentic.

He couldn't have ignored that any more than he could ignore how it had felt holding her close. At that moment, having her in his arms had made him feel whole, complete. Like everything was right in the world.

But it wasn't.

Very little was right in the world right now. They were in the midst of a world war.

He was in the midst of an inner war, too. The person he used to be, the one who had thought he'd been in love with his childhood sweetheart for years, was fighting with the person he'd become, the one who had discovered a new kind of love. A kind that had struck so hard and fast, he was still questioning if it was true.

A part of him was questioning that. The other part of him knew what he felt for Wendy went beyond anything he'd ever known.

And that all led to one conclusion.

It didn't matter if there was barracks housing, where other men lived with their wives and families or not, or numerous other things, because it all came down to him. That part of him hadn't changed. He couldn't commit to Wendy any more than he'd been able to commit to Betty. It wasn't right to expect anyone to be waiting on him when there was a chance that he wouldn't return. His father had told him about the risks of that, and he'd witnessed them himself.

Furthermore, Wendy didn't want to be waiting on anyone, and didn't want them waiting on her. All she wanted was to be friends, to have fun. He was the one that was taking friendship too far.

All of that had come to him after he'd dropped Wendy off at her barracks, where she'd practically leaped out of the jeep and run to the door as if she couldn't get away from him fast enough.

They had spent about an hour at Will's house, where she'd visited with Anda and the baby, while he and Will had talked about the *Nevada*. The ship would need more work than could be accomplished here. Once in dry dock, she'd be repaired enough to make the trip to the mainland and undergo a complete overhaul and modernization there.

He would ask to go with the ship.

Never in his life would he have thought he'd base his actions, his duties, on a woman, but that was exactly what he was doing. Running away from her, because deep down, he knew he could never just be her friend.

He'd come too close to kissing her today.

Forgetting all the consequences and really kissing her. It would have been easy. Too easy, and that wasn't him. War couldn't change him that much.

Nothing could.

Early the next morning, he went to the hospital, knowing it was Wendy's day off. Both Nurse Manning and Dr. Bloomberg examined him and determined bandages were no longer necessary. His burns were no longer painful, but they gave him a supply of ointment for him to apply as needed, mainly to keep the skin supple as it continued to heal. All in all, that felt like the confirmation that he'd needed to convince him that he was doing the right thing.

Part of the right thing included not seeing Wendy for any reason. He'd tried ignoring her before, which hadn't been easy, but this time, he'd make it work.

By working.

The *Nevada* needed his attention, and that's where he kept it. Even on his days off, he was on the ship, overseeing the endless work of getting her afloat. By the following Friday, he geared up to dive for the first time in three months, since that fateful day back in early December.

The weight of the diving gear felt good. He was ready for normalcy to fully return.

Any serious leak could send the ship back to the bottom of the harbor, and he refused to allow that to happen. He personally inspected every bulkhead, hatch, and patch, before okaying the ship be connected to two tugboats to bring her across the harbor to dry dock.

It was a short trip in distance, yet long in other ways. He kept a vigilant eye on the ship as she moved slowly across the water, and he breathed a heavy sigh of relief when the trip ended.

A crowd had gathered at dry dock two, cheering as the ship arrived. Though K.T. was exhilarated and accepted congratulations from Captain Heinz, he couldn't deny a sense of absence deep inside.

Of happiness.

Of Wendy.

He missed the mornings when he'd told her about the recovery efforts and the work that was being undertaken each day, and knew she'd have been cheering louder than others had she been in attendance.

"Your day is done," Captain Heinz said. "The dock crew will take her from here. You've done a hell of a job, Lieutenant. What do you say we round up the crews and take them to the Monkey Bar?"

K.T. appreciated Captain Heinz's style. He was a true leader who expected hard work and success, but he also knew the men needed to be able to celebrate accomplishments. "Sounds good to me."

The crowd around them cheered louder, then, within seconds, men were racing for their barracks to shower and change. They all deserved a bit of celebrating after what they'd completed the past two weeks.

"I'll have some boats rounded up over by the sub base," Captain Heinz said. "The men won't have to worry about curfew."

K.T.'s thoughts instantly went to the race he and Wendy had participated in in order to reach the base before curfew. "They'll appreciate that," he answered. Boats were on the harbor around the clock and weren't patrolled for curfew like the roads. It was assumed anyone on the water had a pass from their supervisor. Heinz was the supervisor for the recovery crews, and was the one providing the boats, which was as close to a pass as any of them would get.

Captain Heinz slapped his shoulder. "See you there."

K.T. agreed and took his jeep to the barracks, where he showered, dressed in his uniform whites, and walked along with the rest of his unit to the submarine base, where a total of five runabout boats were moored to the long dock.

Within minutes all five boats were full of men and motoring around Ford Island toward Pearl City.

The joviality was high, and grew even more as they tied the boats to the several small docks that belonged to the Monkey Bar a short distance up the beach.

George greeted them all as old friends, and once again, K.T. thought of Wendy when the bottles of beer kept being handed out. Evidently, prohibition still hadn't hit the Monkey Bar.

In no time, the jukebox was busy eating coins and spitting out music. K.T. made his way around the room and tables, thanking men for their hard work and taking time to laugh at a few jokes and clink their bottles together in cheers of congratulations.

His thoughts were back on Wendy and he couldn't

help but wonder if he'd ever stop missing her. Not just while here, but years from now, when life was back to normal. Would memories pop up of her and the dance contest, the hospital, the race against the curfew, and would they make him happy or sad? Contemplating if he'd want those memories to make him happy, because there was enough sadness about the attack that he didn't want to remember, he walked through the open flap and out onto the lanai.

It was still early, not even five yet, and figuring he might as well get comfortable because it would be a long time before any of the men were ready to leave, he found himself a cane-backed chair under a palm tree a few steps away from the stone lanai and set his beer on the table next to it.

Another boat had moored at one of the docks and men were walking along the beach, laughing and joking with each other. K.T. knew he could go inside and join the conversations happening at the tables, but that, too, would remind him of Wendy, so he might as well sit here and think about her. About how he was doing the right thing. How cutting ties with her was the smart thing to do. If he accidently bumped into her between now and when he left with the *Nevada* in a few weeks, he'd say hi, explain how busy he was getting the ship ready to take to the mainland.

He'd tell her that's what he was doing. Heading back stateside with the *Nevada*. Captain Heinz had already approved it. Had thanked him for volunteering for the assignment, since he now knew that boat as well as her crew did, and his skills could very well be needed during the voyage.

Once stateside, he'd telephone home. That was allowed only for high level emergencies from here, but on the West Coast, he'd be able to call, make up for the letters he hadn't written. Make up for the ones he hadn't mailed, either. There were two addressed to Betty in his desk drawer. He still cared about her, and hated the idea of hurting her. He would call her, too, talk to her. That would be better than a letter.

It was Wendy that he didn't have a solution for. Even while he was in California, she'd still be on his mind. In his heart.

Wendy scanned the room the moment she walked into the Monkey Bar, but didn't see K.T. at any of the tables. The establishment was full of men dressed in white, some wearing hats and blue neck scarves, some not, but her intuition told her he wasn't amongst any of them even before her eyes did.

Disappointment made her hold in a sigh, even as she told herself it was for the best. She'd spent a lot of hours contemplating many things the past week, and although she hadn't come to any firm conclusions, she needed to show him the letter in her purse.

Not *the* letter that she'd kept hidden from him for months. That one she'd give him right before she boarded the *Solace* in a few weeks. She'd started to wish that Betty would write him again, or that a member of his family would say something about it in a letter, which was as wrong for her to wish as keeping the letter from him. All the justifications she'd come up with, were just that. Justifications. She was so afraid of following in her mother's footsteps, of falling in love and being abandoned, that she'd kept the letter from him. Deep down, she must have thought that would keep him from falling in love with her, or her from falling in love with him. Either way, it didn't make any sense. And now, deep down, she was afraid that once she gave him the letter, he'd never want to see her again.

The official request from the *Solace* for volunteers hadn't been released yet, nor had she asked Gloria about it, but she was certain it would happen, and just as certain that she would be permitted to go.

The letter in her purse was from her cousin. Sid specifically stated that she should tell K.T. that a deal had been struck. Oil had been found on his family's land and Sid's letter assured her it was a win-win agreement for both the family and the oil company. His family might have written him, but Sid's letter said he had permission from K.T.'s family to share the details with her and for her to share with him. She could have just sent the letter to his barracks.

Giving it to him was an excuse to see him, she was sure of that. But it was also a test. Over the past week of not seeing him, she'd convinced herself that she wasn't truly in love with him. She just liked him more than others, and would get over it in time. She had to, because she had never wanted to love any man and now wasn't the time for that to change.

"Aloha, Nurse Smith! Torpedo juice?" George asked as he waved at her from behind the bar.

"Yes, please," she answered, surprised that he remembered her, the place was so full of people.

"I have to get a closer look at those monkeys," Anda said. "Will, get me a soda pop, I'll be around the corner."

Will shrugged and grinned. "She didn't believe me

when I told her about them, and I think she thought you were kidding, too."

"That could be," Wendy said, watching Anda walk around the end of the bar, and wondering what she should do now that K.T. wasn't here.

"Here's your juice," George said, handing over a glass with a straw, "and here's another beer for K.T. He's been out on the lanai for a while and probably needs a refill."

Her heart did a somersault, and she clutched the glass and the bottle tighter to make sure they didn't slip out of her hands.

"I need a bottle of beer and a soda pop," Will told George. "And I'll pay for those two drinks."

George nodded.

Will looked at her. "Take it out to K.T. Figures he'd be out there—he's not much into socializing. Never has been."

"Thank you," she said. "I'll pay you back."

"No," Will said. "They are on me. I owe both you and K.T. more than a drink."

Leaving it at that, she turned and walked through the room to where the canvas flaps were drawn back. There were several people on the lanai, in groups, talking and laughing, and it wasn't until she stepped outside that she saw K.T. seated beneath a palm tree.

As much as she'd told herself that she didn't love him, that she didn't want to love him, her body once again defied her by tingling from head to toe, indicating that every part of her was drawn to him, excited to see him. That certainly never happened when she saw anyone else.

He turned his head, as if hearing her approach, and

his look of surprise made her smile. Even knowing all she did, she was happy to see him.

"Will bought you a beer," she said, holding out the bottle as she arrived near his chair.

He'd stood, and for a moment, didn't say anything, just stared at her as if he wasn't sure what to say. Taking the beer, he said, "Thanks. Is that how you got here? With Will?"

Because she was taking a sip from the straw in her drink she nodded, and swallowed. "Yes, I was at his house when Scott stopped by and invited them to join the rest of you celebrating the *Nevada*'s arrival at dry dock. Congratulations. You must be happy about that."

"Thanks. We all are."

She took another sip of her drink while he tipped his bottle to his mouth. "I...uh... I offered to stay and watch Pearl so Anda could come here with Will, but their neighbor Alice was at their house, too. Her husband won't be off work until curfew, so she said she'd watch Pearl, and Will and Anda asked me to join them." Rather than explain she'd been at Will and Anda's house, hoping to learn when his next day off might be, she said, "I was hoping you'd be here because I have something you need to read."

He lifted a brow. "What?"

"A letter from my cousin Sid. I'm not sure if you'd heard yet, about the surveying company."

He nodded. "Got a letter from my mother the other day, saying they were surveying the property."

Withholding the need to ask if his mother had mentioned anything else in her letter, she set her glass on the table between the two chairs and slid the handles of her purse off her wrist. Opening the clasp, she took out the letter. "Here, he explains it better than I can."

K.T. took the letter and waved a hand for her to sit in one of the chairs. He sat in the other chair and read. "I'll be," he said quietly while flipping the single page over to read the back side of it. "This sounds almost too good to be true."

"Sid isn't the type to exaggerate," she assured him. "Uncle Sy calls Sid a straight shooter, says he tells the truth even when those listening don't want to hear it." She swallowed a sigh, thinking that she should be more like Sid, then continued, "That's what makes him such a good lawyer. That and his ability to argue even the finest points." For no reason other than to assure him of Sid's thoroughness, she added, "Sid went over my Red Cross enrollment agreement with a fine-tooth comb before he gave it his approval. He even crossed out things and made me initial them."

She swallowed, remembering how Sid had pointed out the stipulation that if a Red Cross nurse wanted to get married, she'd have to forfeit the rest of her time with the agency. That had been fine with her then, for she'd had no plans of ever getting married. She didn't now, either.

"It sounds like he was just as thorough with this agreement." K.T. shook his head. "This could be a real windfall for my folks. Their financial worries could be over. Forever." He held the letter toward her. "That wouldn't have been possible without you, Wendy. Without you writing to Sid and him agreeing to help my folks."

Happiness flared inside her for him and his family.

She took the letter, tucked it inside her purse, and set her purse on the ground.

"I don't know how I can ever thank you for that," he said.

She didn't need any thanks, but knowing him and his sense of responsibility, she glanced toward the open flap, where a few couples were dancing to the jukebox music. It would probably be best if she just left now, but this could be the last time she'd see him before leaving on the *Solace*. Having convinced herself that easily, she said, "You could dance with me, Oklahoma. Make this a real celebration."

He looked at her for a few stilled moments before his smile grew into a laugh and he held out a hand. "I can do that, Nebraska."

She laid her hand in his, and her heart had never felt more full as he led her across the lanai and onto the dance floor. There, she was transported back in time, to the dance contest, and once again became Ginger Rogers and he was her Fred Astaire. A complete fantasy, where she had no worries or fears. Was free to just dance.

There was no contest this time, so after a few dances that had held enough dips and twirls to make her dizzy—if she hadn't already been dizzy with pure and simple happiness—they joined a table of companions to laugh, drink, and laugh some more, before making their way back onto the dance floor again.

When they needed to catch their breath after a few more dances, they walked out onto the lanai, where K.T. introduced her to Captain Heinz.

"It's nice to meet you, Nurse Smith," the captain, who wasn't much taller than her and didn't have a single strand of hair on his head, said. "I'm honored."

"As am I, Captain Heinz," she replied. "Congratulations for bringing the *Nevada* into dry dock."

"The congratulations all belong to Lieutenant McCallister," Captain Heinz replied, setting a hand on K.T.'s shoulder. "With his leadership, we're going to see every damaged ship back on the water in record time." With a wink, the captain added, "I won't let California keep him. I've already made that perfectly clear."

Wendy was confused by the comment, but didn't have time to dwell on it, because Captain Heinz was still talking. "George just had a buffet set up. Let's go see what he's feeding us tonight."

Back inside, a buffet table had been set up and hosted a variety of pork, chicken, fish, rice, vegetables, and fruits. Which made her wonder. "Has George not been affected by the rations?" she asked K.T. as they dished food onto their plates.

"I think George has his own suppliers that he's not telling anyone about," K.T. answered.

"Is that possible?" she asked.

K.T. shrugged. "It's happened before, and no one here is going to complain."

Agreeing with that, she scooped a fish filet onto her plate, and thought of the IOU note she still had, for them to go fishing. That wasn't likely to happen now, but it would have been fun. Everything was fun with him.

They found a place to sit at a table with others, and someone brought up the fish and fishing. That caused a round of fish tales from their companions. She laughed at the stories of unbelievable large fish and ones that got away, until her stomach and cheeks hurt from laughing.

The bell rang while they were still eating, and Wendy set down her fork along with others.

K.T. laid a hand on her wrist. "You can finish eating." He then said to Will, "Wendy will catch a ride back with me."

"Aye, aye," Will said, as he and several others headed for the door.

"We don't want to be caught out after curfew," she said to K.T., while observing that a large number of people hadn't left.

"Boats don't have to be off the water by seven forty-five," he said.

She frowned. "So?"

"That's how we got here. Don't worry. I'll have you inside by nine."

If he wasn't worried, she wasn't going to be, either, and finished her meal, before they hit the dance floor again.

The twirling and dipping, high step-kicking, and two-step sashaying across the floor once again made her feel as if she was floating on air. It was unimaginable to believe life could get any better than it was at that moment.

Except for one thing.

The desire to kiss him was so strong inside her, that she feared she might keel over from the want. It was all she could think about. All she could imagine.

If she hadn't withheld the letter from him, that might have happened, but now it never would.

K.T. hadn't forgotten his plan of cutting things clean with Wendy; he was just postponing it. Giving himself one last time with her, and when the second bell rang, he knew it was time for it to end.

It was a sobering thought, but one he accepted nonetheless.

"Time to hit the water, boys!" he shouted.

Outside, Wendy collected her purse from the chairs near the palm tree and he took count of the men in his charge as the crowd made their way down to the docks. Spirits were still high, and assuming the ride to the base would be a fast one, he secured a spot for him and Wendy near the bow of the boat, where it wouldn't be as rough nor would she get wet from the spray of water that would soon be everywhere.

Every boat held more passengers than on the way over, filled with those who hadn't wanted to leave upon the first bell. Tomorrow morning would see people rushing to the Monkey Bar to collect the vehicles left behind tonight.

The boat race that soon ensued wasn't the same as when they'd been in the jeep. This time the boats were fanned out, rather than following each other, and the drivers had an entire load of people shouting and cheering to be the first ones around Ford Island and through the East Loch to the submarine base.

Once again, K.T.'s need to be responsible played havoc inside him. He kept his arm around Wendy, holding her in her seat as they bounced over waves and swerved when other boats got too close. She was laughing and cheering along with the rest, encouraging Adam to drive faster.

K.T. kept his mouth shut, letting the others enjoy the race. It helped to know that this part of the water was free from debris and protected so they didn't have to worry about rogue waves.

He couldn't keep his eyes off Wendy, nor his mind from wondering if someday, when things were different, after the war and after she'd seen the world, if they would meet up again. That could be years from now, but a deep sense of knowing told him that what he felt for her would still be there. His feelings were too strong to ever fade. He couldn't say anything about it, though, because she didn't want anyone waiting on her, and that, too, he fully understood.

Like she had at the table earlier, when fish tales were flying, she was laughing so hard she was holding her stomach when the boat finally came to a stop.

"That was the best boat ride I've ever been on!" she exclaimed.

Others in the boat agreed with clapping and cheering.

K.T. shook his head, even as a deep part of him knew life with her would be an adventure every day. Because she would make it be that way.

She continued to laugh, and joke along with others as they walked in a large group toward the barracks. The sentries manning the guns on the rooftops could see them due to the moonlight, but he still stopped long enough to obtain a flashlight before beginning their walk to her barracks.

"I feel like I'm sneaking around after dark when I shouldn't be," she whispered as they walked.

"Because you are," he whispered in return.

She giggled. "We are." Her sigh echoed in the quiet night air. "Thank you. This was such a fun night."

"You weren't afraid during that boat ride, were you?"

"No. Why would I have been afraid? I know how to swim, but even if I didn't, I was surrounded by seamen, including a navy diver." She looked at him. "You would have saved anyone who went overboard."

He nodded, accepting her belief. "I'm glad you enjoyed yourself," he said, flashing his light briefly at the corners of the building they were approaching. "Thanks for showing me your cousin's letter. I still can't believe it. My folks must be jumping for joy."

"I bet your sister Mavis is," Wendy said. "Now she'll be able to afford to go to college in Oklahoma City."

He felt his brows furrow. "Mavis wants to go to college?"

"Yes, to be a schoolteacher. She considered joining the Red Cross later this year, when she turns twenty-one, but now she can go to college instead."

"How do you know that?" He hadn't known. In his mind, Mavis was still in school, but he had been gone for over three years so that wasn't true.

"Your mother wrote me about it," Wendy said. "She asked about the Red Cross program, and I told her all I know, but Mavis really wants to be a teacher."

All of that was sinking in as they walked off the base. Mavis had sent him several letters over the years, but never mentioned the Red Cross or college. "My mother wrote you about it?"

"Yes, after I added a note to your first letter home, she wrote to thank me, and I wrote back telling her that she was welcome, and then she wrote asking about the Red Cross and I wrote her back telling her—"

"Okay. I get it," he said, laughing because it sounded

like something his mother would do and like she would do. "What else did she say? What else don't I know?"

She was quiet for a moment, then said, "Nothing really, I just mailed her my answers the other day. But she did say that Holly is the one who would like to become a nurse. She could go to nursing school now, too. Become a real nurse, not just a Red Cross nurse's aide."

"There's nothing wrong with being a Red Cross nurse's aide," he said. "I bet you know a lot more than some nurses."

"I don't mind being a nurse's aide, but there are a lot of rules that come along with being a Red Cross volunteer."

"Such as?"

"I'm not complaining. I agreed to everything—there were just a few things that Sid pointed out in my agreement that I told your mother about. We're volunteers, so aren't paid. We receive a stipend and room and board. We aren't part of the military, so there's no credit or acknowledgment for the time we serve. If we'd want to become a nurse after our volunteer time, we'd have to go to nursing school like everyone else. We have to be single. As soon as anyone gets married—" She snapped her fingers. "They're out. We have to agree to go to wherever they want to send you, although, they do give choices. I chose Hawaii."

"In order to see the world," he said, all the while accepting there was one more reason he could never act upon his feelings. She loved being a Red Cross nurse, and was excellent at her job. He could never ask her to give that up.

"Yes," she said. "In order to see the world."

She sounded odd. Not her voice, but the way she

said that. Almost as if she didn't really mean it. She'd never sounded that way before.

"Can I ask you a question?" she asked.

"Sure." He flashed his light toward the upper corners of her building as they turned onto the road leading to her barracks.

"What did Captain Heinz mean about him not letting California keep you?"

Chapter Twelve

K.T. didn't realize he was holding his breath until the pressure in his lungs grew too great to withstand. Letting out the air, he drew in another breath, for reinforcement. "Because I'll be going to California soon. The *Nevada* will be taken there for a complete overhaul and modernization, and I'll travel with her to fix anything that comes up during her transport."

"When will that be?"

"Not exactly sure. A few weeks, maybe. We have to get her in good enough shape that she can make the voyage."

"How long will you be there?"

"I'm not sure of that, either. It'll depend on a lot of things."

They walked in a silence that was so heavy it felt suffocating up to the front of her barracks.

There, she lifted her chin, looked him square in the face. "I suspect I'll be gone by the time you get back."

He felt as if he'd just been kicked in the stomach. "Why?"

"I'm going to be joining the crew of the *Solace* and

sail to the South Pacific. Pago Pago. The Tutuila islands. The Tonga islands, New Zealand, Australia, the Fiji islands, all sorts of places. I'll see them all."

"See the world," he said, though his throat felt raw.

"Yes." She glanced at the door. "Well, I best get inside. It has to be almost nine. Thanks again for a fun evening."

He couldn't come up with a single thing to say. He should be happy for her and wish her well, but all he could think about was never seeing her again. How that hurt, like nothing had ever hurt before.

"Good night," she said.

"Good night," he managed, and waited until she was inside before he began his walk back to his barracks. The desolation inside him was immense, even as he told himself that she was merely doing what she'd said she was going to do since the first night he'd met her. He *should* be happy for her. She'd been happy for him in everything he'd accomplished, yet here he was thinking about himself.

That's all he had been thinking about. Himself. His job, his wants, his desires. Whereas she thought about everyone else. She wasn't even getting paid to be here. She was a volunteer. Doing one hell of a job, too. She was the reason his family would be receiving a very fair deal for the oil on their property. She cared about everyone, and made everyone happy wherever she went. Made them laugh and have fun.

Even him.

It was a good thing she was leaving, that he was leaving. Nothing could ever come between them. Nothing more than the friendship she wanted. That's all he should have wanted, too.

* * *

Wendy didn't go directly upstairs. Helen or Lois could be there and she didn't want to face anyone. They'd see her tears and question her. She didn't have any answers. None that made sense. Her only saving grace was that she'd only need to stay vigilant for a few more weeks.

Then what? She could cry her eyes out and sulk around with a broken heart? That sounded like a downright glorious future.

Like it or not, it was her future. At least for now. She'd get over it. Life had a way of going on. She'd always been grateful for that in the past, and would find a way to be again.

It would just take time.

Her little bit of self-talk didn't do wonders, but it forced her to dry her eyes. Then she used the bathroom, where she washed her face before she entered her room.

Helen and Lois were there, lying on their beds and reading magazines.

"My mom sent a new stash," said Lois, who was from Los Angeles and whose father was a banker. Each month, her mother sent a stack of every woman's magazine she could get her hands on. After the three of them had read every page, the magazines were passed around the barracks, the hospital, and the entire base.

"Great," Wendy said, picking up the top one as if she was excited.

"She also sent lipstick and nail polish," Lois said. "In the box on my dresser, help yourself if you need or want anything."

"I took two of each," Helen said. "We might not get

a chance to get things like that once we set sail for the South Pacific."

Lois set her magazine down beside her on the bed. "I'm going to miss you two." She puffed out air, making her bangs flutter. "I hope I don't end up with a Betty Boop for a roommate. That would get on my nerves!"

"You could come with us," Helen said.

"No, thanks. As soon as my time here is up, I'm heading home." Lois picked up her magazine again. "That was the deal I made with my dad. A year of volunteer work in exchange for him buying me a store. A boutique. In Beverly Hills. I'll be selling clothes to the women you see in these magazines. You two will have to come see me when you get back from the South Pacific. I'll give you the friend's discount."

"You sure have that planned out, don't you?" Helen asked.

While Lois went on explaining everything she had planned out for her boutique, Wendy changed into her nightgown, put away the clothes she had been wearing, and gave her hair a good brushing before climbing onto her bed to read the new magazine.

She half listened to their conversation, half read the pages before her, while in the back of her mind, she fully wondered if anyone ever completely fulfilled the plans they made for themselves, or if things changed and they discovered that their old plan no longer fit what they wanted.

That thought remained with her throughout the night, and she had no plans the following morning to talk with Gloria about anything, but upon entering the hospital for her shift, Gloria met her in the hallway.

"I would like to speak with you in private this morning," Gloria said.

"Is something wrong?" Wendy asked.

"We just need to talk," Gloria replied, without nodding or shaking her head. "Let's sit outside. It's a beautiful morning."

Wendy followed her to the back of the hospital, where a concrete lanai held chairs and tables for hospital staff to use during breaks.

"It's so nice to not smell oil anymore," Gloria said as they sat down.

Wendy hadn't realized that was the case, and took a moment to smell the air, noting a hint of a floral scent along with the fresh smell of the sea. "You're right," Wendy said. "It is nice."

Gloria nodded. "Things change right under our noses and if we don't stop to recognize them, we don't realize them. Don't know when or how they changed."

"That's true," Wendy replied.

"I know you've heard about the *Solace*," Gloria said.

Wendy had to swallow past the lump that formed. "Have the orders came down?"

"Not yet, but they will. Is that something you're interested in? Transferring to the ship?"

The tugging inside Wendy was uncanny. It felt as if her heart was split down the middle, tugging against itself.

"You don't have to answer today," Gloria said. "Nor do I need to say that I'll miss you. You have to know that already. You are a real asset here, and, therefore, I know you'll be a real asset on the ship. If I was to think only of the ship and their needs, I would suggest you first, even before some of the charge nurses. And if I was thinking of the hospital, I'd say we can't let you go. That we need you here."

Wendy didn't know what to say. She didn't truly know what she wanted.

"But I'm not thinking about the ship, or the hospital," Gloria said. "I'm thinking about you, because I have a daughter at home, and I hope that someone right now, is looking out for her."

Surprised, Wendy could only ask, "You do?"

"I do."

"I didn't think nurses could have children and enlist—"

"They can't have children under the age of fourteen," Gloria said. "My daughter was fifteen when I enlisted. My son was seventeen. That was three years ago, when the first invasions started overseas. Eleanor is eighteen now and in college. James is twenty and in medical school. You see, after my first marriage, when I ended up in Kansas City, I was lost. Didn't know what I was going to do. All I could think about was my first husband. The life we had built. It had been a good life before our son had died, and I thought I wanted it back. Wanted my husband to forgive me. That's why I got a job at the hospital, so I could learn things, become good enough that he'd take me back."

"Even after what he did?" Wendy asked.

"Yes. I even went back to the farm once, to see him, but the place was empty, deserted. That's when I realized that we can hang on to what we have with a death grip so we don't lose it, or we can walk away before anyone can leave us behind, because that's what it comes down to. No one wants to lose what they have, but no one wants to be left behind, either. We have to decide which one is right for us."

"What did you do?" Wendy asked.

"I went back to Kansas City. I'd been holding on to something that I'd already lost. I met my second husband, who is an amazing man. One I miss every hour of every day. He, Alvin, is who encouraged me to enlist, knowing how much I wanted what I'd learned to help others. I requested Hawaii, because I thought it would be safe here, would guarantee that I'd return home. Then it gets attacked." Gloria shook her head. "Alvin and I have laughed over that in letters. Just how ironic that is. I know that between him and his family, his mother and sisters, my children have everything they need, but I still miss them terribly."

"I'm sure you do," Wendy said, fully surprised that Gloria had never mentioned any of that before.

"I think that's also why I feel like you're my second daughter, and I want what's best for you."

Wendy was touched, truly, to the point that tears formed in her eyes. "Thank you, that's such an honor."

"You might not think so in a moment or two."

A shiver tickled Wendy's spine. "Oh?"

"I would have to be a fool to not have noticed that you have fallen in love with K.T."

Wendy sucked in air so fast and hard, she choked, and had to cough several times to get her breath back. She also had to wipe at the moisture that filled her eyes.

Gloria was smiling at her. "From someone who has been in love twice, it's easy to see. I'm not going to tell you what to do about that, but I do want to give you some advice."

"I would appreciate that," Wendy said, truly needing it.

Gloria reached over, laid her hand on Wendy's arm.

"I know you promised your mother you would see the world for her, because of the way your father left."

Wendy nodded. She had told Gloria all of that, and more. In fact, there was little Gloria didn't know about her, it seemed.

"This isn't your mother's life, Wendy. It's yours. Yours to live. If you want to see the world more than you want anything else, the *Solace* would be a fine choice. But I'm sure that your mother would never expect you to keep to your promise if it didn't make you happy. No mother would."

The truth behind Gloria's words was sinking in, deep, making Wendy question things she never had questioned before.

"On the other hand," Gloria said, "if you are considering the *Solace* because you are afraid that K.T. might leave you behind like your father did your mother, you need to remember that this is your life, not your mother's, and K.T. is not your father. There is risk in life, and falling in love is one of them. None of us know what the future will bring, we can't. We live in the here and now."

Wendy's heart was thudding hard and fast, and she felt even more confused than ever. She truly didn't know what she wanted, because the things she'd been afraid of seemed different than they used to. Gloria's hand was soft and warm as it patted her arm.

"The official call from the *Solace* for nurses and volunteers will come out next week," Gloria said. "I wanted us to have this discussion so you would have time to think things through before then. Whatever you choose, I'll support you. I'll listen if you want to talk, but I won't make that choice for you, and I won't let anyone else. The only way your name will be added to the list is because it's what you decide."

K.T. had been trying for two days to get his thoughts in order, with very little results. Working wasn't helping. He still did it, without mistakes, but it wasn't at the top of his mind. Not while he was doing it, or afterward, like now when he was attempting to focus on the ship schematics lying before him.

He had fallen in love with Wendy, and tried to convince himself that the reason he couldn't act on those feelings was because they were at war. But the truth was, Wendy didn't want him to act upon them. She didn't want anything except friendship. He had to respect that. Yet, he kept wondering if there was any way to change her mind.

A knock sounded on his door, and he twisted in his chair, to look that way as it opened. Adam poked his head inside. "Someone's here to see you."

K.T. felt his shoulders slump, at the same time his heart kicked up a notch. The last time that had happened, the visitor was Wendy. He wasn't ready to face her.

Yes, he was a coward.

And selfish.

He hated the idea of her boarding the *Solace* and sailing away.

Pushing away from his desk, he stood and then walked to the door.

Adam used a thumb to point over one shoulder.

K.T. instantly stiffened his spine and left his room to meet Captain Heinz in the hallway. "Sir."

"At ease, Lieutenant," Heinz said. "This is a friendly visit. Take a walk with me."

They walked down the hallway and out of the front door, then took a left, walking along the pathway that led between the barracks.

"I've been impressed with your work, K.T.," the captain said. "What you accomplished with the *Nevada* was nothing shy of miraculous. You not only knew what needed to be done, you knew how and in what order things had to be accomplished to make it work. I've let that be known to the commander in chief. As you know, the Salvage Division is a new branch of the navy, and with fighting going on around the world, our division will grow. Fast and furious, I believe, which is why I've requested a second-in-command."

K.T. nodded. "I can see that being needed."

"Good, because you are who I'd like to see in that position."

Taken aback, K.T. stopped walking. "Sir, I'm a welder and diver, I don't have the qualifications or—"

"I believe you do, K.T.," Heinz interrupted. "I fully understand how serious your injuries were and am amazed at how quickly you recovered, but I also see your injuries as a blessing in disguise. I know you met almost daily with Seaman Scott Westman. The instruction and guidance you gave him prior to my arrival was invaluable. Your commitment to participating while still recovering upon your release from the hospital was also vital. I learned from you while sitting in those meetings, and I say that with pride. Yes, I went to the Naval Academy and served on a battleship, studied naval architecture, worked in shipyards, and served on the Bureau of Construction and Repair in Washington, DC, but you're young and fresh off building and repairing these ships. I don't have that knowledge. Together, you and I could build this division into a force to be reckoned with."

K.T. was as honored as he was stunned.

"I fully understand that your commitment of obligation is almost at term. As my second-in-command, you would not be requested to make a long-term obligation. But I would request that it's until the war ends. Whether that be months or years, no one knows right now. Nor can I assure you that your time will be spent here. You may be required to go wherever a ship or a crew needs your expertise. The one thing I can guarantee is that you will have access to receive the highest rank, rate, and grade that an enlisted seaman can acquire."

K.T. had never considered reenlisting. There were too many people to consider when it came to something like that.

"I don't expect an answer from you today," Captain Heinz said. "I just wanted to plant the seed before you leave for California. If possible, I would like confirmation of your decision upon your return. If you need a few days to go home to Oklahoma while stateside, I can make that work, too."

"Thank you, sir," K.T. said. "For the consideration and for the time to think this through. It's an unexpected offer. I would like time to consider the options."

"I knew you would." Heinz glanced toward the barracks. "Between now and then, I'd appreciate if we kept this under wraps. I don't need men bowing at my feet with a hope of moving into a position they aren't ready for, but feel free to talk with those whom your decision might affect outside of the men."

"I fully understand, sir."

Heinz gave a nod. "I'll let you get back to your evening."

K.T. nodded, and remained where he stood as Heinz walked away. This should be enough to get Wendy off his mind.

It wasn't.

In fact, the more he thought about the offer, the more he thought about her. Mainly because he found himself comparing her to Betty, and that wasn't fair. They were two very different people, and they both were full of good qualities.

Betty would be disappointed if he chose to reenlist, whereas Wendy, well, she was too full of adventure for that. Too full of challenges and of fun. That's what life was for, she'd said that when they'd first met, and she'd lived it nearly every day since.

Betty was more cautious and, well, like him. Responsible and set in her ways. That's why they'd always gotten along so well.

Flustered, he turned about, but rather than walking back to the barracks, he went toward the harbor. Between the navy yard and Hospital Point, there was a small section of beach where he'd seen people swimming or just soaking up sun prior to the attack.

It wasn't a long walk, nor was there any barbed wire strung along the sand like the beaches along the outer shores of the island. Others were there, too, couples, families, and a few people who looked like they were there for the same reason as him. To sit and think.

He found a spot away from others, and sat down on the warm, sugar-fine sand. Straight across the water was where the *Nevada* had run ashore, and he couldn't help but think how satisfying the work of getting her afloat had been. It had been a challenge, but mastering those challenges was what brought the satisfaction, and he knew he would relish more challenges like that.

"Is this spot taken?"

Shocked, because he clearly recognized that voice, he glanced up. Seeing Wendy's dimpled smile caused his own to form. "No, it's not," he answered.

"Mind if I sit?" she asked, using the shoes in her hand to point to the ground beside him.

"By all means. I'd offer to brush away the sand, but that would be useless."

She giggled as she sat down beside him, set her shoes aside, and tugged her bright blue skirt over her knees as she buried her toes in the sand. "So what are you doing here?"

"Nothing. You?"

"I'm going to watch the sunset," she said. "I haven't done that since the attack, and I'm not sure why. Before then, I did it every night that I could."

"Curfew, blackouts, the provost court," he said.

She laughed again. "Yeah, that might all have something to do with it." Letting out a soft sigh, she asked, "How was your day?"

"Good," he lied. "Yours?"

She was looking out at the water. "I've had better."

Instantly concerned, he asked, "Something happen?"

"No, I've just had a lot on my mind lately."

There was her honesty again. He could have said just as much, and been just as honest. Even tell her about Captain Heinz's offer, but he already knew what she'd say. She'd tell him to do what would make him happy, because that's what she did, which caused him to ask, "Want to talk about it?"

"Nope. I'm here to watch the sunset and not think about anything except how beautiful it is." She looked at him. "I find that more helpful at times."

He nodded, fully understanding her answer.

Her gaze went from his face down to his shoes and back up again. "Your shoes are going to be full of sand."

"They already are," he admitted.

She giggled. "Then take them off."

"That's all right."

"Come on, Oklahoma, take off your shoes. Live a little."

"I am living, with my shoes on."

She nodded and looked back over the ocean again. "Chicken again."

"I'm not chicken, I just don't want to walk home with sandy feet," he rationalized.

"Your shoes are already full of sand. You just admitted that." Looking at him again, she said, "Take them off and we'll walk in the water. Or are you too chicken to do that, too?"

He couldn't help but laugh. She was so...so her. "Fine." He took off his shoes and pulled off his socks, then leaped to his feet and held out a hand. "Come on."

She grasped his hand and hopped to her feet.

He could have released her hand, but they were friends. She didn't want anything more than that. It was time for him to accept that, and be happy for her. Happy that she was living life as she wanted.

Hand in hand, they walked to the water, then walked along the shoreline, letting the water wash over their feet.

"Doesn't that feel good?" she asked. "I love the way the wet sand squishes between my toes."

He laughed. "You would love that."

"Why not? It feels good."

He clamped his lips together to keep from saying that it wouldn't feel good if either of them stepped on a piece of shrapnel. Why hadn't he thought about that before now? Walking barefoot was not a responsible thing to do.

"Quit thinking about what could be, Oklahoma, and think about what is," she said.

"How do you know what I'm thinking?"

"Because you went stiff and quiet," she said. "You did that while we were racing home from the Monkey Bar in both the jeep and the boat."

That was true. "It's habit."

"Because you're a McCallister," she said.

He'd never thought of it that way, but it fit.

"It's all right," she said. "We need all kinds in this world, but once in a while, it's okay to be different. To just be yourself. Who you want to be, not who others want you to be." She released his hand and spun in a circle, arms out and face lifted toward the sky. "To just be free."

Filled with admiration, because he did admire so many things about her, he watched her spin several times before she stopped and held her hands out toward him.

He took her hands in his, and let her lead him around in a few circles, before he said, "You are going to end up so dizzy, you'll fall in the water."

Her giggle floated on the air. "So? What would that hurt?"

"You'd get wet," he warned.

"I've been wet before."

He wasn't sure what possessed him, but without questioning the desire, he tugged her closer, released her hands, and picked her up. With one hand around her back and the other under her knees, he carried her deeper into the water.

She wrapped her arms around his neck. "What are you doing?"

"I'm going to let you get wet," he teased.

Her hands tightened around his neck and she pressed her body tight against his. "You are not going to drop me in the water!"

"I thought you wanted to get wet."

"Wet! Not dunked!"

He laughed and slowly lowered her legs, until her feet touched the ground. Water swished around their shins. His hand was still around her back, holding her close, and he scanned her face. Every inch of it. Her ocean-blue eyes. Perfectly shaped nose, her dimples, and petal-shaped lips.

What he wouldn't give to taste those lips. Feel them pressed against his. Friends, though, didn't kiss on the lips, even if he was sure that she would kiss him back if he gave in to his desires.

In an attempt to bury those burning desires, he said, "I've never met anyone like you, Nebraska."

She stared at him for a long time, before she sighed, and then leaned forward. The blood that was already pounding in his veins heated up more in anticipation.

Her hands went around his waist and she laid her head against his chest. "The feeling is mutual, Oklahoma," she whispered.

A hug wasn't the same as a kiss, yet he found a great deal of satisfaction in wrapping his arms around her and holding her close as they stood there. If he could be who he wanted to be at this moment, it would be a man who could freely love her. Forever.

Chapter Thirteen

Wendy wished she could stop time. That she could remain right here, in K.T.'s arms forever. Of course, that wasn't possible. They'd eventually need to eat, go to the bathroom, sleep, go to work. Live.

She'd been surprised to see K.T. sitting on the beach. Actually, she'd thought she was seeing things when she'd first arrived. He was so embedded in her mind she had images of him floating around day and night.

There were other thoughts in her mind day and night, too, and she still hadn't decided what she was going to do. Letting out a sigh, she released her hold on his waist and took a step back. Because she didn't believe in spreading unhappiness, she found the ability to smile up at him. "We don't want to miss the sunset."

"No, we don't."

The warmth of his hand as he took a hold of hers, and the firmness of his hold as they walked out of the water made her wonder how something so simple could feel so right. Or was it not that simple? Nothing about her life felt simple right now.

Arriving where they'd left their shoes, they sat down,

facing the water, where the sky was already glistening with shades of yellow and pink. Oranges and reds would come next, and reflect off the water. It would be a sight to see. She knew, because she'd seen it before, but it never got old. Much like K.T. Seeing him would never get old. It was understandable how she'd fallen in love with a man so perfect, so honorable and respectable.

"What is it in the world that you want to see?" K.T. asked.

Bewildered, she could do nothing but turn her gaze to him. "No one has ever asked me that before."

He grinned, gave a slight nod. "What do you want to see?"

Her mind was blank. "I guess I'm not really sure."

Using his hand, he gestured, pointed to things surrounding them while asking, "Sunsets, people, the ocean, buildings, flowers, landmarks?"

"I really don't know," she answered. "But I didn't know what I wanted to see here, either, until I arrived and discovered all the things there are to see."

He nodded and looked out at the sunset. "That makes sense."

"Does it?" she wondered aloud. "I mean, shouldn't I know what I want to see? Shouldn't I really want to see something specific?"

"I don't know," he said. "I guess that's up to you."

Frustration had her saying, "People sure are good at offering advice that doesn't have any advice in it."

Frowning, he asked, "What?"

She shook her head and sighed. "Nothing. Just thinking aloud."

He scooted closer to her and put an arm around her

shoulder. "Well, then, my friend, let's just sit here and watch the sunset."

Even though she knew what she felt went deeper, she leaned her head against his shoulder and looked out over the bay. "I like being your friend, Oklahoma."

"I like being your friend, Nebraska."

They sat in silence, complete, comforting silence as the setting sun filled the sky with a bright golden haloed prism of red and yellow that reflected off the water, turning it into a matching prism. She couldn't help but wonder if she'd given him Betty's letter back in December if he'd be interested in being more than her friend. The desire to be more to him was very much alive inside her, and she doubted it would ever wane, no matter where she was or what she was doing.

Others around them left, but they sat there until the sun had completely disappeared, leaving behind nothing but a horizon of fading colors as darkness slowly rolled in like a huge sky blanket tucking the world in for a good night.

He gave her arm a pat before removing his arm from around her shoulders and reaching down to put on his socks and shoes.

She picked up her shoes and waited until he was done before standing. They walked to the road, where she paused to slide on her shoes, and he removed his, one at a time and emptied the sand from them.

It had been so unfair of her to keep Betty's letter from him, and she wanted to tell him she was sorry, but was still so afraid. Not just of being abandoned like Gloria said, but of how her life could change. If by some miracle, he did like her more than a friend, everything could change. She could be evacuated to the

States, she couldn't be married and continue with her work; all sorts of things could change that she didn't want. Letting out a sigh as they began walking again, she asked, "How are the repairs on the *Nevada* coming?"

"Good, but there's a lot to be done."

"Tell me about it."

"It's a lot, technical stuff, boring."

"Not to me." She missed the mornings when she'd put a bandage on his back and he'd tell her about the things he had to do that day. "I like hearing about it. What part of the ship are you working on?"

"All parts, her steering system was destroyed, her rudder damaged, and the saltwater played havoc on miles of wires that will need to be rewrapped for her electrical mechanics."

She asked more specific questions about the things he said, and listened as he explained things, answering each question more thoroughly. Everything he said was interesting, but it was how he said it that she was hearing. There was pride and excitement in his voice. She didn't want things to change for him any more than she wanted them to change for herself.

Their conversation didn't stop until they arrived at her door. "Thank you for telling me all that, and it wasn't boring. Not at all. It sounds complicated and I'm amazed by how much you know about so many different things. I'm also happy that you are doing something that you like so much."

He reached up and softly brushed the hair off the side of her face. Her entire body was tingling again, from head to toe, as it always did when he was near. But it increased in unique and exciting ways when he looked at her like he was right now. It made her breath stall, and her heart thud.

"I'm happy that you are doing what you want to do, too," he said. "Seeing the world. Good night, Nebraska."

She hid her disappointment over the fact that she'd wanted him to kiss her, even though she knew he never would do that. Not while believing that Betty was at home thinking they were still dating. What she'd done was so wrong. "Good night, Oklahoma."

As always, he waited until she was inside before he turned and walked away, and as always, she watched him walk down the road. A thought shifted in her mind. When Gloria had talked about holding on to something so you don't lose it, she assumed Gloria was talking about her promise to her mother, but that's not what Gloria had meant.

She'd been holding on to that letter so K.T. couldn't fall in love with her, because if he could fall out of love with Betty, he could just as easily fall out of love with her. Then she would become her mother. Left with a heart so broken she would never be happy again.

Her stomach knotted.

She'd been holding that letter over his head like some sort of invisible weapon, without him knowing it.

Only an awful person would do that.

A truly awful person.

That was her.

She had to stop thinking only of herself and put things right.

The following day, after her shift had ended, she changed out of her uniform, put the letter in her purse, and left the barracks. She didn't know when K.T. would get off work, so she'd just wait at his barracks until he did arrive. Knowing what she'd done, and why, was making her physically sick. Her stomach was so upset, she hadn't dared to eat anything all day, and her head ached. For months she'd told herself that she hadn't given him the letter because she didn't want to see him hurt, but she'd only been trying to save herself from being hurt the entire time.

The rumble of a vehicle behind her had her stepping to the side of the road before she turned around.

Her heart leaped with joy at recognizing the driver. Then dropped to her stomach remembering why she was on her way to see him.

"I was coming to see you," K.T. said as he stopped the jeep beside her.

"Oh." She swallowed the lump in her throat. "Why?"

The guilt inside her was increasing over how she'd wished at times that someone else would write him, tell him about Betty. That, too, had been selfish. No one else had written him because unlike her, they didn't stick their noses in where they didn't belong.

"To talk," he said. "Where are you going?"

She could feel her courage slipping away. "To talk to you," she said quickly, before losing her last nerve.

"So you heard?" he asked.

"Heard what?" She shook her head. "I haven't heard anything."

He glanced around. "We can't talk here, in the middle of the road. Climb in and we'll go down to the beach."

Fear alone caused her to hesitate for a moment, before she climbed in the jeep and clutched onto the handles of her purse, knowing that what it held was going to change everything. The one thing she hadn't wanted to happen, she had caused to happen.

"I went to the hospital," he said, "but they said you'd already left."

"I got off a few minutes early. It was a quiet day."

It was a short drive to the beach, and once there, he parked the jeep facing the water, but made no effort to climb out after he'd shut off the engine. Twisting in his seat, so he was looking at her, he asked, "Why were you coming to see me?"

She tried, but couldn't speak.

"Is the *Solace* shipping out?"

The hard knot that was still in her stomach twisted even tighter, and she shook her head while trying to find her voice. "No. Not yet. Sometime in March."

He nodded. "Well, I—I wanted a chance to say goodbye, in case you're gone when I return, and… uh…to say…"

Not expecting that, her heart thudded so hard, she interrupted, "Return? I thought you weren't leaving for weeks."

"Plans changed. I'm leaving tomorrow morning."

She couldn't think of a thing to say, or maybe it was simply that her throat was burning and her mind knew it wouldn't work if she tried speaking.

"Not on the *Nevada*," he said. "It'll be weeks before she's ready. It's another ship. Going to the mainland. A couple of the men from the Salvage Division that were scheduled to sail with the crew in the event that repairs were needed enroute came down sick and Captain Heinz asked me to fill in for them. I'm taking Adam with me. We'll be gone for possibly two weeks, maybe three, and, I—I wanted you to know. I wanted to say thanks for all you've done."

She pinched her lips together. All she'd done? He had no idea all that she'd done.

"I'm glad we met," he said. "Very glad we met, and I—I… Well, um…"

A sob bubbled in her throat and she squeezed her eyes shut against the tears.

His hand, warm and familiar, so familiar, touched hers. "Wendy, I want you to know that while I'm in Calif—"

"I have something you need to read," she blurted out. With trembling hands, she opened her purse and pulled out the envelope.

"Another letter from your cousin?"

"No." She handed it to him.

The moment he saw the front of the envelope, his name, he frowned.

She closed her eyes again, unable to look at him. She heard the paper, heard the soft clink of the necklace chain. His intake of breath.

"What the—" He went silent.

He was reading it. That was obvious. Covering her mouth to hold in any sounds, she told herself that she should leave now. Just leave. But she had to apologize first. Still not able to look at him, she whispered, "I'm sorry. So sorry."

"How long have you had this?" he asked.

It hurt to breathe. Every part of her hurt and she didn't know if the pain was for herself, or for him. "Since you were in the hospital. I started to read it to you, but you said to wait, and by then, I'd seen the necklace, read the first paragraph to myself. I—I just couldn't—" Her thoughts were sporadic. Weren't clear even to her. "You were in such pain. I didn't want to cause you more. I just hid it. Kept it."

He didn't say a word, but she could hear him breathing. Heavily.

What more could she say?

"You've had this for three months?" he asked.

"Two and a half," she clarified. Foolishly clarified! As if two weeks made a difference. She couldn't justify what she'd done. Nothing could.

"At any time in the past *two and a half months*," he asked, "did it ever occur to you that I might want to know—"

"Yes," she interrupted. "It occurred to me all the time, but I—I'm sorry, I can't explain why I didn't give it to you." She sucked in air to compensate for the tears and sobs making her voice tremble. "I'm just so sorry."

There was nothing more she could say, or do. Hooking her purse over her wrist, she climbed out of the jeep.

"Wendy, wait—"

"I have to leave." She swiped at the tears streaming down her face, and blinked trying to see him through the blur. "Please take care of yourself. Be safe. And—and, have a good life. A very good life. Have fun." Nodding, because that's what she wanted for him—a good, fun life—she added one last truth. "I just wanted to be your friend and couldn't stand the thought of… Oh, never mind." Then, she turned and ran.

Didn't stop until she was in the bathroom in the upstairs of her barracks. Then, like she had the night of the attack, she stripped down and climbed in the shower and cried her eyes out.

First thing tomorrow morning, she'd tell Gloria she wanted to leave with the *Solace*. Because this was it. This is what it felt like to have a broken heart, and she'd done it all by herself.

It took two days before K.T. was able to think beyond the insurmountable anger that had consumed him. The fact he was in the middle of the Pacific Ocean, on a damaged ship that looked more like an overgrown PT boat rather than a battleship, had helped in some ways, not in others. He'd ignored the anger while focused on the work at hand.

The USS *Shaw*'s bow had been blown apart in the attack. The temporary one that had been attached to get her to the mainland was rough at best. The bow was a stubby thing, half the size as it needed to be, so the ship was plowing through the waves straight on, which made for a constant rough ride. Her crew were seasoned men and half of them were seasick because of the never-ending jarring. Six days of this was going to be hell, and he hoped they all lived to see Mare Island.

That could be part of why his anger was mellowing into a simmer. He didn't want to go out of this world mad at anyone. Not even himself.

The ship's engineering machinery hadn't been damaged in the attack and was moving the ship slowly across the ocean, with a destroyer on each side, escorting them all the way to California. He'd call home from there. Talk to his family, let them know that he was reenlisting.

He should have questioned not receiving a letter from Betty harder. Should have figured something had changed. It had just been easier to pretend that it hadn't, because if he'd known, he would have asked Wendy to marry him. He was sure of that, and just as sure of what her answer would have been.

She'd have said no. Right from the start, she'd made it clear that she only wanted to be friends. That's why she never gave him the letter.

A letter that had been more of a relief than a disappointment. Betty's letter had said that she hadn't expected to fall in love with someone else, had never imagined it was possible, until it had happened.

He could relate to that, because that's exactly what had happened to him. He'd tried to not let it happen, but it had.

All the guilt over that, and the pain of fighting the feelings he'd had for Wendy, of fighting the desires he'd had for her, had made him so mad, he hadn't been able to think straight when he'd first read Betty's letter.

Even with all that anger, Wendy's tears had affected him, and he'd almost followed her, until her final words had settled into his mind.

He'd heard all of her reasons for just wanting to be friends, but it hadn't made a difference. He'd fallen in love with her anyway.

That's where his anger came from now. From how foolish he'd been.

Yes, Wendy was the prettiest woman he'd ever seen. The nicest. The sweetest. Her free spirit alone was enough to make any man fall for her.

But she hadn't wanted anyone to fall in love with her.

Another thing she'd told him more than once.

She'd also told him that if she wanted to keep her job, her volunteer position, she had to remain single.

Unaware of his own selfishness, he'd ignored all the signs, all the things she'd said. It was a good thing that she'd given him the letter right when she had, before he'd made a fool of himself by telling her that when he was in California, he'd planned on calling Betty and telling her that he'd fallen in love with someone else.

He'd been about to confess everything when she'd given him the letter.

It was a good thing that she had, before he made a complete fool of himself.

A knock roused him from the bed he was lying on, and he smacked his head on the bunk above him. Rubbing the spot, he left the bed and opened the door.

"Sorry, Lieutenant," a shipmate said. "Got water. Don't know if it's from hitting the waves so hard or if there's a leak."

"I'm coming," K.T. replied, not minding the interruption at all. Work, staying busy, was exactly what he needed right now.

Four days later, just as the sun was setting, they arrived at Mare Island. The ship had held up with only minor repairs along the way, and thankfully, no enemies on the water or in the air had spotted the damaged battleship.

Upon disembarking, K.T. accepted a sleeping unit at the barracks, took a hot shower, then fell into bed, where he slept for ten hours straight. The first thing he did, after applying some ointment to his back the best he could because his skin was itching and aching, and after getting dressed, was to find the common room and the telephone.

He asked the operator to connect him to the Tillis Feed

Store in Guymon, Oklahoma, and waited through a series of clicks, clacks, buzzes, and several rings before a voice came on the other line.

"Ed?" he asked into the telephone receiver.

"Yes, who's this?"

"It's K.T.," he answered. "K.T. McCallister."

"K.T.!"

Ed's shout echoed through the line so loud that K.T. held the earpiece away from his ear for a moment.

"Golly! You calling all the way from Hawaii?"

"No, I'm at Mare Island."

"Where? What Island? Is it near Hawaii?"

"No, it's in California, I'm only here for a few days and would like to talk to my folks. Could you get a message to them? Tell them that I'll call them back at your place around this time tomorrow morning?"

"Of course, I can! I can have them here in less than an hour, if you'd like. It sure is good to hear your voice K.T. What are you doing in California?"

"I had to bring a ship back here to be worked on," he said, explaining things in the simplest way.

"One that was hit during the attack? We were all glued to the radios that day. You had a lot of prayers going up for you that day. Every day. We are all awfully proud of you. Say, Wendy's not with you, is she?"

K.T. pulled the receiver away from his ear again, just long enough to stare at it, wondering if he heard correctly or not. "Wendy?" he asked, putting the phone back to his ear.

"Yes, your nurse, Wendy."

"No," he answered. "She's in Hawaii, at the hospital, working." At least he assumed she still was. He still hated the idea of her sailing away on the *Solace*, but it was what she wanted and he had to be happy for her.

"Oh, I guess that figures." Ed sounded disappointed.

"How—" K.T. stopped himself from asking more.

Ed however, still had plenty to say. "The whole town sure would like to meet her someday. Sorry things didn't work out between you and Betty, she's a fine gal and all—we all miss her, but it sounds like you got yourself a real fine gal, now. We've all met her cousin. Sid Williams, that lawyer from Nebraska. He's a smart man. Did you know lawyers have to have licenses to practice in other states? Sid got permission to work here with some Oklahoma lawyers and he didn't let those city slicker lawyers from the oil company trick anyone into signing anything. Folks were all able to keep the mineral rights of their land. Going to get royalties for every gallon of oil pumped out of the ground. 'Bout time we had some good luck around here. Your ma says that was Wendy. She was our good luck. Yours, too. Hear tell she really nursed you back to health."

His mother would say that, and taking advantage of Ed sucking in air, K.T. quickly said, "I have to go, Ed, but I'll call back tomorrow morning. This same time."

"Got it! I'll have your whole family here by ten in the morning. Probably the whole town. Everyone will want to hear what you have to say!"

K.T. rubbed his forehead, even though he had to grin. The whole town probably would be there tomorrow morning, and they probably did want to meet Wendy. They'd like her. It was impossible not to. "Thanks, Ed. Goodbye."

"Goodbye, K.T. Talk to you tomorrow."

The line went dead and he stared at the phone for

a moment after hanging up, knowing one thing for sure. He was going to have a hell of a time forgetting Wendy. Even after he went back home. Whenever that might be.

With a head shake, he stood, and made his way outside, and then to the docks to have a look around. There he met men from the *Shaw*, as well as others and it was several hours later before he made his way back to the barracks. All the while wondering about Wendy, and when the *Solace* would be sailing. Whether she wanted anyone waiting on her to return or not, he'd had the suspicion that he'd be waiting the rest of his life hoping to see her again.

Adam was at the barracks, sitting in a chair with his feet propped up on another reading a magazine. He reached into his breast pocket. "Hey, they gave this message to me, to give to you."

It was a slip of paper, telling him to call a telephone number as soon as possible.

"Thanks." Figuring it had something to do with the ship, K.T. went back to the common room and dialed the number.

It was answered on the second ring, by a woman who merely said, "Hello?"

"I'm not sure if I have the right number. This is K.T. McCallister and I was—"

"K.T., it's Betty."

He shouldn't keep questioning his hearing, yet asked, "Betty?"

"Yes. I live in San Francisco, now. Ed stopped by my folks' house after going out to your house, and my mother drove into town and called me, told me that you are at Mare Island."

"I am." He shook his head. "You live in San Francisco?"

"Yes. Can we meet?" she asked. "I'd really like to talk to you. See you."

He had no hard feelings toward her. In fact, it would be good to see her, find out when she'd moved. "Sure."

"Wonderful! When? Do you want to meet someplace? Should I pick you up?"

"Just tell me when and where, I'll get a ride."

Chapter Fourteen

Despite the melancholy state she'd been in for days, a smile slipped onto Wendy's lips as memories formed. She was cleaning up an exam room where a plaster cast had been placed on a sailor's leg who had slipped and fallen while running to get in his jeep last night at the Monkey Bar, but who hadn't come in until this morning, because he hadn't thought he'd broken anything.

He had broken his ankle, and was still lying in the gurney, waiting for the plaster to dry, and wondering how much trouble he was going to be in from his supervisor.

"Did you see the monkeys?" she asked the sailor while wiping plaster spattle off the work cart tray with a wet cloth.

"You've been there?" he asked.

"I have." She rinsed out the cloth and wrung it out. "It's a fun place."

"It was." He let out a long sigh, staring at the cast. "How much trouble do you think I'll be in?"

"I don't know," she admitted. "But I do know that we all make mistakes." Big ones. Ones that people regret for the rest of their lives. She certainly would.

"Seaman Westman could have my head for this," the sailor said.

"Seaman Scott Westman?" she asked. "Is he your supervisor?"

"Yes, for now. I'm assigned to the USS *Cassin*, but they haven't decided if they are going to repair her or scrap her, so we've all been temporarily assigned to different units in the yard. I know how to weld, so Lieutenant McCallister put me under Westman."

Just the sound of K.T.'s name was enough to make tears form. She closed her eyes for a moment, giving them a chance to dry up.

"Do you know Seaman Westman?" the sailor asked.

"Yes, I do." Her mind wasn't on Scott, or the sailor, it was on K.T. But that wasn't anything new. She wiped the last few drops of white plaster spattle off the floor and set her cloth on the cart. "I have a suggestion if you'd like to hear it."

"Sure."

"Once that plaster is dried, you'll be given some crutches, and I'd suggest that you find Seaman Westman, tell him yourself what happened. Ask him if there is something you can do while healing." She thought of all the things K.T. had told her about. "If there are some blueprints you can study, or schematics, or supply inventory reports, anything that will help your unit until you have the use of both legs again."

"That's a good idea. There are all sorts of things I can do. I know there are."

She was glad to see him smiling. "Good, then offer to do them."

"I will. Thanks."

"You're welcome." She rolled the cart around to wheel it out the door. "Good luck."

"Thanks!"

She pushed the cart to the nurse's station to put away the unused supplies, sanitize the tray, and restock the bottom shelf for the next use, and was in the midst of that, when Gloria entered the station.

"How's the broken ankle patient?"

"He's doing fine," Wendy replied.

Gloria leaned back against the door frame and crossed her arms. "Official word from the *Solace* arrived. She'll be sailing in five days. Do you still want to be on her?"

Wendy had thought she'd hardened herself, thought she was prepared for that news, but the sharp pinch in her heart was painful enough to make her flinch. Yet, she had made up her mind. "Yes, I do."

"Do you still not want to talk about it?"

"No." Confused as ever, Wendy shook her head. "I mean yes, I still don't want to talk about it."

"I wish you would."

Wendy put the last pack of gauze on the cart shelf and pushed it near the wall where other carts were lined up. "There's nothing to talk about."

"Yes, there is, and pretending there's not won't change it."

Nothing would change anything. Not what she'd done. Not how she felt.

Not what she had to do.

Straightening her spine, because she needed some sort of fortification as she met Gloria's gaze, she said, "I suspect there are things that need to be done here, to get ready for the patient transfers from the *Solace*. Where do you need me to start?"

Always professional, thinking of the hospital and patients first, Gloria nodded. It was what she did next that surprised Wendy. Before she even realized it, Gloria's arms were around her, holding her in a tight hug.

"I would like you to start at the beginning," Gloria said. "Tell me why you are running away. Because that's what you're doing, and that's not the way to fix a problem."

Wendy's entire body slouched, wanted to crumble onto the floor. She couldn't do that, so she wrapped her arms around Gloria. "There's nothing to fix."

"Yes, there is." Gloria held her for several moments, before she leaned back and cupped Wendy's face with both hands. "But I can't help, if I don't know what happened."

Even as the shame of what she'd done washed over her, Wendy couldn't stop herself from telling Gloria about the letter she'd kept hidden from K.T. for months. She continued her babbling ramble that included a few hiccups and sobs, by explaining that she knew K.T. could never forgive her for that. It had been wrong. So wrong.

"Well, now," Gloria said. "That does appear to be a problem, doesn't it?"

Wendy sighed and because she was no longer holding on to Gloria, she stepped back and leaned against the counter for support. "Yes."

"And, where there is a problem, there is a solution."

Wendy shook her head. "It was just like you said. I was holding on to him, because I didn't want to lose him, I didn't want to have a broken heart."

"It does appear that way, doesn't it?"

"It is that way." She'd gone over things a hundred

times in her head, and fully understood what she'd done, and why. "I was only thinking of myself."

"Everyone thinks of themselves, Wendy. We have to. We depend on ourselves." Gloria let out a small sigh. "Let's start at the beginning and go through it again. You didn't give him the letter at first because you didn't want to see him in more pain while he was in the hospital, correct?"

"Yes, and then I didn't give him the letter because I was already falling in love with him and I didn't want that. I've never wanted that. My mother was so unhappy, and that was why, because she fell in love with my father and he left."

"This is your life, not your mother's, so tell me why you didn't want K.T. to love you."

"I just told you what happened—"

"To your mother," Gloria said. "Why do you think that would happen to you? You know other couples who love each other. Who are happily married. Some for many years. Like your aunt and uncle."

"Well, yes, but…"

"But?"

Wendy didn't know the answer, and searched for one. "I'm not their daughter."

"What difference does that make?"

Wendy didn't know the answer to that, either.

Gloria stepped forward, then turned about and leaned against the corner next to her. "What if it wasn't K.T. that you were holding on to, but bits and pieces of your old life that you didn't want to lose? Things that aren't even true anymore? Aren't even there?"

As Wendy contemplated that, her thoughts wandered to Gloria's life. "Like you? Your first marriage?"

"This is your life, not mine, but there could be similarities. I was afraid to leave my old life behind. Afraid of finding a new one, because I didn't want to fail again."

Goose bumps formed on Wendy's arms.

"But we all fail, we all make mistakes," Gloria said. "And we all have the choice to try again or give up."

Wendy shook her head, because she didn't have a choice to try again.

"If things were the other way around, if K.T. had withheld information from you. Vital information, would you forgive him?"

"Of course." Wendy didn't need to think about that.

"Then why aren't you giving him that same opportunity? He deserves that, doesn't he?"

Wendy pinched her lips together, knowing that K.T. deserved far more than that.

Gloria pushed off the counter. "Five beds will need to be made up on the second floor for patients being transferred from the ship. I trust you'll see to them?"

Wendy nodded. "I will."

Gloria walked to the door, but before leaving, she turned. "And I trust you'll give me your final answer about the *Solace* by tomorrow."

Wendy nodded again. "I will."

"I want you to have it," K.T. told Betty. "I bought it for you." There had been no rhyme or reason why he'd added her letter and the necklace to his duffle bag when he'd left Hawaii, but he had bought her the necklace and did want her to have it. Nearly every day that he'd been in California, he'd had dinner with her and her husband, Jim Jackson, who was a real okay guy. Jim worked for a company that made seismograph equipment used to explore for oil. That's how he'd ended up in Oklahoma, and had met Betty.

"Thank you," Betty said. "It's lovely." She let out a laugh. "I hated sending it back to you, because it was so lovely, but I didn't feel as if I could keep it."

"Now, you can feel as if you can keep it," K.T. said. "Even Jim agrees."

Jim, who was tall, with dark hair and dressed like a real city slicker in his three-piece suits, smiled at Betty. "Yes, even I agree." He then shook K.T.'s hand. "Send us a postcard now and again. We'll be wondering how you're doing."

"I will," K.T. replied. "And remember what I told you. Leave the city duds behind when you go to Oklahoma. They make you stand out like a sore thumb."

Jim laughed. "I wished I'd met you before my first trip out there. It would have saved me from getting run off with a shotgun from more than one property."

K.T. laughed at the image that formed in his mind. Betty had told him all about how she and Jim had met. How they'd eloped, and how she was afraid to go back home, fearing that everyone would hate her for what she'd done. He'd told her that they wouldn't and he'd told his folks, and half the town who had been listening in on his telephone call, that they all should be happy for both him and Betty. Things had worked out just as they should.

That's what he was telling himself, too.

Betty gave him a hug. "It was so good seeing you. We've been friends since we were born, and I hated the idea of losing that."

It seemed he was destined to just be friends. "Me, too. It was great seeing you. Really great."

"We made the right decision to wait on getting engaged," she said. "Neither of us had experienced real love. You'll know what I mean when it hits you. It'll consume you and you'll be unable to wait for anything."

He already knew that feeling, but kept that to himself. "I have to get down to the shipyard before the boat leaves without me. You two take care."

"You, too! Write when you can!" Betty shouted as he walked away.

"I will," he shouted while climbing in the jeep he'd borrowed from the base.

He started the engine and waved while driving away. She was still the Betty he'd always known, and he truly was happy for her. Seeing her had confirmed that he'd never truly been in love with her. He liked her, but seeing her hadn't made his heart go wild, nor had he felt any sense of jealousy over Jim being her husband instead of him.

He'd almost mentioned Wendy several times while talking with them, but hadn't. Just the thought of her made his throat swell up. There was no telling if she'd still be in Hawaii when he got back or not. He and Adam were catching a ride back on an ocean liner, a cruise ship that had been converted into a supply hauler, so the trip would be faster and smoother, but he still would have been gone for over two weeks when they arrived.

Two of the longest weeks of his life.

Which proved to be very true during the voyage back across the Pacific. At least while on the *Shaw*, though rough as that ride had been, he'd had work to keep him busy. There was nothing for him to do on the ocean liner, except think.

Think too damn much.

The first place he was going to go was the hospital. If she wasn't there, he'd go to her barracks. Or maybe he'd go there first, depending on what time they arrived and disembarked.

If friendship was all she wanted, that was fine. He just had to make things right between them. Like he had with Betty.

Who was he trying to fool?

Friendship was fine with Betty, but Wendy was different.

He loved Wendy too much to ever just be her friend. He missed her. So much.

That was something he might have to get used to. She could have already sailed on the *Solace*. He had no way of knowing. Wouldn't have any way of knowing until he arrived at the harbor.

If she hadn't sailed yet, he was going to talk to her about that. He didn't want her floating around the ocean. Not without him. There had to be a way they could figure something out.

Figure out if maybe someday, she'd want to be more than friends. Much more. He'd find a way to show her the world. Find a way to give her anything, everything, she'd ever want.

Those thoughts swam in his head day and night. Night and day.

Right up until twenty knots outside of Hawaii, when the sighting of another ship was announced. Like many other passengers, he went to the upper deck, anxious to catch sight of something except for the water they'd been looking at for days.

It was midmorning, and between the sun shining on the water and distance, the other ship was little more than a ghostly outline, but the vicinity alone said she was either leaving from or sailing to Hawaii.

He stood, waiting to see if he could make out more, until he heard a shout. Then, it felt as if his world shattered. Along with his heart.

"It's a mercy ship! A hospital ship!" echoed over and over in his mind until the ship was completely out of sight.

There were other hospital ships, but he knew that had been the *Solace*.

Knew with all his heart.

An emptiness formed inside him, and grew until it fully encompassed him. It was heavy, too. Heavier than his diving suit. That's what it felt like, as if he was trying to walk on land while wearing weighted shoes. When his ship finally pulled into port, it took effort for him to put on the white Dixie cup hat that went with his blue uniform. More effort to lift up his duffle bag, and more to walk to the gangway, still more to pretend that he was happy they'd arrived.

He forced himself to conjure up good thoughts for Wendy. He did want her to be happy, and hoped she enjoyed seeing the world.

One thing was for sure, she'd make other people happy wherever she went.

Adam elbowed him as they stepped off the gangway.

K.T. glanced over, to see what Adam wanted.

Adam nodded his chin toward the end of the dock. "Looks like you have someone waiting for you."

This time it wasn't his hearing K.T. questioned, it was his eyes. There could be a number of reasons for a nurse to be standing at the end of the dock, but he knew this one. Knew that perfect shape, that dark hair. Knew she was the only woman who would ever make his heart pound hard enough to break a rib.

He wiped at the smile that formed on his face with one hand, then handed his duffle bag to Adam. "Take this for me."

His heart was racing faster than an electric motor and it was all he could do to keep his feet from running. He was happy, very happy that she wasn't on the *Solace*, but warned himself that he didn't know why.

That was the first thing he wanted to ask when he stopped before her, with his hands in his pockets because they were itching to touch her, but again, cautioned himself. "I saw the *Solace* out on the ocean."

She nodded. "It left." Then she shrugged. "I couldn't go."

Her ocean-blue eyes held a sparkling gleam, and her signature dimpled smile was on her beautiful face, yet, he was concerned that she was hiding her disappointment. "Why couldn't you go?"

She reached into her white apron pocket and pulled out a slip of paper. Holding it up, she said, "Because you haven't given me my Christmas present yet. One fishing trip."

He'd never felt the degree of happiness that he did right then. A single chuckle rumbled in his throat. Then another at the thrill that shot through him. "There's one other thing that I haven't given you yet."

"Oh? What's that?" she asked.

The wait was over. He wasn't going to fight the desires

that had damn near been killing him for months any longer. He was going to take a chance and figure things out later. "This." He wrapped an arm around her, and dipped her backward over his arm like he had done so many times while dancing with her, but this time, he lowered his head and covered her lips with his.

The softness, the sweetness, of her lips was more than he'd imagined. Because no one could ever imagine something so perfect.

Her arms looped around his neck as she returned his kiss, touch for touch. Glide for glide. Pressure for pressure.

He kissed her a long time. A very long time, trying to make up for all the times he'd wanted to kiss her and hadn't.

It wasn't until an ounce of reality formed, that he eased his lips off hers, and gave them a final quick peck, before he lifted his head.

Her smile was still there, even before her eyes fluttered open. "That was a pretty nice present, too," she whispered.

He laughed. "I've missed you."

"I've missed you, too."

He eased her upright, pulled her close, into a long hug, and kept her there as he whispered, "I know you just want to be friends, but I'd like to talk about that."

She leaned her head back, looked up at him. "I never wanted to just be your friend. I was afraid."

"Of what?"

"Of leaving my old life behind, entering one I knew nothing about." She laid a hand against his cheek. "I'm so sorry that I didn't give you Betty's letter sooner, I knew it would change everything, and I was afraid of that. So afraid."

A tear slipped from the corner of her eye. He wiped it aside with his thumb. "It would have changed everything."

She nodded. "Do—do you think you could ever forgive me for that?"

He kissed her forehead, the end of her nose, her lips. "I already have."

A soft sob escaped her lips before she pinched them together, and looked at him with tears shimmering in her eyes.

"If you don't want me to be your friend, what do you want?" he asked, half afraid of her answer. Yet, also excited to hear her response.

Never breaking eye contact, she asked, "What do you want me to be?"

"My wife," he answered without hesitation.

For a good thirty seconds, at least it felt that long, she stared at him, before asking, "You do remember that I don't know how to cook? Or sew? I'm not very good at ironing, either."

"We'll eat at the mess hall. I've sewn on buttons for years, and I have my own iron." He touched his forehead to hers. "I know you can dance, and I want us to keep dancing together. Forever and ever and ever."

She threw her head back in laughter and then stretched upward and kissed him. Not a simple, soft kiss. This one was filled with all the enthusiasm she put into everything she did.

He picked her up, and with their lips still locked together, twirled around in a circle. Several circles, before he stopped. He didn't lower her so her feet could touch the ground, just kept holding her. "Is that a yes, or do I need to ask again?"

Wendy had never felt so wonderful. She was no longer conflicted about anything. She knew exactly what she wanted. "It's a yes." She kissed his lips, an action that she'd never get tired of doing. "A very big yes."

"I love you, Nebraska," he said.

"I love you, Oklahoma," she replied. "I love you so, so much."

They kissed again, and again before he lowered her so her feet touched the ground, and his smile slowly slipped away. "Will they really make you quit your job when we get married?"

She nodded. "Yes, but it doesn't matter. Gloria said I can become a hospital volunteer. That's what Faye does."

"You won't mind?"

"No, not at all."

They were still at the end of the dock, with other people walking around them. He seemed to realize that at the same time she did. Laughing together, they clasped hands and walked toward the road that led to the exit of the base.

"What would you think about me reenlisting?" he asked. "Until the end of the war?"

"I think you are very good at what you do and the navy would be lucky to have you. Besides, you love it. You love a good challenge." It was amazing how crystal clear things had become once she'd thought through all of Gloria's advice. Or perhaps it was pure wisdom. Either way, she would forever be grateful for Gloria's assistance in helping her understand things. All sorts of things, but mainly, that this was her life.

"Captain Heinz asked me if I'd be interested in being his second-in-command," K.T. said. "That could mean that I'd be assigned to different shipyards, all around the world, and I'll take you with me, so you can see everything that you want to see. And if there are places that we don't go, I promise, I'll do whatever I can, so you can see them. See the world."

She stopped walking, and waited until he turned toward her. She took a single step in order to look him square in the face. "I'm looking at *my* world." The truth of that filled her with confidence. She was no longer vulnerable to old thoughts, old beliefs. "I'm looking at the only thing that I want to see for the rest of my life."

He held her chin with one hand. "So am I. You caught my eye the night of the dance contest. I'd never seen anyone so full of life or so beautiful, but I know you. You're too adventurous to only want to look at this mug for the rest of your life."

That was another thing she loved about him. The way he made her laugh. "Well, as long as you mentioned it, there is one place that I do want to see."

"Where?" he asked. "I promise to take you there, wherever it is. However long it takes."

She stretched on her toes and touched her lips against his as she whispered, "Oklahoma. The state. Specifically, the town of Guymon."

He laughed. "There's not a lot to see, but everyone there wants to meet you. They claim you are their good luck."

"No, they don't."

"Yes, they do." He draped an arm around her and

they began walking again. "I talked to my folks while I was in California, and I talked to Betty. She and her husband, Jim, live in San Francisco."

"Husband? She's already married? And living in California?"

"Yes." As they walked, he told her how Betty had learned that he was in California via the feed store owner, and that he'd met Betty and Jim, more than once, and was happy for them. He'd given her the necklace back.

"You weren't upset with her?" Wendy asked.

"No. Not even when I read her letter, because I could completely understand exactly what happened. It had happened to me, too. She hadn't planned on falling in love, and neither had I, but I did. I know I love the right woman. You."

She bumped his shoulder with her head. He truly was a remarkable man. "I love the right man, too. You." They reached the road, and she asked, "Where are we going?"

Stopping, he looked both up and down the road. "I don't know. Do you have to go back to the hospital?"

"No. Gloria said I could have the rest of the day off. Do you have to report for work?"

"Not until tomorrow morning." His smile grew. "Want to go fishing?"

"Yes!" She wanted to go fishing with him, but would have said yes to anything because she didn't want to be separated from him. Not ever. She'd never missed someone so badly in her life. "I have to change and get my camera. And we have to get your lures, and find some fishing poles, and…"

Chapter Fifteen

"I think I'm going to cry," Lois said, fluffing the short veil that was attached to the small white pillbox hat atop Wendy's head. "It'll make my mascara run, but you look so adorable."

"Here." Wendy handed Lois her handkerchief.

"I can't use that," Lois said. "That was your mother's. It's your something old."

"That doesn't mean it can't be used." Wendy wrapped the handkerchief back around the bouquet of flowers in her hands, because Lois was using her pinkie to wipe the corners of her eyes. Her something new were pearl earrings, a gift from K.T. Borrowed was the penny in her shoe from Lois, and blue was a lovely flowered broach that Gloria had given her and was pinned to the front of her simple, short-sleeved, knee-length white dress.

"Are you nervous?" Lois asked, having crossed the room to peek out the door.

They were in the chapel at the base, where her wedding would take place in minutes. "No," Wendy replied. "I'm happy, excited, and growing impatient."

"For the wedding night?" Lois asked, giggling.

"Yes," Wendy answered. The past two weeks had been amazing, but she was more than ready to share all of the love inside her with K.T.

"When a nifty number makes your pulse throb, that's not love, it's sex," Lois said, repeating one of the lines they'd read together from a magazine.

"My entire body has been throbbing for months," Wendy said. The magazine hadn't been the only advice she'd been given on sex. Gloria had not only offered plenty, she'd seen that a contraceptive diaphragm had been prescribed.

"Children can come once the war is over," Gloria had said, and once again, Wendy had accepted that as good advice. She didn't want there to be any reason for her and K.T. to be separated.

He'd accepted the second-in-command position for the Salvage Division, and Captain Heinz had said that having her travel with K.T. would be like having their own private nurse on staff.

The captain had also seen that they were given housing. A beautiful house in the officers' residential quarters because K.T. was now a member of a new program that had been formed for the navy to appointment enlisted men to the rank of officers. The house was furnished and full of their belongings, just waiting for them to arrive later today.

"I think everyone is here," Lois said. "The music should start at any moment."

Wendy wanted to throw open the door and march down the aisle. Get all the pomp and circumstance over with. She'd have been fine with just going to the justice of the peace in Honolulu, but everyone had wanted a wedding.

Everyone meaning all the friends they'd acquired here in Hawaii. There were plenty. And she appreciated each and every one of them very much.

However, she adored K.T. and all she wanted was for him to be her husband.

Forever more.

That finally happened. Lois opened the door, and Captain Heinz walked her down the aisle, where she never took her eyes off K.T. as they vowed their love and honor to one another.

As soon as the minister pronounced them man and wife, K.T. lifted her veil. Not caring that everyone in the chapel was watching, she flung her arms around his neck and kissed him like the world was about to end.

She knew it wasn't. It was just beginning.

Minutes later, they were splattered with rice as they left the chapel and climbed into a gray jeep that had a just married sign hanging on the back, along with strings of cans.

"Ready?" he asked while starting the engine.

She held her bouquet of flowers over her head. "I'm always ready!" She'd already tucked her handkerchief into her purse, so as they began to drive away, she tossed the bouquet into the crowd. Then spun around to see who caught it.

Lois looked stunned, then held the bouquet over her head as if it was a trophy as she ran toward another jeep.

A line of jeeps was soon behind them, honking as they drove through the base toward the sub base, where they would board boats to go to the Monkey Bar so no one would have to worry about being off the roads by seven forty-five.

People working at the base stopped long enough to wave or salute the jeep.

"Join us at the Monkey Bar!" she shouted and waved.

"You will have the entire base there," K.T. said, laughing.

"The more the merrier!" She hugged his arm. "And I couldn't be any merrier! I'm married!"

He laughed. "So am I!"

At the dock, they quickly left the jeep and boarded a boat that already had a driver, who took off as soon as they sat down.

"More people can fit in here," she told K.T.

He kissed her. "There are plenty of other boats, and I like having you all to myself."

"Ooh, la, la," she said, while wrapping her arms around his neck for a kiss that lasted until she felt a tug on her hair.

She broke this kiss in time to see her hat and veil flying through the air. There were several boats behind them and one swerved beneath the hat. A sailor reached up and plucked the hat out of the air. The entire boat, and those beside it, cheered at the accomplishment.

At the docks, that boat landed beside them and the sailor offered her the hat. It turned out to be the one with the broken ankle, still wearing his cast. "Keep it," Wendy said, grasping K.T.'s arm with both hands. "I have what I want."

The smile on K.T.'s face confirmed what she already knew. He loved her as much as she loved him, and that was the best thing ever.

Rather than walking up the beach to the bar, K.T. turned, so they were walking along the beach.

"Where are we going?" she asked.

"I have something you need to read," he said.

"What?"

He stopped and pulled a folded piece of paper out of his white dress uniform pocket. "This."

She looked up at him, then unfolded the paper. "It's a telegram."

"From Sid."

"I've never received a telegram before." Excited, she read the typed note:

> *Congratulations Wendy and K.T. We all wish we could be there. A luau has been requested to continue your celebration. Send us pictures.*
> *With love,*
> *Kent McCallister and Sidney Williams*

She looked at K.T. "A luau?"

K.T. loved the way her eyes shimmered, the way her dimpled smile made her entire face shine, and her. All of her. "Yes, a luau. Compliments of our families." Sid had sent him a separate telegram last week, asking for information about paying for the wedding. Her family felt it necessary, and had stated that his family wanted to provide money for the wedding, too. The contract with the oil company was already paying off. He'd agreed to a luau, but kept it as a surprise for her.

"That was so nice of them." She tucked the telegram in his suit coat pocket, then wrapped her arms around his neck. "Oh, Oklahoma, we are going to have the best life. The absolute best life."

He ran his hand up and down her sides, loving how her curves fit perfectly in the palms of his hands. "Yes, we are."

Because of her, he no longer felt that he needed to control everything, amongst other things. She'd shown him how life was meant to be lived. To its fullest every day. Starting tonight, they'd live their nights to the fullest, too. He kissed her, long and deeply, a precursor for what was to come.

"With kisses like that, I might be convinced to forgo the luau," she said.

He lifted a brow.

She giggled and took a hold of his hand and gave it a tug. "We can't miss the whole party. We'll leave after we've learned how to hula dance."

"Men don't hula dance."

"Yes, they do. They dance like warriors, I read about it but haven't seen it. I'm glad I gave Lois two rolls of film so I can send some pictures to our families. They should have received the pictures of us fishing by now."

"Probably," he answered. They had caught a couple of fish, and had taken many pictures, but they'd spent most of that day lying on the beach, kissing, and talking, and kissing some more.

"Oh, I can hear the music and smell the food," she said. "This is going to be so much fun. So. Much. Fun."

Hours later, the dancing, food, music, drinks, and camaraderie were still in high gear, when he and Wendy were once again showered, this time with floral leis, as they took their leave. The crowd continued to cheer as they hurried, hand in hand, down to the dock and climbed in the boat where a seaman was ready to drive them across the harbor. K.T. felt like the luckiest man on earth that she loved him as much as he loved her.

"Look at that," she said. "The sun is setting and we're going to ride right through it." Leaning her head on his shoulder, she sighed. "This has been the best day of my life."

"Mine, too." He agreed.

She lifted her head. "I love you, K.T. McCallister."

"I love you, Wendy McCallister."

"Oh, I love my new name. Love everything about my new life. I don't know why I was afraid of all this."

"Everyone is afraid of something."

"Not you."

He ran a finger down the side of her face. "I was afraid of never seeing you again. So afraid, that if the *Solace* had been closer to the cruiser that day, I would have dived in, and swum to it."

"Thank goodness you didn't, and thank goodness Gloria refused to put my name on the list."

He frowned, having never heard that. "Why did she refuse?"

"She told me that I had to give you the chance to forgive me, and I agreed, but I was still so ashamed of not giving you Betty's letter, that I told Gloria to add my name to the list. She refused. Told me that she wouldn't approve a transfer for me to anywhere until I learned a valuable lesson."

"What was the lesson?"

"How to forgive myself. Gloria said it wasn't easy, but that's where forgiveness starts. That if she hadn't learned to forgive herself for her son's accident, she would have never become a nurse. Never have done anything with her life, except wallow in pity. I figured if she'd been able to forgive herself, I could, too."

"Forgive yourself for what?"

"For the way I behaved. How I kept Betty's letter from you, for lying to you about only wanting to be friends. I'd never done anything like that before, and I was so ashamed. I'm normally a very honest person, and I promise to spend the rest of my life making that up to you."

He kissed her forehead. "There is nothing for you to make up. We both had things we needed to work out. The day you gave me Betty's letter, I was going to tell you that while I was in California, I was going to call Betty, tell her that I wouldn't be coming home because I loved you. But I didn't tell you any of that, because all along, I'd been telling myself that I couldn't commit to anything, couldn't commit to loving you, because the world is at war. We don't know what tomorrow might bring, but while in California, I realized that not loving you was a far greater risk. One that I couldn't live with."

"Oh, K.T." She laid a hand on his chest, right above his heart. "That's what I realized, too. You are everything I ever wanted, all rolled up in one. You are my world."

"And you are mine." He kissed her, but just a fast kiss because the boat was pulling into the dock, and he was anxious to share the love that was boiling over in his heart with her.

The drive to their new home in the jeep wasn't overly far, and once there, he lifted her into his arms and carried her over the threshold.

"You can put me down now," she said, once the door was closed behind them and she'd flicked on the light.

"Nope, I'm carrying you straight to the bedroom."

She laughed and kissed the side of his face. "What are we going to do there?"

He carried her down the hall. "I don't know? What do you want to do?"

"We could hula dance," she whispered. "With no clothes on."

"You're full of challenges, Nebraska," he said, clearly recalling how he'd told her that the night of the dance contest.

"You love challenges," she replied, just as she had before.

He walked into the bedroom. "How do you know that?" he asked, again, just as he had that night.

"You married me," she said.

He dropped her onto the bed, gently, but enough that the bed bounced and it bounced again as he dove onto the mattress beside her. "You're right, and it's the smartest thing I've ever done."

The need for the ultimate physical connection between the two of them had been boiling inside him for a long time, and he knew she felt the same. She put her heart and soul into everything she did, and once again proved that as she held nothing back when her lips met his with an open-mouthed kiss.

That kiss created a firestorm of desires and emotions so charged they couldn't get their clothes off fast enough. Couldn't get enough of touching each other, kissing each other. All the dreams he'd had about her, all the fantasies his mind had created, didn't compare to the real thing.

His life had changed the moment he'd met her and despite the route they'd taken to get to this moment, he knew it had all been worth it. He would never have understood that nothing was stronger than true love if he hadn't lived through finding it.

All of their nearly frantic kissing, tasting, caressing, and teasing, had brought them to the ultimate moment, and the mere idea of how close he'd come to losing all of this, to never experiencing all of this with her, momentarily brought him down to earth.

He paused, his gaze locked with hers and his body positioned over hers.

She bit down on her bottom lip and cupped his face, splayed her fingers into his hair. "This is us, Oklahoma."

Nodding, because only she would know what he was thinking and why he'd paused, he said, "I know. I'm just in awe at how lucky I am."

She pulled his face downward, so their lips were almost touching. "One more thing we have in common."

The instant their lips touched, the emotions and desires filling the room were reignited, flaring hotter and brighter. He lost his ability to do anything but feel when her warm, moist body fully accepted him as he slid inside her. Together, they embarked on a union focused on nothing except giving and receiving undiluted pleasure.

Every movement, every thrust, brought a new dimension to gratification, driving them to a conclusion that struck with a brilliance and left them clinging to each other, gasping for air.

As the waves of satisfaction washing over him slowed to ripples, he rolled onto his side, still breathing hard.

"Holy cow!" she said, throwing an arm across her forehead. "No wonder there are so many articles about that in magazines."

He loved her honesty, and humor, and absolutely everything else about her, and wasn't in the least surprised that she'd read articles on the subject. Propping his head with one hand, he used his other hand to trace a line from the base of her neck all the way down to her stomach, already contemplating round two. "How many articles did you read?"

"A few." She twisted her neck, gave the length of him a slow appraisal, moving nothing but her eyes, before rolling onto her side and draping a leg over his. "But I'd rather do than read and I think that's something that we may need to do again." She kissed him. "At least once a day for the rest of our lives."

"Just once a day?"

Pushing his shoulder, encouraging him to roll onto his back, she climbed on top of him. "Not just, at least. Life is all about having fun."

She had taught him that, and though their first encounter had been amazing by no stretch of the imagination, he knew that with practice, it was only going to get better and better.

Just like his life.

Their life.

Epilogue

February 1961, Guymon, Oklahoma

Wendy closed the bedroom door, and took a moment to appreciate the sight before her. K.T. was on the bed, bare chested, sitting up with pillows propped behind his back and a book on his lap. The fluttering in her stomach made her smile, after nineteen years of marriage, that still hadn't changed. If anything, he thrilled her even more now than before, in many ways.

He was an amazing husband, an incredible father, and an extraordinarily successful inventor. After their time in the navy, they'd moved home, to Oklahoma, where he'd begun creating things. It had all started with the oil company, and the pump engines on the McCallister properties. They were always breaking down for one reason or another, so he had built one. One that to this day was still working. He'd gotten a patent on the engine and sold it.

That had been just the beginning of the things he'd created, built, patented, and sold. There were days when the mailbox was packed full of nothing but royalty checks from his inventions.

Yet, he was always working on the next one, and she loved it. She loved working in the shop beside him. Loved how sometimes, in the middle of the day, when the right song came on the radio, they'd stop working and dance.

Just dance.

"Are you going to stand there all night?" he asked, flipping back the covers on her side of the bed.

"No." She untied her bathrobe as she walked toward the bed. "I was just admiring you, thinking how lucky I am."

"One more thing we have in common," he said, watching her lay her robe over the foot of the bed.

Wearing only a long silk nightgown, she climbed on the bed and kissed him. "Yes." She tucked her feet beneath the covers and scooted up next to him, sharing the pillows stacked behind his back. "What are you reading?"

"Not reading, looking."

She realized then that it was a photo album on his lap. "Our wedding pictures."

"Yes." He pointed at a picture. "Remember that?"

The picture was of Harvey Clemmons, with her veiled pillbox hat atop his head and a cast on his foot. "Yes. He wore that hat all night after catching it when it flew off my head."

He flipped to the next page. "What about that?"

She laughed at the picture of her in her white wedding dress amongst all the other women in grass skirts. "I was a pretty good hula dancer back then."

His lips touched her temple. "You still are."

Although contentment washed over her, she said, "You have to say that. You're my husband."

He chuckled. "Marrying you is still the smartest thing I ever did."

"What made you pull this out?" she asked. "Our anniversary was last week." As if she was a model, she held her right hand before his face, showing him the gorgeous mother's ring that he'd given her last week. The gold band held three shimmering stones for each of their children. Roger, their oldest, was fifteen and much like his father. Overly serious at times and intelligent. Sharon, who was thirteen, was more like her. Meaning, she couldn't cook, either—which was why they had a live-in cook and housekeeper—but loved seeing people happy. And their youngest, Tad. He'd just turned ten and was a mixture of the two of them. A free spirit who could fix anything.

K.T. took a hold of her fingers and kissed the back of her hand, but didn't say anything. Which made her know he was up to something.

Looking at the album again, she flipped to the next page. Sure enough, there was an envelope. "What's this?"

"Something for you to read."

She picked up the envelope and lifted the unsealed flap. "Airline tickets? Where are we going?" Not so remarkably, because he'd promised to show her the world, they'd been on every continent since getting married. Some while in the navy, others because he'd sold his inventions, and others still, just because they were places they'd wanted to see.

"Read them."

She pulled the tickets out of the envelope, and her heart leaped. "Hawaii?"

He nodded. "It's time to revisit where it all started."

"Oh, Oklahoma, that will be so wonderful." She glanced at the tickets. "These are for next month! It's going to be so warm and beautiful there!"

"There's something else in the envelope."

She set the airline tickets aside and pulled out more tickets, smaller ones, and read them. "Elvis Presley?" She let out a squeal. "In concert?"

"Yes, he's performing at the Bloch Arena. It's a fundraiser for the memorial they are building at Pearl Harbor. I thought we should be there."

Tears formed in her eyes as she thought of the time they'd spent at the harbor, all the good times, and even the tragic ones. Blinking didn't clear her vision, but that was just fine. She set aside the tickets and the photo album, and wrapped her arms around him. "K.T. McCallister, I love you. I love you so very, very much."

He pulled her on top of him as he slid down on the bed, until they were lying down. "Prove it."

She laughed, because she loved a challenge, and she also remembered the first time she'd said that to him at the Bloch Arena, where it had all started. They both had proven many things to each other over the years, but she didn't mind doing it again.

And again.

And again.

* * * * *

*If you enjoyed this story,
then make sure to read Lauri Robinson's
Southern Belles in London miniseries*

The Return of His Promised Duchess
The Making of His Marchioness
Falling for His Pretend Countess

*And why not pick up one of her other
brilliant stories?*

An Unlikely Match for the Governess
The Captain's Christmas Homecoming
A Family for the Titanic Survivor
Diary of a War Bride